SAY YOU'LL BE NINE

LUCY LENNOX

Cover Art: Cate Ashwood Designs

Cover Photo: Wander Aguiar

Editing: One Love Editing

Proofreading: Lori Parks and Victoria Rothenberg

Beta Reading: Leslie Copeland, May Archer, Shay Haude, Molly Maddox, and Chad Williams.

DEDICATION

Special thanks to May Archer for motivating me to work hard and focus during such strange times. May also read early parts of *Say You'll Be Nine* and gave me enough encouragement to know I was on the right track.

May, this one's for you, because you deserve every cinnamon roll in the bakery case.

KEEP IN TOUCH WITH LUCY!

Join Lucy's Lair
Get Lucy's New Release Alerts
Like Lucy on Facebook
Follow Lucy on BookBub
Follow Lucy on Amazon
Follow Lucy on Instagram
Follow Lucy on Pinterest

Other books by Lucy:
Made Marian Series
Forever Wilde Series
Aster Valley Series
Twist of Fate Series with Sloane Kennedy
After Oscar Series with Molly Maddox
Licking Thicket Series with May Archer
Virgin Flyer
Say You'll Be Nine

Visit Lucy's website at www.LucyLennox.com for a comprehensive list of titles, audio samples, freebies, suggested reading order, and more!

1

NINE

"Nine will help you carry those out to the car."

I glanced up and smiled while Walt handed Mr. Purcell his change. Mr. Purcell was one of several customers who still paid in cash, even when he was shelling out for half a pallet of potting soil like he was today. Walt's assurance of my help was one I'd heard thousands of times in my life.

Nine will help. Nine will carry that. Nine will do that for you. It was a familiar refrain both at work and at my family's farm.

As I made my way to the front of the store, I ignored the buzz of my phone in my pocket. My mother had been messaging me all day to remind me of the leaky bathroom faucet she needed me to fix after work, and my brother Eli was no doubt texting me to remind me it was my turn to buy beer for poker night this weekend. As if I'd forget. The first Friday of the month was my night to buy beer. Lord only knew why I drew the first Friday when I was the last boy out of the ten of us, but there it was. It was fine. I didn't complain. I never complained, and I always helped out.

It was what I was known for, and honestly, I enjoyed helping people. I liked knowing something I did made someone else's life easier.

Mr. Purcell turned to me with a smile. "There he is. Been recording any more of them videos for me? I was hoping you might do one on repairing roof flashing. Now that the weather's turning, I'd like to get up there and patch everything. Be great if I could do it myself without having to call in John over at the roofing company, you know?"

I gathered up several of the bags of potting soil from the counter and threw them over my shoulder. "I did the one on switching out your door locks like you asked, but I haven't done any roofing ones yet."

"Oh! Well if you did the door locks, let me go back in and pick those up and I'll get 'em knocked out this afternoon. I'd like to break off my key every time that damned thing jams up."

He opened the rear hatch in his old Suburban, and I loaded the bags of soil before turning to get the remaining bags of soil, seeds, and starter pots he'd purchased. I pointed him in the direction of the locks and told him I'd be right there to make sure he got the right items. As soon as I'd closed his SUV up, I joined him on aisle four.

"Didn't you say you needed one for the tool shed too?" I asked, scratching the back of my neck and trying to remember our conversation from a few weeks ago. "Oh, and Debbie's place now that Nate left. Can't be too careful after a breakup."

Mr. Purcell snapped his fingers. "Damned right, Nine. Thank you. I tried to get her to move back home with her mom and me, but you know how girls can be. Stubbornly independent, that's how." He reached for the set I pointed out. "Hey, speaking of independent women, I saw your sister working a shift at the hospital. She's pregnant again, isn't she?"

"Yes, sir. Beth and Matt are expecting their third. You can imagine my mom is thrilled. Already knitting up a storm. This will be her seventh grandchild."

His eyes sparkled. I already knew that half the items he'd purchased today were to help his own grandson with a 4-H project. The Purcells were as close as my own crazy family. "What about you,

Nine? When are you going to join the club and start making your mama happy?" he asked with a wink, but I knew he was serious. I was only twenty-four, but because my oldest brother was thirty-seven, people tended to think of me as somehow way behind the eight ball when it came to settling down.

I swallowed. I'd never been all that comfortable with personal questions and being the center of attention. "Well, sir. I guess when the right woman comes along. In the meantime I'm pretty happy with just me and Nacho, you know?"

The dog heard his name and perked his head up behind the checkout counter. I heard the telltale jingle of his collar and tags.

Mr. Purcell laughed. "Man needs more than the love of a good dog, son. You oughta ask out that new girl who works at the diner. Debbie said she's a sweetheart, not like that woman who married the vet. She's a piece of work if you don't mind my saying."

I did mind him saying. Lauren had been nice enough when we'd dated, and I knew for a fact she was happy as a clam now that she was with Eric Pender. It had turned out for the best all around when she'd dumped me for the new "doctor" in town. I got more time to make my how-to videos, and she got to do her pageant wave in the town parade with a nice big rock on her finger.

"Yes, sir," I mumbled, turning to help him carry his new lock sets to the front counter. Walt was nowhere to be found, so I rang up the new purchases and bagged everything before carrying them out to the Suburban. "That gonna do for you today, Mr. Purcell?"

He clapped me on the shoulder. "Sure is. Can't wait to look up the video when I get home. I'll give you a call if I have any trouble."

I nodded and stepped back after closing the hatch again. As soon as he'd pulled out of the drive, a bright yellow VW Beetle pulled in and out popped Beverly Abbott. "Just the man I wanted to see," she said with a bright smile. "I came across your video about building a raised vegetable bed and wanted to pick up some supplies. Can you help?"

"'Course," I murmured, holding the front door for her. I noticed

Walt watering the hanging baskets several yards down the storefront. He'd obviously overheard Bev because he beamed at me. Ever since I'd started doing the videos to help out our customers, he'd heaped praise on me for the accompanying boost in business.

I didn't pay much attention to the increase in sales since it didn't particularly benefit me other than providing basic job security, but I had to admit I enjoyed helping people. And of course I was happy for Walt's increase in business because he was a hard worker and he ran a good shop. I'd been doing the DIY videos for about a year now, and they'd been very popular. There were even people all over the world who'd stumbled across them and found them useful, to the point I'd gotten requests to translate measurements into meters and help people find alternatives for products that weren't available in other countries.

It was a nice peek outside of the small town of Wheatland, Wyoming, for someone who'd never even been across state lines. The process of learning how to take and edit video had become more fun than I'd expected, even though my sister Delia made fun of me for thinking that.

"You've always liked figuring out how things work," she'd said over family dinner one night. "Tech equipment is no different than complex power tools."

My dad and brothers had hooted about that, but she was right. It was fun figuring out how to optimize a project with the tools you had at your disposal. Of course, it always made you want better tools, but that was the same case with anything. My dad had been half in love with a brand-new automated combine for the farm for years even though his income couldn't justify the expense.

I helped Beverly find everything she needed and got it loaded up in her little car before saying my goodbyes to Walt for the day and whistling for Nacho. Walt knew Thursday nights were family dinner night at the Winshed Farm, and my parents didn't take very many excuses to miss it.

When I loaded us both up in the truck, I checked my phone to see if any of the messages were my mom needing something from the store. I was surprised to see one of the missed calls had come from an unknown number. The voicemail said it was a man named Clay with Stallion Tools.

I glanced up at all of the brand-name signs in the windows of Walt's hardware store. The Stallion Tools logo was the biggest one with its orange script and stylized outline of a horse. My very first power tool had been a little battery-operated Stallion electric screwdriver that Santa had brought me straight from my wish list when I was seven years old.

How had Stallion gotten my personal cell phone number instead of calling Walt at the number for the store? I clicked the button to listen to the voicemail.

"Hi, Nine, we're big fans of your YouTube channel here at Stallion, and we'd like to pick your brain regarding a new sponsorship opportunity. Please give us a call back at your earliest convenience to discuss or have your agent reach out to us."

I let out a soft snort. Agent. Ha. My DIY and nature videos were hardly the stuff of internet fame. Granted, they'd picked up crazy-big subscription numbers, but I tried not to notice. If I did, it made me clam up the next time I tried shooting a new video.

So, for now, I simply focused on genuine interactions with curious viewers who asked interesting questions and had great suggestions and requests for future content. My YouTube videos gave me an excuse to get outside and away from the obligations of work and family, and you really couldn't put a price on that anyway.

I didn't want to think about having to say no to some exciting offer just because I was legit terrified of talking to new people. The idea of working with the marketing department of some big corporation made me want to hide behind the mountains of chicken feed that had just come in. There was a reason I'd never gone to college like most of my siblings had. I wasn't really a people person, and I didn't have grand expectations of a big life.

All I needed was a job that paid me enough to keep my own place and splurge every now and then on new camera equipment and tools. I'd worked at Walt's hardware store since I was sixteen, and after eight years there, I'd finally amassed a good collection of used tools and DIY supplies I used for my videos. My next goal was a place of my own in the woods. Even a little fixer-upper would suit me fine, something full of new challenges and projects with plenty of room for Nacho to roam and far enough away from others to give me the solitude I craved.

Before I even realized what I was doing, I'd headed northwest up toward where Sybille Creek split from the Laramie River. My favorite parcel of land wasn't too far from my family's farm which was how I'd found it all those years ago. The old place had finally been processed by the state after the old man who owned it had died, leaving no heirs.

Sure enough, there was finally a For Sale sign on it.

My heart thumped and my hands shook as I pulled up the real estate listing app. Fifty thousand dollars for thirty acres of gorgeous fertile land with creek frontage and plenty of hardwood trees and wildflowers that bloomed all summer. It didn't sound like much, but I only had ten saved up. It was enough for the down payment, but then I wouldn't be able to afford to put a house on it for a while.

I closed my eyes and took a breath before doing a U-turn and heading to family dinner. When I pulled into my parents' driveway, I knew I needed to suck it up and call the Stallion guy back to get it over with and off my mind.

Unfortunately, he was still in the office.

"Nine, so glad to hear from you," he said in his big businessman voice. "We stumbled onto your YouTube channel recently and are very impressed with the DIY content you're providing. These simple how-to videos have clearly gone viral, and we see your subscribership is hitting impressive levels."

My heart was already hammering before he mentioned subscribers. Now it was about to crack right out of my chest.

"Thank you, sir," I said, grateful my voice sounded much more in control than I felt.

There was a pause. "You're up in Wyoming, right?"

"Yes, sir. North of Cheyenne."

"I don't suppose you know many other YouTubers who do what you do?"

Movement out of the windshield caught my eye. My bossy sister Dee was tapping her nonexistent watch at me. "No, sir. Not really. I mostly just film the videos and upload them. I don't really... engage in the community all that much."

I knew this was probably the thing that would turn him off considering me for a sponsorship of any kind. Usually companies liked to partner with social media stars who worked their numbers hard, the ones who had Instagram, Facebook, Snapchat, and whatever the hell else there was out there.

I didn't do any of that.

"So... let me ask you something." He sounded hesitant and weird all of a sudden.

"Yes?"

"How do you feel about gay rights and all that?"

What?

"I'm sorry, I... I don't understand what you're—"

"Our new focus for this sponsorship is reaching the LGBTQ community. We've been challenged by one of the professional athletes we sponsor to create a project dispelling some stereotypes about the kind of men who use tools."

I thought about all of the *women* who used tools, but it wasn't my place to correct him. If he was putting together a campaign to make power tools and DIY more accessible to any minority community, that was a good thing.

"That's fine," I said without thinking. I hadn't meant it was fine and I'd do the project. I'd only meant to say LGBTQ stuff was fine with me. I didn't have a problem with gay people. Despite my upbringing in a pretty conservative place and family, I'd spent more than my fair share of time on the internet and watching television. I wasn't a complete hillbilly despite what some people thought.

"I don't suppose you... nah, well, anyway, I can't really ask you that. But I wonder if you might know of someone... someone LGBT or like that, who does what you do. We're looking to sponsor content like yours that's being done by someone in the LGBT community. So if you or anyone you know might be interested in something like that, say... fixing up a place and broadcasting it using Stallion Tools... please get in touch with us, alright?"

I didn't say anything while my brain ping-ponged around wondering what exactly he was saying. This was certainly not the way I'd envisioned the conversation going.

He began speaking again. "Tell you what, Nine... why don't you think about it, talk to your friends in the business, and get back to me. Does that sound good?"

At this point my sister was having a full-blown fit on the front porch for me to come inside.

"Uh, yes, sir. That sounds fine."

After the call ended, I had to admit to being a little disappointed I didn't meet their sponsorship criteria. I daydreamed of making enough money to put a down payment on a piece of property. I fantasized about having the latest tech from one of the best power tool companies around. And being able to get my hands on a new drone for taking aerial shots? Man, that would have been tempting. But even then, I couldn't really stomach the idea of performing for others, and I was sure they'd probably have rules about what I could and couldn't post. Just the thought of that made me uncomfortable and nervous, and I wasn't even in the running for their sponsorship.

I climbed out of the truck and made my way into my family's sprawling ranch house. My mother needed some help in the kitchen, and then we were all taking our seats around the giant dining room table and beginning to pass dishes. She'd made several large pans of lasagne, and one of my sisters had made the special garlic bread that went with it. After letting out a contented sigh, I reached for the bread basket. This was one of my favorite meals, and if I had to put up with my family's chaos to enjoy it, I would do it happily.

After a few minutes of plates clinking and murmured please and thankyous as we all served ourselves, my mother led a prayer blessing. I bowed my head and did what I always did: took a slow, deep breath and centered myself. I wasn't much for Jesus anymore, but I still loved to take a minute to calm down when everyone else around me was saying their prayers at the table or when I got roped into joining Mom and Dad at church. It was kind of like the shower I took every night before bed—gave me a chance to wash off the day's dirt and start again fresh.

Finally it was time to eat, and we dug in like animals. Lord only knew how my mom had kept us all fed all these years. It always amazed me when I saw how much food the twelve of us ate. Only now the table was over twice as full with spouses and kids. My nieces and nephews mostly ate in the kitchen at the big table in there, but a handful were old enough to join us at the adult table now. Sometimes I couldn't believe I had nieces and nephews almost old enough to graduate from high school when I myself still felt like I'd just gotten out.

"You given anymore thought to college, Nolan?" My mom's face lit up the way it always did when she focused on her favorite grandson. "If you stay here and go to UW, Grandpa and I are willing to chip in half the tuition."

She was desperate to keep him local, and I got that. I did. Only, she'd never bothered to send me, her own son, to college with that kind of offer, not that I'd really wanted to go or anything. Most everyone I knew agreed I wasn't exactly college material. Instead, she and my dad had made it very clear that the only two people they could afford to help with college were my two oldest brothers. One was expected to study agriculture and return home to help on the farm, and the other was expected to become a doctor because my mother was batshit crazy. Colt was never, ever going to be doctor material. Quite frankly, we were lucky he was car mechanic material. My sister Beth, on the other hand, was definitely doctor material. But since Mom didn't believe in "lady doctors," Beth had contented herself with becoming a nurse which was probably for the best because she loved her job and her patients adored her.

As everyone chattered around me, I thought back to my conversation with the corporate guy. He'd asked if I could recommend a vlogger like me who was LGBT. Hell, I only knew one gay person in real life, and to be honest, he and I didn't get along all that well. But I remembered he was doing something with social media these days, so maybe he'd know who I could talk to.

"Hey, Eli," I said, leaning forward to find my brother midbite.

"Ngh?"

"What's Cooper up to these days?"

He swallowed and crinkled his forehead at me. "Same old. Why you asking?"

My brother's best friend from college had moved out to LA after graduation to become an actor. It hadn't worked, and I wasn't really surprised. The guy was a total know-it-all with opinions for days. Now he was trying to become an Instagram star or something. I only knew because my niece had mentioned it, not because I stalked him or anything.

"He still in California?"

Eli shook his head. "Nah. Had to move back home to Colorado which is probably for the best. His brother's going through some shit right now. Health stuff. They don't know what the problem is though."

I felt a pinch in my gut. Even though I strongly disliked the guy, I hated to hear about anyone going through a health scare. I remembered hearing about his brother, Jackson, enough to know they were close. Cooper had stayed with us during some of the school breaks at UW since he hadn't had a car to drive home. I remembered being annoyed by his constant chatter and never-ending perky energy.

After one of his visits, I'd asked Eli how the hell he'd ended up friends with a drama major in the first place, and Eli had told me Cooper was more than he appeared. I'd never understood what that had meant, and honestly I hadn't cared enough to ask. As far as I was concerned, Cooper was all buckle and no belt.

But now I wondered if he'd be willing to let me ask him some questions about gay stuff on social media so I could help the Stallion guys out. Although, I wasn't sure what exactly that could be. Maybe Cooper knew a guy who did YouTube videos with tools who might want the sponsorship opportunity. If I could help Stallion find an LGBT vlogger, maybe then they'd keep me in mind when they had other sponsorship opportunities come up.

My brother Tip smirked at me from across the table. "Why you asking? You got a crush on him or something?" Tip always made a big fucking deal about Cooper being gay, so any discussion of him invariably led to a bunch of bullshit.

"Hell no, *Francis*," I said, calling him by his real name because I knew he hated it. "I just..." I blinked at everyone staring at me from around the table. "There's this sponsorship at Stallion Tools, and—"

My dad's attention perked up from his spot at the head of the table. "Stallion? They looking to do more at Walt's?"

I shook my head. "No, this is for my YouTube stuff, not the store. They—"

Dad's forehead creased in confusion. "Why would a tool company care about some how-to videos?"

My sister Dee rolled her eyes. "Dad, they care because it's a way of advertising. Lots of companies run ads on YouTube now. Maybe they want to sponsor Nine's show."

Dad was suddenly interested. I could practically see the dollar signs in his eyes. "They fixing to give you money, son?"

I fidgeted in my seat. "No, no. At least I don't think so. I got a call today from a guy there who—"

More interruptions. This time it was Eli. "What's this have to do with Cooper?"

I felt my face heat. I hated being the center of everyone's attention. "Um, well, they said that they're doing a big sponsorship or something to reach out to the LGBT community about using tools."

My nephew snickered, but I ignored him and continued. "And I just thought if I knew anyone who..."

Dee rolled her eyes again. It was her favorite expression. "Jesus. Is Cooper Heath the only gay person you know or something?"

I looked around the table. "Uh, yeah?"

And this was where it all went downhill. It started with Nolan. "My Spanish teacher at the high school is gay. Señor Hopkins wears bright pink running shoes. I saw him one time at the park jogging."

Suddenly I was no longer the target of Dee's annoyance. "Pink shoes don't make the man gay, Colby. Christ."

Mom shot her a look. "Language."

"Sorry," Dee muttered. "Surely you all know Linda Wieler. She's gay."

Mom *tsked*. "Just because a woman raises chickens, doesn't mean she's gay, Cassandra."

More eye rolling. "Mom, she and her partner Pam have been together for years."

My dad's brows furrowed. "Linda down at the bank? I thought Pam was her sister."

My niece Twyla grinned at me with a big mouth of neon green braces, "You should do it, Uncle Nine. That sounds cool."

Me? Hadn't she heard the part about needing to be gay? "No, I—"

Eli's eyes widened comically. "You totally should! How much money they offering?"

"I have no idea since I'm not *gay*." I pushed my plate back from the edge of the table and crumpled up my napkin.

My parents studied me for a beat before my dad went ahead and said it. "But you could pretend."

Were they insane? "No. No way. That's fraud."

"Pfft." Eli looked like the cat with the canary. "It's hardly fraud. Haven't you ever heard of 'gay for pay'?"

"Eli!" My mother gasped as if this was all some kind of blasphemy.

My sister Beth patted my hand. "Are you sure you're not gay? Or maybe bi?"

"Emily!" Mom's shock reflex was getting a workout.

Beth turned to my mother with her typical serene demeanor. "Mother, it's not the end of the world if Nine is gay or bisexual. I'm only asking because he's never really dated anyone. Maybe—"

Mom sat forward in her seat and looked smug. "What about Lauren? And Cherry Kelly? They dated in high school."

I pinched my lips closed. This wasn't something I was willing to discuss, and as it was, my stomach was already hurting from nerves. I hated when everyone looked at me.

"Oh yeah," Colt said with a laugh. "I know they had sex because poor Cherry came into the Superette looking for a pregnancy test after they went to prom together. Remember that? You dodged a bullet there, little brother."

Now I was mortified on top of nauseous.

"Isaac Denton Winshed, is this true?" My mother had suddenly notched her voice up to the level that silenced all other communication in the house. You could have heard a pin drop.

I lowered my head, trying to sink inside myself. I didn't want to contribute to gossip about Cherry Kelly, but at the same time, I could hardly lie to my mother after she'd asked me a direct question. Thankfully, before I had a chance to answer, my father stepped in.

"This is hardly the kind of conversation appropriate for the dinner table."

When everyone started talking again, Beth leaned over and whispered, "Is it true? Did you and Cherry have sex in high school?"

I swallowed and nodded, but I didn't tell her about me insisting on using not one, but two, condoms because I was so scared of getting her pregnant. When I found out she'd had a pregnancy scare, I'd known she'd probably been sleeping with Bobby Hilden even though she'd told me they were long broken up. It was fine by me. The sex had been awkward and awful. It had turned me off trying it again for a long time.

"Huh. I was wrong, then. Sorry about that. Not that there's anything wrong with being gay." She ducked down to meet my eyes even though I was trying real hard to keep mine on my lap. "You know that, right? There's nothing wrong with any kind of sexuality that involves legality and consent. And I will love you no matter what—"

I couldn't take this anymore.

"I gotta go," I blurted, shoving my chair back. "Sorry. I forgot I have to drop something off at... someone's house, and, uh... yeah. And I gotta go."

As I raced out the door, my mother got one more chance to gasp in shock. "What about my leaky faucet?"

Before I could get out to my truck, Eli stopped me. "Hey, wait. Gimme your phone."

I blinked at him in confusion. "Why?"

He held out his hand and gave me the look that all older brothers had, the one that said *do what I say or get a knuckle sandwich.*

"Fine, here," I said, slapping it into his hand. He tapped around in it for a bit before handing it back.

"I put Cooper's info in there for you. Give him a call. He's desperate for extra work right now and could really use the money."

I was not suggesting Cooper Heath for this sponsorship. He was about as likely to know how to use a Stallion tool as he was to know how to replace a crank shield on a hay baler. The very idea was ridiculous. Last I'd heard, the man had been cast in a commercial for Crest Whitening Strips.

Eli stared me down. "I mean it, Nine. His brother's in bad shape. If they can't earn enough money for a bone marrow transplant, he could die."

"What do you want me to do, Eli? Lie and tell Stallion the guy's a DIY YouTuber when he's not?"

Eli studied me for a minute. "No, but... if I can figure out a way for us to help him, you'll do it, right?"

I sighed and looked up at the darkened sky. My brother already knew the answer to that question.

Nine will help.

It was what I was known for. Stranded on the highway with a blown tire? *Call Nine.* Need someone to pick up a bag of ice before the party? *Nine will do it.* One of the Wise Men in the pageant called in sick? *That costume will surely fit Nine Winshed, and we all know that man doesn't say no to anyone in need.*

"Of course I will," I muttered before whistling for Nacho to load up in the truck. Even if I didn't much care for Cooper Heath, I was a sucker for someone in need. His brother deserved a healthy life. And if it was in my power to help him get it, well, I'd do whatever I could.

I always did.

2

COOPER

I wondered if there was a place in hell for nurses who used the phrase "Just a little poke" before jabbing a needle into your skin.

Just the sight of it made me feel faint, so I dropped into the nearest visitor chair by the window.

My brother's wince was almost imperceptible since he took great pride in acting like this was all just a normal walk in the park. It wasn't. It had been a horrible slog through muddy waters for nearly two years while we struggled to find a diagnosis for his chronic fatigue and fevers. But now we had one.

Aplastic anemia, most likely caused by the CMV virus. So far, the doctors had tried blood transfusions and immunosuppressants, but they weren't working well enough. They wanted to do a bone marrow transplant. The good news was, as his identical twin, I was definitely a match. The bad news was, it would end up costing us a minimum of ten grand.

We didn't have ten grand.

My mother's version of hand-wringing was clicking the end of a click-top pen. Over and over and over again. Which meant I was going to have to kill her at some point.

"You okay, Pooh Bear?" she asked Jackson. From the date of his diagnosis to now, she'd reverted to treating us both like we were five.

"Mom," Jackson said with a sigh. "It's fine."

Click, click, click.

Jacks shot me a look. *Make it stop.*

"Mom, why don't we go grab some lunch? Jackson said he's desperate for sushi today."

Her head snapped toward me. "He can't have raw fish. If he got food poisoning..."

I reached for her arm. "I know. That's why we're getting the cooked stuff and veggie sushi. There's a place right down the street."

Mom shot another look at her poor, pitiful baby laid up in the hospital bed. I couldn't blame her. It wasn't fun to see him like this. He'd lost a lot of weight and looked pale and weak. It was a striking contrast to the tan, muscled guy he'd been only two years before.

"All right," Mom said on a sigh. "I guess I could go for a California roll myself."

It was the only roll she knew. She liked to call it by name to sound cool, like she was a trendy, young hipster who ate sushi like the rest of us.

She didn't. She ate the California roll and six pieces of ebi, cooked shrimp that may as well have been hibachi shrimp on the plate, cooked for her by a performance chef. Which, let's be honest, she'd prefer.

As we walked out of the hospital, she dug in her purse for her pen so she could click her way down the street. "Ten thousand dollars," she muttered. "They might as well have said a hundred thousand."

"Not true. Between the three of us, we can come up with it."

"I could kill your father."

"Me too." Not that I wanted to start this conversation again. There was no point to it. What was done was done. The man had fucked us all over time and time again, despite having fucked us over the first time by leaving years and years ago. Little had we known, he'd taken copies of our birth certificates and social security cards to use as a financial credit free-for-all. It had left all three of us not only broker than shit, but also in the credit score basement. Meaning... we couldn't get a medical loan, and we didn't have credit cards.

I held the door open for her and followed her across the parking lot to our car.

Mom was still clicking. "They said he can get another couple of blood transfusions to give us time to save up. Six months maybe."

"Yeah." I opened the door for her and closed it once she was settled. I didn't trust her not to accidentally shut her long skirt in the door and drag it down E. Colfax Avenue. "I've got some things in the works with potential sponsors, but if it doesn't work out..."

I didn't want to say it out loud, but it was time to face facts.

"I meant to tell you I got my job at Bolt's back."

"Oh honey. I hate that you have to give up the Instagram thing to bartend again," she said. "But maybe Bolt would let me take some of your shifts in addition to—"

"*No.*" Not only no, but hell no. Our mother already worked her ass off at a med spa doing laser hair removal. In our tiny town of Caswell, Colorado, it was considered a good-paying job. And it was. But after losing her house and car to her asshole deadbeat ex-husband, the money didn't go as far as it used to. Now she had a car payment on an older Prius and rent on her own damned house that was now owned by a real estate investor.

I chose not to correct her when she called my social media company an "Instagram thing" because I knew she didn't fully understand social media content and the concept of influencers. Jackson did. I'd created plenty of content for the website of the coffee shop and bakery he owned with his best friend, Marchie. They'd gone through a sales slump when a diner opened up nearby, so I'd talked them into letting me take over their social media channels for a little while to help. It had really worked, enough that they'd started paying me to keep me on long after the sales slump was over. Now it was an effort not to spend more time on their accounts than my own, since theirs was a paying job with a steady income while mine was just a wing and a prayer at this point.

I'd even considered starting a brand-awareness and content business instead of trying to build my own influencer brand, but that would be like saying goodbye to my pursuit of acting altogether, and I wasn't ready to do that at the age of twenty-nine. Yeah, I knew my time for breaking into the business was running out, but I still loved performing with everything I had. I was desperate to find a way to do it. My dream of being in the entertainment business went practically back to the womb.

"You doing okay, sweetheart?" Mom's concern turned to me since Jackson was no longer there to focus on. "I know seeing your brother like this can't be easy."

"He's going to be fine. Last time they gave him a transfusion he was as good as new." I didn't mention it hadn't lasted, but at least he'd be able to work again and he'd look less like a skeleton and more like the old Jackson.

"Yeah." She blew out a breath and plastered on a smile. "Yeah, you're right. He's strong and we have time. All we need to do is be really careful with our expenses and try to get creative. The good news is, work is picking up since we're getting closer to bathing suit season. You wouldn't believe how packed the appointment book is." As she continued to catch me up on work, I opened the door to the restaurant for her and followed her to take our place in the order line just as my phone rang.

I glanced down to see it was my best friend, Eli. He'd been researching what new tires I should get for my brother's car since I was shit at anything having to do with cars and one of Eli's brothers was a mechanic. Even though it would be a bitch of a drive to meet up with him, I hoped he could get me a good deal on the set.

After I asked my mom to order for me and handed her my wallet, I stepped back outside to take his call.

"Hey, bud," I said. "How's Crystal? She pregnant yet?" He was more in love with his favorite mare than his girlfriend.

His warm laughter came through the line. "No. Shut the fuck up. That damned horse I put her with must be shooting blanks. I need to look into alternative plans."

"Too bad you can't be the donor. That would be perfect." I

grinned, picturing his wide smile and warm brown eyes set in a weather-worn face. A face just like every other good-looking man in his family, including one that flashed in my mind's eye damned near every night whether I wanted it to or not. *I will not think of Nine. I will not think of Nine.*

"Yeah, yeah. You're not the first person to make that joke. But listen, that's not why I'm calling." He took a breath and blew it out. "I know this is gonna sound crazy, but my brother Nine has this, uh, tool company who's been calling him about a sponsorship for his YouTube stuff."

Dammit.

"Okayyy...?"

"Yeah, so anyway, apparently this company needs to find some, uh, gay people." I could hear the sound of him swallowing. Despite being my best friend outside of my family, Eli had never been all that comfortable about my sexuality. "It's only offering the sponsorship to the LBG...L...Q... community. Or whatever."

"Why does it surprise me you doubled up on the lesbians and left out the poor trans folks?" I teased.

"What? Oh. Yeah, you know I don't know much about all that stuff."

His words started sinking in. "Wait. Are you saying Nine is LGBTQ?"

"What? No! No. That's not what I'm saying at all. Christ."

I rolled my eyes and wanted to call him out on his homophobic freak-out, but I bit my tongue. "Then get to the point. I'm about to have lunch with my mom."

"I thought maybe you could help him pretend."

A car honked at the red light out on the main road, distracting me for a beat. "Pretend what?"

"To be gay. For the money."

"Wait. Wait. You want me to help your asshole, weirdo brother—the one who hates me by the way—pretend to be gay so he can defraud a company of YouTube ad money?"

Silence for a second. "You don't have to make it sound like that.

All you'd have to do is help him renovate a little cabin in the woods and take video of it for his video blog."

That didn't sound right. "Help him renovate? That's it? What's the catch? And how does this make Nine LGBTQ?"

"Well, I mean... I kind of told them you two were a couple, so you'd have to pretend—"

I cut him off. "No. *No*. Wait... *you* told them?"

Eli was quiet for a minute. "I... kind of snuck the guy's phone number and pretended to be Nine's agent. It's cool though. The guy was really excited about it, and as soon as I—"

"Excited about your straight cowboy brother and a noticeably not-straight actor from LA and pretending to be in love and also particularly handy with power tools. Is that about the sum of it?"

"Uh, yeah?"

"Dude, even if I was up for it, there's no way in hell your brother would agree to it." I thought of those chocolate-brown eyes that reminded me of the baby cows on their family's farm. Suddenly, I remembered the one sure thing about Isaac Winshed.

He never said no to someone in need.

Eli made a noise of disagreement. "Are you kidding? He's already agreed. That kid once gave his brand-new sleeping bag—the one he'd gotten for his birthday so he could go on the Boy Scout camping trip —to our local pastor after a reading of Matthew's gospel about hospitality. He wanted Father Bryant to give it to someone in need."

That sounded like the guy I knew. Honestly, their entire family was pretty generous as a rule, but there was something specifically selfless about the youngest brother. "I find it hard to believe there's a homeless problem in Wheatland, Wyoming," I said.

Eli chuckled. "Which is why the bag turned up on the front porch the following day with a note from Father Bryant telling him a couple of Saturday mornings helping weed the flower beds at the senior home would be more appreciated. Said Matthew also did a bit in the gospel about flowers in the field or some shit. Nine lapped it up. Hell, he's probably still in charge of keeping those flower beds weed-free."

I needed to spend time with a sexy *straight* do-gooder like I needed a hole in the head.

I sighed. "The answer is no. Forget it. And why me?" The minute the question was out of my mouth, I knew the answer. I was the only gay person they thought they knew. "Never mind. The answer is still no. Hell no."

Just as I was yanking the restaurant door back open and considering hanging up on him, his voice cut through the line again.

"Even if it paid you twenty thousand dollars for only a summer's work?"

I froze in place. My sneakers made an awful screeching sound on the tile floor, causing my mom to look up at me. She looked exhausted and worried, the way she'd looked for months now. She was working her fingers to the bone to try and provide my brother with his best chance at a long and healthy life.

Twenty thousand dollars. *Twenty thousand dollars*. I could pay for Jackson's surgery and still have enough left over to commit to my own business full-time. I could buy new camera equipment and costumes for the impressions and skits I did.

My brain was going a mile a minute. I sure as hell wasn't going to stand on my high horse while my brother was in a hospital bed. Belatedly, I realized Eli was still talking.

"And I'm waiting for one more estimate before I'll have information on the tires for you."

I nodded. "Oh, yeah. The tires."

"And you'll think about the thing with Nine?"

Isaac. His name is Isaac.

"Yeah. I'll think about it."

But of course, there was nothing to consider. If I could get my hands on the money for Jackson's surgery, I was all in. I had to be.

Even if it meant spending time with Isaac Fucking Winshed.

3

NINE

My hands shook and my T-shirt was plastered to my lower back with sweat despite my truck's air-conditioning being turned up to full blast for the past five hours. Even though it was June and he had a full fur coat, poor Nacho was probably frozen solid in the back seat. He'd be relieved when he was finally able to hop out and run free at the cabin.

The team at Stallion had been a little vague about the property. They'd mostly just said it was a mountain cabin set on a hundred acres near the White River National Forest that needed a makeover. The idea was for Cooper and me to spend the summer turning an old hunter's cabin into a luxury retreat while vlogging the process as the gay couple we were. Rather, as the gay couple they *thought* we were.

Which was why I'd spent the past two weeks unable to eat. The very idea of pretending to be gay made me feel extremely uncomfortable. But doing it in front of Cooper? How the hell was I supposed to do that when I barely even knew the man?

Another reason I was deeply uncomfortable was because I'd been having thoughts. Lots of thoughts. Ever since my family had pointed out my lack of relationship experience, I'd thought back through the last ten years and second-guessed everything. I remembered going to the rodeo when I was fourteen and getting a boner when I saw the cowboys in chaps. But I'd also gotten a boner that weekend in church when the choir sang, so that wasn't saying much. Then there was the time I caught myself staring at the men's baseball team in their uniform pants in high school when they walked past me in the parking lot to the game field. I remembered thinking how amazing their bodies had looked, but at the time I'd thought it was a kind of appreciation and envy, not like... not like perving on them or whatever.

But I also had to agree to not being all that thrilled by girls necessarily. At least, not as much as my brothers always seemed to be. It was always "boobs" this and "hooters" that. And talk like that made me uncomfortable. Still did. I'd had some nice women friends over the years, but none I'd really wanted to do things with all that much. It had gotten to the point where I simply thought maybe I wasn't as sexual as the next guy. Maybe I was missing something that they all had, or perhaps I was what my grandma called a "late bloomer." As long as I was still in my twenties, I hadn't worried too much about it. I wasn't sure who in Wheatland would want a hardware store clerk as a husband anyway, so what was the point?

Thinking about Cooper though... well, that did something to me. It made me annoyed, mostly, but for some reason that annoyance made itself known through what I'd begun to think of as "angry dick." Yes, thoughts of arguing with Cooper made me hard. And since I was fixing to spend the entire summer sleeping near, fighting with, and pretending to kiss and hug the man, this was going to be a problem.

"Keep it together," I grumbled under my breath. Nacho's ears perked up in the rearview mirror. "Oh, not you, baby. You're fine. Go back to sleep. Daddy's just having a sexuality crisis, no big."

I remembered one time when Cooper was staying over during a spring break, I'd come home late from helping a neighbor fix his tractor shed and run right into Cooper pouring himself a glass of ice water in the darkened kitchen. He'd been standing there in nothing but navy-striped boxer briefs, and I'd stared at him like he was some kind of alien.

"Nine," he'd said slowly. "Didn't know you were out this late."

I'd glanced my fill of his entire body, curious more than anything about what another man outside my family looked like without his clothes on. Since I'd helped my dad on the farm and worked at Walt's, I hadn't played school sports and had the locker room experience like some others had.

I remembered the air getting weird between us and his underwear getting bulgier as we stood there. Had it been possible he was getting hard for me? I'd known he was gay, but this was something else.

"Uh, yeah," I'd croaked. "Was working at the farm next door. Sorry." I'd scooted past him and raced for my room, kicking myself for apologizing for being in my own damned kitchen. After that, every time I'd seen Cooper I hadn't been able to help but look at his fly to see if he was getting hard for me again. It had been this inappropriate addiction I'd had that had pissed me the hell off and started the odd discord between us. Was it ego? Did I really care if some gay guy found me attractive?

So yeah. I was sweating buckets and probably going to puke and faint at the same time the minute I saw him at the renovation cabin. Super-duper.

When I finally pulled off the deserted mountain highway and onto the road where the property was located, I wrenched my truck into Park and upchucked into the weeds at the side of the forest. Nothing like christening a new place with a little vomit.

Nacho whimpered and whined from the half-open window, so I waved my hand at him to let him know I was still alive. I used some napkins from the side pocket to wipe my mouth and then swished with water from my water bottle. Finally, I popped in some mint gum from the console and tried to take a deep breath. At least now I wasn't going to puke when I saw Cooper.

Not many people knew I'd never been out of the state of

Wyoming, and I didn't need to give the guy more reasons to think I was weird.

I made my way several more miles until I found the gravel turnoff marked only with a tiny black sign and the handprinted number 6793 on it. The truck bumped its way down the overgrown drive and around a corner shaded by large, overhanging pine trees. When I finally came to a break in the trees, I legit snorted.

This wasn't a hunter's cabin. It was a ramshackle mess made up of half-rotten old timber and hope. There was no way I was going to be able to rebuild this place if the only help I had was a preening actor who probably thought framing referred to taking the perfect selfie rather than creating the wall structure of a house.

We were in a shit ton of trouble.

Once I got clear of the trees, I saw a shiny new beige and brown RV off to the left, parked along the edge of the forest. I knew from the emails that had flown back and forth that Stallion had arranged for Cooper to pick up the RV so we'd have somewhere to live while we worked on the cabin. I'd stupidly thought it was a luxury they were offering to sweeten the deal, but now I wondered if it hadn't been a necessity since the cabin wasn't livable.

I parked the truck and let Nacho out. He took off like a bumblebee, buzzing from tree to tree sniffing everything he could get his nose on. Meanwhile the door to the RV opened and there stood the man I hadn't seen in at least two years.

He looked taller than I remembered, but that was probably just the smaller door of the RV making him look like a giant. The last time he'd been to visit Eli, Cooper had come up to my nose almost exactly. I was a big guy, so that probably made him a little shy of six feet. The sun hit him full-on, lighting up his bronze skin and picking up coppery bits in his brown hair. He wore old jeans that looked like they'd been sculpted to his body after years of constant use. Slices of bare skin peeked out from frayed holes here and there, and my eyes traced over them like I needed to map them to memory for some reason.

I blinked and shook my head before turning back to the truck to get something, anything, to keep myself busy while I caught my breath.

"Well, hello to you too."

His voice was laced with its usual humor. For some reason, hearing it reminded me of the time he told a story about finding a litter of kittens in a cardboard box backstage in a community playhouse. He'd described how each kitten was a different color, and it had brought home how terrible he was in science class since he couldn't wrap his head around how two cats could produce four different color kittens. My whole family had been in tears of laughter listening to him tell the story just like they always were when Cooper was around. He was the kind of guy who stole the show. When he was around, the oxygen left the room and the rest of us struggled to breathe.

"Mpfh," I replied. After grabbing the duffle bag with my clothes in it, I headed toward the door of the RV. "We staying in here?"

What? Of course we were staying in here. Where else would we be staying? *Idiot.*

The corner of his mouth quirked up which drew my eyes to his lips. They were full and surrounded by the dark whiskers of late-day stubble even though it was only noon. It looked good on him, but then again, Cooper always knew he was a good-looking guy. I was honestly surprised Hollywood hadn't gone nuts for him. At the very least I would have thought he'd be discovered by a model scout or something.

"Yeah, *Nine*. We're staying in here. Unless you wanted to sleep with the termites and possums? Guy like you probably loves sleeping in nature, what with that Grizzly Adams thing you've got going on these days."

I felt my nostrils flare. Not all of us were as blessed with good looks as the jackass in front of me. Some of us had to disguise our ugly mugs with thick beards and shaggy hair. Just because I wasn't some kind of movie star like most of the other people he knew, didn't mean—

"Stop standing there and get in here. I need you to open a jar for me. If I do it, I might break a nail."

I glanced back up at him in surprise. "Oh, you think your manicure is going to survive this mess? That's adorable."

He glared at me, but I could see the hint of a smirk underneath. The apples of his cheeks reddened in frustration. "Believe me, it brings me no joy whatsoever to ask you for help. But if I don't have a pickle with my sandwich, my entire day is going to go to shit. I can just feel it."

He stepped back to let me enter the place, and the first thing I noticed was how expensive everything looked. The RV was clearly brand-spanking-new. The seats were a buff leather, and the floors were a laminate made to look like hardwoods. The kitchen appliances gleamed and the entire place had that new-car smell. I wondered how long that would last with two sweaty men and a dirty dog living in it.

After tossing the duffle on the nearest captain's chair, I turned to him and rubbed my hands together. "Muscles ready for action."

As soon as the words were out of my mouth, I felt my cheeks incinerate. Cooper's eyebrow shot up and he opened his mouth, no doubt to say something snarky, but I growled a warning before he had a chance to get it out.

He laughed and turned to the small kitchen area where it looked like he'd been in the middle of unpacking groceries. I spotted the jar of pickles next to a pair of half-made sandwiches and popped it open on the first attempt with no problem.

Cooper stared at me. "That's it? Just like that?"

I shrugged. "Just like that." I moved past him to check out the rest of the RV. As I brushed against his side, I caught a whiff of something medicinal. Suddenly, I remembered my manners. "Shit, how's your brother. I'm sorry. I didn't think to ask."

Cooper turned to me in surprise. "Oh, uh... yeah. He's doing okay. He got a blood transfusion which will help him get back to work for a little while. Thanks for asking. I would have gotten here sooner if I hadn't wanted to drive him home from the hospital this morning."

I nodded and peeked into the bedroom. There was a huge king-sized mattress in the back, and Cooper had already thrown his stuff all over it. I guess I was sleeping on the sofa. "Eli said he's been sick for a while. Is that why you moved back home from California?" I asked, turning back toward the kitchen area.

His body seemed to tense at my question, and I realized it was really none of my business. When he didn't answer right away, I muttered, "Sorry. Just trying to make conversation."

"No, it's fine. Yeah, um, my mom's on her own, so..."

I began opening cabinets to see if there was room to store everything we had. There were several bags of groceries in the back of my truck too. "So you planning to go back there after this?"

The space was so tight, I could feel the air move every time he shifted on his feet as he made the sandwiches. Beneath the scent I now suspected was hospital hand soap, a smell I remembered from when my sister gave birth to my nephew last year, I also detected something unexpected. Gardenia. I'd spent the summer of my freshman year in high school planting gardenia bushes all around our house because my mom couldn't get enough of the smell. She'd gotten a perfume sample at the mall that had the same scent and had decided she wanted the yard filled with it every summer. Why in the world did this man smell like gardenia?

Didn't matter. What did I care what he smelled like? What a ridiculous thought.

"Don't know. Hopefully something big will come out of this, and that will determine where I go. But I at least need to be here in Colorado when Jacks has his procedure since I'm the donor."

I shouldn't have asked him such personal questions. It really wasn't any of my business, and I'd sort of decided not liking him was probably for the best. If I learned too much about him being a nice guy, that wouldn't help all the angry dick problems I was having.

I headed toward the door, intent on checking out the cabin and leaving the man to his lunch when he surprised me.

"Here." He held out one of the sandwiches partially wrapped in a paper towel. The sandwich was made out of thick wheat bread and had layers and layers of meats and cheeses in it. It looked delicious.

I couldn't believe he was offering me half his lunch. "For me?"

Cooper's smile was like the bright beam of the sun bursting out from behind dark clouds. It nearly blinded me. "Yeah, for you. It sure as hell isn't for Nacho out there. Last time I gave him a sandwich—which wasn't voluntary, mind you—he nearly killed me with dog farts. I'm not risking a repeat while we're in close quarters like this."

I couldn't help but let out a chuckle as I reached for the sandwich and murmured my thanks.

"He laughs, ladies and gentlemen," Cooper murmured with a grin. "Imagine that."

4

COOPER

I was well and truly fucked. Isaac "Nine" Winshed was the sexiest bear of a man I'd ever laid eyes on. The minute he'd stepped out of that truck with his thick, dark beard and overgrown hair flipping up over his ears, my dick had gone straight for him. He wore a soft-looking flannel shirt open over a white undershirt. The button-down was rolled up over muscular forearms that were somehow bronze already even after a winter spent stocking shelves inside Walt's Hardware.

The jeans hugging his beefy thighs had a job I'd pay big bucks for. They cupped his package like a lover and ran all forty inches down his damned legs to edges frayed over beat-to-hell work boots.

This was not the awkward gangly teenager I'd first met when I'd spent freshman year winter break at the Winshed house. That kid had been awkward and damned near silent. He'd spent more time in the barn than the house. He'd barely made eye contact with the members of his own family, much less me. And when I'd come back again and again through the four years of college, he'd only grown oddly flippant and distant toward me. He'd gone from meek and sweet to full of barely restrained attitude. If he even bothered to talk to me at all, it was to say something passive-aggressive like how beneficial a drama degree was or how helpful my observation of the fence repair was to morale. When I'd pointed out my lack of knowledge of repairing farm fences, he'd smiled sweetly and muttered something about using my drama degree to *act* like a helpful farmhand.

The last time I'd seen him, he'd been barely legal to get into the local roadhouse with his brothers and me to drink a few beers. Now here he was, all grown up and stroking all the lumberjack fantasies I'd never known I'd had.

Was it okay to want to punch him *and* fuck him? Because I wanted to do both. *Hard*.

I bit into my sandwich as he took his outside to wander around. I could see him through the window over the sink. Nacho pranced around him trying to lure him into sharing a bite of his sandwich. The early-afternoon sun dappled through the trees, laying out a path of lighter spots here and there for him to follow toward the hellhole we'd been tasked with renovating.

The place was a disaster. We'd for damned sure been baited and switched by someone at Stallion Tools. They'd told us that the property had been previously used as a hunting cabin, but it looked like the last hunters to use it had been hunting wild buffalo on the plains with bows and arrows. I'd taken one peek inside and scampered back to the land of the living. I had a feeling I was going to be spending plenty of time hugging the modern facilities of this RV and praising Stallion's generosity for arranging it for us.

A loud whistle blasted through the air. My eyes shot to Nine's face and noticed the thumb and forefinger in his mouth I recognized as the Winshed Whistle position. It bugged the shit out of me when Eli did it, but I sure as hell wasn't going to let Nine summon me that way. I wasn't a dog.

I continued eating my sandwich.

The whistle rent the silence again, making me jump and knock the mayo-covered knife onto the pristine floor with a clatter.

"Cut that shit out!" I shouted as I leaned down to pick up the knife. "I'm not your beck-and-call boy!"

I tossed the knife in the sink and cleaned up the splotch of mayo from the floor with a paper towel. Then I went back to eating my sandwich with shaking hands and my shoulders up to my ears.

Sure enough, that fucker turned right around and stared at me through the window as he whistled one more time. Now my nerves were on edge, and every molecule of my being wanted to obey and go to him. I refused. That would set a precedent that would doom me from day one.

"Knock it off," I cried. Nacho's ears perked up at my voice, and he took off at a lope toward the RV, his happy smile wide enough to allow his tongue to loll out one side. He was going to love living in the woods all summer. I could only imagine the mischief that dog was going to get up to.

"Hi, baby," I cooed, leaning down to scratch his ears. "Miss me? Did you miss me, sweet boy? Yes you did."

By the time Nine gave up his alpha male bullshit and came back inside, I was on the floor in full-on dog snuggle mode.

"Have a little pride," Nine muttered. "Don't you know where that tongue has been?"

Before I could defend my love for his dog, Nine met my eyes with a smirk and finished his sentence. "Nacho."

"The man's a comedian, everyone," I said with an eye roll. "I'll have you know this tongue hasn't been anywhere in a very, very long time."

Time stood still for a moment while we locked eyes. Why had I said that? It was none of his business. Now I sounded like a loser.

"Not for lack of opportunity," I added stupidly.

Shut up.

"Good to know. And here I was wondering what your tongue had been doing." He narrowed his eyes at me. "Not. Feel free to keep your sex life details to yourself."

I felt a flip in my gut. He'd never been overtly homophobic to me, but I needed to remind myself he was from small-town Wyoming. Nine and Eli's family was traditional, salt-of-the-earth Christian conservative. They hunted on Saturday and praised Jesus on Sunday. Even though Eli had never been intentionally homophobic toward me, it was still obvious his upbringing had tons of built-in ignorance regarding anything LGBT related. It was a detail that could really come back to bite us in our current situation.

I returned his glare. “Considering you *are* my sex life right now, I don’t think I’m going to keep it to myself.”

The surprise on his face was comical, as if he’d just now put two and two together to realize it added up to sex. “We’re dating, remember? You’re my boyfriend and we’re in love. Two little lovebirds renovating a cabin in the woods for their luxury love nest.” I stepped closer to him until our chests almost brushed. Nine sucked in a breath as I leaned in and drew the tip of my index finger down the center of his chest. “Right, sweetie?”

He made a choking sound in his throat that almost made me bark out a laugh. I bit my tongue instead and turned around to gather my composure. I hadn’t expected to notice the warmth of his body through his cotton undershirt or the muted crinkle of what had to be thick, delicious chest hair beneath the fabric.

I squeezed my eyes closed for a second and reminded myself that straight men usually didn’t take kindly to flirty gay guys, even if it was clearly a joke. Even though Nine was a giant guy with jacked-up muscles, I knew enough about him to know he’d never hurt me. Nine Winshed had a reputation in Wheatland and in the Winshed family for being a gentle giant. If they hadn’t already given him the nickname “Nine,” they would have called him Snow White because of how damned sweet he was with animals and how much he loved being outside with them.

But everyone had their limits. I knew from experience not to make assumptions, and to be honest, it wasn’t like I knew Nine *that* well. He wasn’t much of a talker on his best day, and even Eli had told me he kept himself to himself mostly. I couldn’t imagine that. I was the opposite. In fact, the idea of spending all summer stuck out in the middle of this godforsaken place with only a repressed lumberjack for company was depressing as hell.

Keep your eye on the prize.

I needed the money this job would bring. Stallion had made us a very lucrative offer with bonuses and accelerators based on how big we could grow our subscribership for the vlog. Hopefully Nine was as money motivated as I was because I was going to work this opportunity for everything I was worth. My goal was to blow the roof off the income potential of this. I wanted my brother taken care of. I wanted my mom's house back. And I wanted the opportunity to start a new chapter. This vlog was my chance at the kind of exposure and freedom I hadn't been able to find in LA.

I took a breath and pulled my phone out of my pocket. "Speaking of our relationship. I think we should make our first post right now and get this party started."

After nudging him back out the door to the RV and into the clearing between the RV and the rubble pile formerly known as a cabin, I positioned him the way I wanted. "Okay, stay right there."

I turned around and backed up against him until my back rested against his front. His entire body tensed. I leaned my head back against his shoulder and reached for one of his hands to pull it around my waist in an embrace. It was like trying to mold a brick of stubborn ice. "Relax," I muttered. "I'm not going to take advantage of you."

"Nfh."

His grunt made me laugh, so I took the opportunity to capture it on film, clicking my phone while trying to make sure the rubble pile was also in the frame. Even on my small phone screen, I could see Nine's discomfort.

"Act like you're not disgusted by me, you oaf." Now he was starting to piss me off. "This is never going to work if you look like you'd rather be having dental surgery than touching me."

I felt the warm air of his exhale against the side of my neck seconds before his beard brushed the same spot. He nuzzled into my neck with his beard and his lips, nearly bringing me to my knees with shock and pleasure. I hoped to god that tiny whimper was only in my head.

"You smell like pickles," he murmured against my neck. "I like pickles."

My breathing came in short, shallow pulls as his arm tightened around my middle and the bulky fly of his jeans brushed against my ass.

Oh dear god.

"Me too," I breathed.

"You too what?" he asked.

"Like pickles. A lot." I closed my eyes and begged for strength. "A lot, a lot. Like… a lot."

What was I even talking about right now?

The deep rumble of his laughter vibrated against my back just before he stepped away and turned to walk toward the rubble. "I think you got enough shots for now. Let's see what we've got."

I watched the round globes of his ass being lovingly attended to by those jeans as he walked away. He'd stripped off the flannel, leaving only the tight, white undershirt. It highlighted the massively wide shoulders and every rounded muscle in his back leading down to his narrow waist and championship ass. The man was god's definition of masculine perfection.

Okay, he was at least *my* definition of it. I couldn't look away. My dick was as hard as the sturdy pine trees at the edge of the forest.

His gruff voice snapped me out of my lumberjack fantasy. "Stop staring at my ass, and get over here with that camera."

"I was only looking at your ass because you sat in something brown," I said. "Looks like you shat yourself. It's disgusting."

He looked back over his shoulder to see if I was joking. And that's when it happened.

Nine's eyes traveled down my body like the hands of an attentive lover before landing on my dick and staying there for a long moment. When his eyes moved back up to meet mine, they were filled with undeniable heat. I couldn't breathe. My throat had turned to dust, and my heart didn't know how to beat. What the fuck was happening?

"Based on the state of your blue jeans," he drawled, "I don't think you find me disgusting at all. Now get your ass over here and start taking pictures. *Sweetie.*"

5

NINE

The cabin wasn't as bad as it looked. The structure was sound, and I realized my first impression had been based on some rotten boards on the fascia over the front door and the disintegrating shutters blocking the front windows. The windows were broken, of course, which had reminded me the first thing I needed to do was make a list of things that needed to be ordered. Windows would take time to get here.

I spent a couple of hours walking around with a pencil and a notebook while Cooper got started creating our social media accounts. We'd emailed back and forth a little bit to hash out some essential details before arriving here. Of course, I wanted to stick to YouTube only, but Cooper had insisted on doing an Instagram account too. Since that was the platform he was trying to build a following on for his own career, I couldn't deny him that opportunity. Plus, I figured I could take the lead on the vlogging and video while he handled most of the still photos and Instagram.

Since I didn't much care about the details of things like branding and whatnot, I stayed outside and got to work on the important stuff while he gave the internet hotspot a workout. I still couldn't believe the money Stallion had been willing to spend on this project.

They'd supplied us with the RV which had solar panels and a generator for electricity, a pair of mobile hotspots for Wi-Fi, an open credit line at the nearest home supply store which was about forty minutes back the way I'd come, and a giant stack of new camera and video equipment that was currently stashed in the lockbox in the back of my truck. It was such high-end stuff, I was almost too scared to use it.

Instead, I sketched out the dimensions of the cabin and began taking stock of what we had to work with. At one point, Cooper came to find me.

"Thought you might be thirsty, and I made some lemonade."

I glanced up at him in the dim, shadowy light filtering through one of the cabin's broken windows. "Oh, uh, thanks. Yeah. That's nice."

He stepped forward and held out an insulated water bottle. "I put it in here with some ice in case you were planning on being out here for a while longer."

He looked unsure of himself which wasn't at all like the cocky Cooper Heath I knew. I took the bottle from him, unscrewed the cap, and took a long swig. It tasted amazing. "God, that's good. Thank you."

"It's just a powder mix. Nothing special. I'm not a fan of plain water, so I have a bunch of different flavors of the sugar-free mixes."

Was he babbling?

He turned in a circle like he couldn't decide to stay or bolt. "Anyway, that's all. I just wanted to—"

"Wait." Suddenly I didn't want him to leave. "There's an ice maker in that thing?"

"What? Oh, yeah. Totally cool. It's connected to the drinking water line I guess. I don't know much about RVs, but the guy gave me a kind of training session when I picked it up. There's also a big-ass instruction manual if we need it."

I took another sip. "I just need to know how to work the shower and turn the sofa into a bed and I'm all set."

Cooper's brow crinkled. "What sofa?"

"You know, RVs always have like a sofa that turns into an extra bed. Don't they?"

"Well, maybe. But this one doesn't. It has recliners."

I remembered seeing the big leather captain's chairs in front of the flat-screen television. "Shit. Where am I supposed to sleep?"

He shrugged. "Well, the banquette turns into a bed for a toddler. I think it's about five feet long. Maybe you could try that."

"I'm six four. Didn't you think to ask them for the kind that had an extra bed in it?"

Cooper placed a hand on his hip. "Yeah. So my *boyfriend* and I could keep a healthy distance from each other at night. No, Nine. I didn't tell them we needed separate beds. I assume it's hard enough for the folks at Stallion to believe their beloved lumberjack poster boy is actually queer, and any evidence to the contrary might not be a great idea."

Uh-oh. Now he was pissed.

"Fine. I'll sleep outside."

His jaw dropped. "I don't have fucking rabies, you asshole. It's a giant king-sized bed. I thought we could share it. But if you'd rather sleep outside with the wolves and bears, then by all means."

Before I knew it, he'd stormed out.

Shit. I'd only meant that… I hadn't wanted to impose on him and assume we'd…

I sighed. The truth was, there was no way I could imagine myself sharing a bed with Cooper. I didn't even want to share a bed with one of my own brothers. How the hell was I supposed to wake up with morning wood next to a guy who… who… And what if he had morning wood too? What if our morning woods… touched?

I felt my dick begin to act out the scenario. Not helpful.

"Isaac!" Cooper's terror-filled scream shot through the cabin. I bolted out of the small space and into the fading sunlight. Cooper stood in the center of the clearing staring at the open RV door. His hands were propped on his knees, and he was practically hyperventilating.

"What? What is it?" I put him behind me and kept my eyes in that direction, expecting a bear or a mountain lion, or something else equally threatening rattling around inside. I'd brought my rifle, but it was still in the truck's locked storage box and my keys were on the RV's kitchen counter.

"There's a bat in there." His voice shook. "Fuck! There's a giant fucking bat in there." He shuddered. "It came right at me like it wanted to eat me or something. It fucking touched me, and now I'm going to have to burn my clothes and my skin. Bats have rabies, don't they? Do I have to get shots in my stomach now? Shit. If I have to do the shots in my stomach because some bitch-ass flying demon did a drive-by on my face, I'm going to—"

I poked my head in the RV. All was quiet for a minute until I caught movement from the front windshield area.

It was a tiny brown sparrow clearly terrified and trying to escape through the large clear window.

"C'mere, little one," I murmured, trying to get close enough to cup him between my hands. But he was too frantic for that. I finally found one of the paper shopping bags and flattened it. After closing the bedroom and bathroom doors, I returned to the front of the RV and used the bag to direct the bird out the main door. It took a little while, but it finally worked.

When the little sparrow flapped its way out the front door, Cooper let out another squawk of fear. I laughed at him from the doorway.

"Dude, it was a tiny songbird. Hardly the grim reaper. And I can assure you if you have rabies, it's not from Tweety Bird over there. That poor baby was terrified."

Cooper threw up his hands. "Thank you, Steve Irwin. New rule. The RV door stays closed at all times. If I wake up with wildlife all up in my business, we're going to have a problem."

This was the Cooper I was familiar with. Prissy and bitchy. Even though he wasn't born and raised a city boy, he may as well have been. The man wouldn't even visit our horses when he stayed with us since he claimed they "gave him the stink eye."

I chuckled. "Something tells me you're going to have a long summer, princess."

He shot me a look. "Not all of us grew up with baby chicks as pets."

He'd use any excuse to bring that story up. "Take that back. Sir Pecks-A-Lot was a faithful companion. I loved her."

Cooper's dimple appeared. I hated to admit I wanted more of it. "She was a chicken. Who lived in your closet. You were fourteen."

"My dad wanted to eat her. What else was I supposed to do? You don't know what it's like developing feelings for an animal whose only purpose is to feed your huge fucking family."

"So when he couldn't find Sir PAL, what happened? Your family just went without dinner?"

I grinned at him. He already knew the answer to this because he'd been there. "He killed Cupcake. Which was fine with me because that chicken was a total bitch."

He threw his head back and laughed. It made me feel light-headed. Maybe I was just happy to give him a lighter moment while he'd been worried about his brother, or maybe I was happy to make anyone laugh for any reason. But it was like a drug. Addictive. I wanted another hit.

"Is the internet stuff working?" I asked. "I need to put in a supply order now that I know what we need."

So much for making him laugh. I wasn't naturally funny. I was naturally boring as hell.

His smile dimmed even though his eyes still danced. "Uh, yeah. It's good. Better than I expected all the way out here."

I nodded and moved back toward the RV. "Then let's get back to work."

"Yes, master," he muttered from behind me. "Whatever you say, master. Even though I just had a near death experience and everything. You should be tucking me into bed and singing that Warm Kitty song. But nooooo, someone wants to get his precious order in. Why, back in my day—"

I didn't hear the rest because I slammed the RV closed between us, shutting him out.

"What the hell?" he shouted from outside.

"You said to keep the RV door closed at all times," I replied. "I don't make the rules."

THAT EVENING after we'd destroyed a couple of rotisserie chickens I'd picked up on the way in, and Cooper had made all kinds of Sir Pecks-A-Lot jokes, we ended up sitting across from each other at the little dinette table with our laptops. I'd already placed the order, but I needed to enter all of the items into a spreadsheet to keep them straight for cost purposes. Cooper was busy working on figuring out a logo for our new brand, and he kept muttering to himself under his breath.

It was kind of endearing.

"Not purple. No one likes purple," he said.

"I like purple."

He didn't bother to look up. "You don't count."

"Mpfh." I went back to my spreadsheet. After a few minutes, I finished that and moved on to typing up a list of projects and tasks that needed to be done first before I could get started on the cabin work itself. If I didn't make a plan, I'd be all over the place and unable to focus.

"I'm going to mount a few cameras around the clearing," I told him.

Cooper finally lifted his head. "What for?"

Was he joking? "For capturing video."

"Of what?"

I rubbed my hands over my face and scratched my fingers through my beard while I swallowed down my initial response.

"Of our work on the cabin. Of our lives here. Of us." He still looked confused. "The *v* in vlogging stands for—"

Cooper shot me a look. "I get it. But I thought we'd just take video as we went along."

I shook my head. "No. We need to time-lapse the entire project from several different angles. That's the video that will bring in the most subscribers. Haven't you seen Shawn James?"

"Who?"

"My Self Reliance? The guy in Canada who hand-built a log cabin by himself and vlogged the whole thing?"

"My YouTube watching is a touch more... shall we say... comedic than that."

I huffed. "Well, watch it. It's a great vlog, and the videography is well-done. I spent some time scrolling through how other people have set up cameras for this type of project, and I sketched out a plan if you want to see it."

"Yeah. I guess that would be a good idea. I wouldn't want to stumble over to a tree to take a piss and not realize it was being recorded for posterity."

I sifted back through my notebook until I found the right page and then shoved the spiral across the table, pointing to the big rectangle in the clearing. "Here's the RV. You actually parked it exactly where it will be the least distracting in the shots, so that's good. I think if we put the three mounts here, here, and here, we'll cover most of the angles we need. I have a drone we can use for the aerial shots, of course, but the main stuff will be shot with this killer Sony camera and a Zeiss lens."

Cooper tilted his head at me and smiled. "Listen to you, chatterbox. Did you accidentally snort some coke or something?"

I felt my face heat. "No, I just... I really like this stuff. It's mechanical, you know? Like tools. Like fixing stuff. Once you learn the settings, it's not as scary. Like when I was little and I picked up my dad's chalk line out of the toolbox. It looked like the weirdest thing ever. How could a chalky rope be useful? But then I saw him snap it on a piece of plywood for the first time, and suddenly I got it. This camera stuff is like that."

Why wasn't I shutting up? And why did this RV seem so small all of a sudden? I could feel the heat from Cooper's legs against mine under the table. Cooper's hand ran lazily through Nacho's coat where the dog lay sprawled on the bench seat with his big golden body pressed against Cooper's hip. Nacho's legs hung off the seat in all directions, but his head was happily propped on Cooper's thigh. He was clearly in heaven.

I clamped my lips together and focused back on the sketch. "Um, so that's about it. I thought when we get some good sunset light, I could do a drone flight over the property and capture some 360-degree views and stuff. People seem to like that."

I could feel Cooper's eyes on me. "How would you know?"

My eyes flashed up to him. Acid popped in my gut as I felt the stirring of angry defensiveness. I wasn't stupid. Plenty of people thought I was because I didn't say much, but I knew stuff.

"Because I run one of the top DIY channels on YouTube," I said angrily. "Asshole."

Oddly, his smile was triumphant. Just what the hell was he playing at?

6

COOPER

Half of me wanted to recoil in fear at the look of anger in the big man's eyes, but half of me wanted to laugh. He was so easy to rile.

"Calm down, Grizzly Adams. I didn't think you paid much attention to things like rank and subscribers."

He clamped his jaw. "I don't."

"Then how do you know what your subscribers like? How do you know how popular your videos are?"

"Because I'm not an idiot. Contrary to what *some* people think."

I sat back and stretched my arms above my head. "I don't think you're an idiot. But I also don't think you're doing as much as you could to boost subscribers and get to the next level."

"Fuck you."

"Nice. Mature. Don't ever let anyone tell you you're not erudite, Isaac Winshed."

Smoke came out of his ears. "This isn't going to work. I don't know what I did to piss you off way back when, but I don't deserve to be treated like I'm stupid." He stood up and moved toward the bedroom before remembering that's where I was going to sleep too. When he had to walk past me to get to the door of the RV, I reached out and grabbed his wrist.

"Wait."

His jaw clenched and he kept looking straight ahead.

"Isaac. I don't think you're stupid. I'm sorry. I went about this all wrong. Will you please sit back down?"

He looked at me with suspicion in his eyes, but he slid back into the booth across from me.

"Thank you. Now, I was trying to make the point that you run a crazy-popular channel without even putting effort into growing your audience. You focus on your videos, your equipment and settings, your instructions and helping do-it-yourselfers, but you don't seem to spend much time growing your business."

"I don't really look at it like a business. I just like making the videos, helping people."

I nodded. "Yes. I totally get that. Up till now, you've done it for fun. But in order for this to work, we have to really push the business side too. So I propose that's how we split the work. You keep focusing on what you were just saying. Frame gorgeous shots—because you do take gorgeous shots—and I will work the popularity angle online. Does that make sense?"

He hesitated before nodding, but he was clearly still skeptical. "But I'm going to need help with the actual renovation work too."

"Well, I have bad news for you. I've never even used a hammer before. Not that I'm not willing to learn."

Heavy sigh. "Shit."

"Yep," I said perkily. "Lucky us. The good news is, I think we can use that."

He lifted an eyebrow. "How do you mean?"

"Well, how cute would it be if my boyfriend had to practice eminent patience while he taught me how to do simple things? People would eat that shit up. Especially if you were all… 'not like that, sweetheart. You turn the screwdriver this way. That's it. I knew you were good at screwing,' wink, wink."

Nine's eyes widened. "Me?" he squeaked. "Saying that? To you?" The high-pitched sound coming from the mountain man made me laugh.

"Unless you're too chickenshit. But if you're going to have a problem pretending to be my boyfriend, you'd better say so now." I acted like I was teasing, but the truth was, I absolutely could not allow him to give up on this. I needed the money from this project. I wasn't about to let him ditch me.

His jaw tightened again. "I don't have a problem, and I'm not a chickenshit."

And then I said something utterly ridiculous. "Then prove you're not a homophobic Neanderthal and share the bed with me for god's sake."

As soon as the words were out of my mouth, I wanted to take them back. What the hell had I been thinking? What if I rolled over and cuddled the shit out of him in my sleep? Or worse... what if I dry humped him?

My heart sped up. What if I *wet* humped him? Oh god. This was a big mistake. Huge.

"Um," I began, frantically searching for a way out of my big mouth's stupid gaffe.

"No, you're right. It's fine. I certainly don't relish the idea of waking up covered in mosquito bites. It's better if I stay inside. Besides, I'm not homophobic. And if you imply I am one more time, I'm going to... to... prove it."

He kind of winced at the stupid conclusion to his rant. Meanwhile, all I could picture was how someone would prove he wasn't homophobic. By kissing me? By letting me suck him off perhaps? By sucking me off?

Fuck.

"Yeah, uh... no proving necessary. Let's just... um..." I swallowed. "Let's go over the accounts I set up today and the logo choices I put together."

He blew out a breath. The tips of his ears were deep red. He was even cuter when flustered. "Yeah. Good."

I turned my laptop around so we could both see it.

"Cooped Up With Nine?" he asked incredulously. "That's what you're calling this?"

"Cute, huh? I thought it was a fun play on our names. Besides, part of what we're going to be vlogging is living together in this small space, right?"

He sighed. "Fine. What else?"

I clicked to another window where I had a selection of logos I'd made. "Do any of these jump out to you? I mean, they're rough, so… if I need to change or try something else…"

The side of his lips curved up and his entire demeanor softened. "Yeah. This one." He pointed to a line drawing I'd done on my iPad of a cute cabin outline and comic versions of us and Nacho standing in the clearing. Nine had his arm around me and was kissing my cheek. A tiny cartoon heart floated up above the kiss. It was by far my favorite too, but I was surprised to see him react so positively to seeing himself embracing me that way.

"Oh. Okay. Yeah. Good. That's done. Now…" I thought of what else I needed to ask him about, but he reached over and grabbed my hand before I could think.

"Coop. That's amazing work. Truly." He looked from the logo up to my eyes. "Do you think we can find someone to animate it to put it at the beginning of each video?"

My heart leaped up at his enthusiasm. "Yeah. Uh. I have a buddy from LA who can probably try it. He works for an animation house there."

"That would be killer. It would look really professional, wouldn't it?" His grin was contagious. Sometimes he seemed like an eager puppy. The man was mercurial as hell, but I kind of liked the unpredictability.

I nodded. "Okay, what's next?"

We continued sorting through plans for a couple more hours until it was nearing midnight. Both of us were probably subconsciously avoiding bedtime, but it had been a long day and I was going to fall asleep on the kitchen table if I didn't move to the bed.

"I'm going to brush my teeth and crawl in bed," I said, nudging Nacho off the bench so I could get out. "Want me to let this guy out for a final pee?"

Nine stretched and slid out of the booth as well. "Nah. I'll take him out while you're in the bathroom. Then I'll get my turn."

Once the two of them were outside, I let out a deep breath. How the fuck was I going to manage this? When I'd first met him, Nine had been a gangly teen, but when he'd graduated from high school, he'd suddenly bulked up and sprouted even taller. That was when I'd taken a different kind of notice of him. Since he was still Eli's kid brother, I'd avoided him like the plague. But now? With that fucking hair and beard and those jacked muscles? How was I supposed to keep myself from climbing him like a tree? He was pure bear, and he even smelled like honey. So help me, if he slept shirtless and had a big chest full of hair, I was going to stroke it whether I wanted to or not.

And I wanted to.

After brushing my teeth and washing my face, I changed into flannel pjs and an old ratty T-shirt. Better to cover everything and look unappealing. As if it mattered at all to Nine. Whatever. If I felt unsexy, maybe it would make me less prone to sexing all over him.

Earlier this afternoon I'd made the bed up from washed sheets my mom had sent along. As I slid between the covers, I smelled the familiar laundry detergent from home. I'd texted Mom and Jacks when I'd arrived, but I hadn't called to check in. Hopefully they were fine. Since Stallion was allowing us to keep the internet hot spot on all the time, I felt more confident that they'd be able to reach me if something came up.

When Nine came back in the RV, I heard him mumble something to Nacho, and the dog raced into the bedroom and launched himself onto the bed with me.

"Hey, buddy." I laughed and leaned down to pet him. "You gonna be our chaperone tonight? Huh?"

Nine poked his head into the small room. "Sorry about that. He's used to sleeping with me. He'll sleep on my feet and shouldn't bother you, but I can kick him off if you want."

"No, no. I like it. It's fine."

He smiled a sweet little smile and turned to squeeze himself into the bathroom. I heard the water in the shower turn on and tried not to picture his big ass naked in that tiny cubicle. Lucky fucking shower stall.

My cock got hard of course. I wondered if there was any possible way I could rub one out really quickly, but before I could even think it through, the water turned off. Stupid RV water conservation. I guessed we weren't going to take long, luxurious showers all summer. Damn.

We're also not having sex all summer.

Oh wow. Now that was a kick in the balls. Maybe there'd be a weekend we could go to town and find some action or something. I wondered if he had a girlfriend back home in Wyoming. Eli had laughed when I'd asked him, but it was possible Nine didn't tell his brother everything.

But if he did, wouldn't she have forbidden him from acting gay with a guy in public like this? What would all of her friends think?

The door opened and some steam billowed out. I'd already turned most of the lights off, so his figure was mostly in shadow. A thick towel wrapped around his waist as he stepped up to the sink to brush his teeth.

His ass bubbled out from his lower back. God was either teasing me or tempting me. Either way, it was mean.

As he shifted the weight on his feet, the towel clung to his flexing glutes. I whimpered just a little bit.

"Hmm?" he asked, turning to look at me with the frothy toothbrush still in his mouth.

I cleared my throat. "Nothing." It came out croaky like a thirteen-year-old saying the word "boobs" for the first time.

His brow furrowed, but he turned back to the sink. Holy fuck was he a specimen of masculinity. His body was muscular as fuck, but I knew he'd probably never entered a gym in his life. Tan lines exposed the truth of his lifestyle. His trunk and shoulders were pale while his arms and neck were dark honey brown. And sure enough, his chest was a pleasure garden of fur for men like me.

I closed my eyes and turned toward the wall, scooting as close as I could to my edge of the bed without tipping onto the floor. When I heard him come closer, he muttered, "Being straight's not contagious, you know."

Did he...? Did that man just make a joke?

I turned to glance at him over my shoulder, and the motherfucker winked at me.

Oh god.

I was going to fall in love with my best friend's straight brother, wasn't I?

7

NINE

One minute I was referring to myself as straight, and the next I was questioning everything I'd ever known about myself.

I lay in bed on my back as stiff as a board, trying like hell not to disturb him. But every single micro-movement he made lit up my entire body. I was hyperaware of him, but not in the way I would have been if I was sharing a bed with one of my brothers. This was different.

Very different.

I wondered what he had on under the covers. I wondered how long it would take before the sheets carried his faint gardenia smell. Most of all, I wondered what it would feel like to spoon someone for the first time. Yes, I'd had sex before, and not just that time with Cherry. I'd been set up on a blind date by one of my sisters two years ago and had dated Lauren Orville for a grand total of one month before she'd realized I was the most boring human being on earth and dumped me for Eric Pender, our local veterinarian. I couldn't blame her. Eric was good-looking and successful. He was the total package, and I was just some guy who worked at a hardware store and was easily lulled to sleep by conversations about makeup contouring and hair highlights.

The sex hadn't been that great with her either, but at least I'd felt a little more sure of myself since I'd had some time to watch porn and whatnot in the intervening years since Cherry.

But now... now my brain went in a thousand different directions. When I'd had sex with Lauren, I hadn't lain there wondering what her lady parts looked like. I hadn't imagined what her naked butt looked like. If pressed, I would have said all butts looked the same. But for some reason, I thought Cooper's butt probably didn't look the same as mine. It probably looked nicer. And from what I could tell by looking at him in his blue jeans, it probably looked nicer than both Cherry's and Lauren's put together.

And I wondered what his dick looked like. Did it look like mine? Kind of thick and ruddy? Or was it whiter, creamier? Was he circumcised? Did he, like... shave down there? Did gay men do that? Manscaping, I thought it was called. Did he manscape? Should I manscape?

"If you don't stop thinking, none of us are ever going to get to sleep."

I turned my head to face him. "Do guys manscape?"

The whites of his eyes shone in the dark room. "Um, I'm sorry. What?"

"Never mind. Forget I said anything. That was stupid." I turned around onto my side and faced away from him. "Good night."

The silence wasn't as uncomfortable as I expected. After a little while, Cooper's warm hand landed on my shoulder, making me jump. "Hey. Turn around. Ask me what you want to know."

I took a breath and turned around. "It's just... I mean, my brothers don't talk about this shit, and I don't really have guy friends or anything. I keep seeing these ads on my channel about something called the Lawnmower, and at first I thought it was an actual lawn mower. But it's not. It's a shaver for like, your dick. And it just made me wonder if all guys are doing something I should be doing."

Thank goodness for the darkness because my face was going to melt off.

Cooper took my question seriously. "This is kind of like asking what kind of clothes you should wear. It's definitely a personal choice, but I would say het guys are probably not as likely to be paying much attention down there as gay guys do. Gay guys run the gamut. Some wax, some shave, some just keep it super-trimmed."

I wanted to ask him what he did, but my throat was too clogged to get the question out. I also didn't want to think about how he knew what so many gay guys did. Had he been with that many people? Had he seen that many dicks?

Cooper shifted closer. "Nine, have you gotten comments from the women you sleep with? Is that why you're asking?"

Ha. As if there was a whole line of them in my past to survey. "No. I just assumed if someone was attracted to me in the first place, they'd know I was... I mean... it's not like it's a secret I have thick hair or anything."

"Do you want to know what I think?"

I swallowed. What if he told me I was disgusting? "I guess."

He leaned across and ran his fingertips through my beard, tugging it a little to make his point. "I think your hair is hot as shit. I think anyone would be an idiot to let a little body hair turn them away, especially when it's this glorious, thick, shiny brown hair. If you ever find someone who's bothered by the way you are, drop them in a skinny minute and look for someone else."

He let go and leaned back. The ghost of his touch lingered in my beard, and his words settled in my chest. I felt more relaxed and began to doze off. Cooper's words broke into my haze.

"Shit. You know what we should have done? A recap post for the day. Like a little video saying what we got done today and how we're feeling about it."

"Mm."

He shifted. "No, for real. Wake back up. We need to do this. You don't ever get Day One back."

"Huh?"

He flicked on the light switch, causing me to grunt and squeeze my eyes closed. "I'll just use my phone and we'll knock it out really quickly. Here, lean in."

I leaned in to the center of the bed. Our heads ended up on the same pillow. I could smell the scent of Cooper's toothpaste breath. Gradually, I was able to open my eyes. "What're we going to say?"

"Leave it to me." He moved closer until his head was on my shoulder, but then he sighed and sat up, pulling my arm out before settling back down in the crook of it with his head on my shoulder again. I wrapped my arm around his shoulder automatically. It felt awkward and strange, but not in a bad way. More in a foreign way.

When he turned the camera image to face us, we looked like a real couple. His wavy hair already looked tousled by the pillows, and my eyes looked squinty with sleep. I wondered what my family would say when they saw me like this with him.

Cooper hit the Record button. "Hi, everyone, Cooper and Nine here. We just wanted to say good night. We spent the evening sketching out plans for the cabin, and Nine placed a big order for supplies. The design looks amazing." He turned to look up at me, and I realized what a good actor he really was. The man looked at me like I was the most precious thing in the world to him.

My breath caught.

He looked relaxed and happy. "You're really talented, babe."

I was frozen in a combination of fear, nerves, and shock. Surely, I looked like I'd just been goosed by a wild monkey. Cooper's laughter rang out while he turned back to the camera. "He's shy, but you already know that about him. He's also humble as hell. My guy's not all that comfortable with praise. We'll have to work on that."

He was so good at this, so natural. He really made it seem like we were a couple. What could I do to help? I didn't know what to do more than lie there and gawp at him.

When he turned his head to smile at me again, I leaned in and pressed a kiss to his forehead, mumbling *thanks*.

Now Cooper looked like the one who'd gotten the monkey treatment. It took him a second to return to normal and face the camera again. "So, ah, yeah. Stay tuned for much more. We traveled today which made for a long, tiring day. All I want to do is snuggle up with this guy and get some good sleep. As you can see, Nacho is already snoring." He panned the phone camera around to show Nacho curled up on my feet. Sure enough, little doggie snores were loud enough for the camera to pick up. I didn't realize I was grinning until he turned the camera back on us.

"G'night, everyone. Say good night, Nine."

I couldn't resist. "Good night, Nine," I said.

He hit the button to end the recording just as he snorted with laughter.

Bright Cooper eyes met mine as his lips still turned up. "That was perfect. We're going to rock this." His smile faded. "Listen... I'm sorry about earlier. About treating you like you were a homophobe. You did great just now, and... and that kiss was... it was good. People will love it." He took a breath. "You did good, Nine."

I clamped my lips together and nodded my thanks. He'd said people would love it, but what about him? Had he loved it? And why did I care? It was a damned peck on the forehead. Hardly a sex move or anything.

He put his phone away and turned off the light again. After a little while, I noticed his breathing had steadied. I turned my head and watched his dark form against the lighter background of the sheets. My lips could still feel the warm, smooth skin of Cooper's forehead. The gardenia smell had come from his hairline, and I wondered if it was a styling product he used. He had Hollywood hair. Probably paid more money for his cut than the ten bucks I paid Big Mike at the Shave Shack. Every time he came to visit my family, I was struck by how fashionable he looked. I'd always chalked it up to some kind of gay thing, but that was shitty of me.

Then I thought maybe it was a Hollywood thing, but I guess that was shitty too. Stereotyping wasn't fair. But whatever it was, I liked it. I liked that his hair was always styled and he seemed so put together with stylish clothes on. He stood out from all the other guys in Wheatland. It was a refreshing change.

I fell asleep to thoughts of him and wound up dreaming about Cooper giving haircuts to thousands of different men. Only, they wanted haircuts to their pubic area too. So he'd cut their hair and then ask them to strip so he could use a mini version of an actual lawn mower to cut patterns into the hair around their dicks. And all the dicks we're different. Light, dark, big, small. Hard, soft. One guy had so much hair, Cooper shaved a design into it until it resembled a family of bats swooping down toward his dick.

When I woke up in the morning, hard as a fucking nail, I was mortified by my brain shenanigans. The only saving grace was the empty bed next to me. Thankfully, there was no witness to my tent pole.

I took several deep breaths to try and get my dick to stand down before I could stumble to the bathroom. When I finally finished getting dressed, I heard the RV door open and Nacho came running. I hadn't even noticed he was gone.

"Coffee's ready," Cooper called from the kitchen area.

I ducked through the little hallway separating us and was surprised to see Cooper handing me a mug of coffee already prepared just the way I liked it. I mumbled a thanks, but I couldn't look him in the eye after my dreams last night.

"Sorry you have to duck in here. That must suck. I told them we needed one with high ceilings, but this was the best they had."

I glanced up at him. "You did?"

He nodded and took a sip of his own coffee. "Yeah. I remembered that time you drove Eli's old Camaro and had to hunch over like a granny."

I carefully stretched to my full height to show him that the ceiling was, in fact, high enough in most areas of the RV. "It's really just the hallway and the bathroom because of the fan. So, uh, thanks. That was nice of you."

He smiled. "Okay, good. That's good. Wouldn't want you to be stiff and cranky all summer." He turned back around to the food he'd set out on the counter. "I'm making eggs and toast. How do you like yours?"

This was the second time he'd offered to feed me. It was nice. I'd kind of envisioned us doing our own thing, but I guess it made sense to work together. More efficient that way.

"Any way is fine. I'm not picky." I took a sip of my coffee and accidentally let out a groan. "Fuck, what'd you put in this? It tastes amazing."

He grinned. "It's just really good coffee. A friend of mine got me hooked on it and sent me a bunch of it when he heard I was going to be living in the backwoods all summer. Oh, and I put flavored creamer in it too."

He went back to cooking while I savored the hot drink and continued waking up. I could tell from the dish on the floor that Cooper had already fed Nacho. I thanked him and then kind of felt awkward when silence fell between us again.

"So, I'm going to set up those cameras after breakfast and then—"

I heard the sound of a picture being taken and glanced up. Cooper finger typed onto the screen and then slipped the phone back in his pocket. "Sorry, continue." He turned to tend to the eggs before reaching over to push the bread in the toaster down.

"What was that for?"

"You just look really cute right now. I wanted to post a pic."

I blinked at the back of his head. "Oh, uh, okay. Um..."

He glanced at me over his shoulder. "You seriously don't know why your subscriber numbers are as big as they are, do you?"

"People like to learn how to make stuff."

He laughed so hard I thought he was going to pull a muscle, and then he didn't say anything until the scrambled eggs and toast were on plates. Once we sat down at the dinette, he reached across and squeezed my arm.

"You're sexy as fuck, big guy. I'll bet if we did a deep dive into your subscribers, we'd see a very small portion of them actually own a hammer. They're probably mostly drooling women and jacking-off gay guys."

I almost choked on my eggs. "No. You have a mixed-up view of the world. You've been in California too long."

He shook his head and dove into his own breakfast. "And you're adorably naive. I will bet you a thousand dollars—which I obviously don't have, so this is symbolic, mind you—that this sleepy beefcake pic gets more likes than the time you posted that handy feet-to-meters conversion trick."

"Pfft."

He shrugged and sipped more coffee. "You'll see. And the comments will be obscene, mark my words."

I grunted. "I don't read the comments." The sound of his laughter was something I could get used to with my morning coffee every day.

"Of course you don't." He took a few more bites of his food before asking, "Did you sleep well?"

I felt my ears go hot, but I kept my eyes on my toast. "Mm-hm. You? You, ah... you... I mean, nothing happened or... I didn't do anything, did I?" I realized how that sounded, so I quickly tried to clarify. "I mean, like hog the bed or kick you...?"

Cooper didn't say anything at first, so I risked a peek at him. His nostrils were flared, and his eyes danced like he was holding back a laugh. "Nine, sweetie. *Baby*. What happened last night, hmmm?"

"What? Nothing."

"Then why did you just eat a forkful of air?"

I looked down at an empty plate and wondered when I'd run out of eggs. "I was pretending you'd cooked me enough eggs," I grumbled.

More laughter. I wanted to bathe in it regardless of how embarrassed I was. Why did he affect me this way when no other man did? When no other *person* did?

Cooper slid out of the booth and came back with two bananas and a piece of string cheese. "Here. I forgot I was feeding a growing boy."

I ripped open one of the bananas and slid it into my mouth, stupidly taking that moment to glance over at him.

He stared at me with his mouth open. For a split second, the moment hung heavy between us. I had a giant banana halfway down my throat, and Cooper was looking at me like I was his next meal.

8

COOPER

I scrambled out of the booth and gave the rest of my breakfast to Nacho. "Welp, lots to do today," I said quickly. "Better make hay while the sun shines."

What the fuck? That was not a phrase I'd ever used in my life.

I was sure if I'd looked back at Nine, he would have been smirking at me for sounding like a cowpoke. Didn't matter. I grabbed my laptop and bolted from the RV, intent on checking out the long, thick log at the edge of the clearing. Apparently everything in my life right now was phallic. Whatever, I planned to use the fallen log as a bench so I wasn't stuck inside all day.

I sat down and got to work, trying desperately to ignore Nine as he began moving around the clearing mounting his cameras. I certainly did not look at his bubble butt when he was up on that ladder.

When he got everything where he wanted it, he pulled out his own laptop and took a spot on the log next to me. I glanced at his screen to see him pulling up remote feeds for the cameras. He spent some time resetting each one until he got it just right. After he returned to the log, he typed some more. It was kind of cute watching his big overgrown frame hunched over the tiny computer. His fingers were like sausages on the delicate keys.

"We should take a video," I said, clearing my throat. "Like... like an introduction of ourselves to our followers. My followers don't know you, and yours don't know me."

He didn't say anything or even look up. His forehead creased as he stared at something on his screen. I felt his entire body tense up right in front of me.

"Are you even listening to me?"

He glanced up at me, and I noticed his scowl was tempered by the worry in his eyes. "Sorry."

"What's wrong?" I scooted over so I could see his screen better. He had his email pulled up, and it was full of vile homophobic slurs from shocked and pissed-off Nine fans. "Oh shit."

"It's fine." He moved the cursor to select the entire column and hit the delete button. "There, gone."

I grasped his arm. "Isaac..."

He shook his head. "No, really. I expected this. I don't even read email from fans normally. In fact, I usually have it set to send any fan emails straight to the trash folder, but... I did this tutorial on how to install window flashing on oddball window shapes, and it was kind of complicated. I told people they could email me if they had trouble with it."

He seemed so deflated. I leaned my head onto his broad shoulder and squeezed his arm even tighter. "You're a good man. I'm sorry you're getting unfairly painted with the gay brush or whatever."

He slammed the top of his laptop a little too hard. "No, dammit. That's not fair. It's not fair that someone can just... can just call you names for being the way you are, whether that's tall or short, or Spanish or Indian, or... or..."

"Gay or straight?" I smiled up at him in hopes of calming him down.

Nine reached up and used the tip of a finger to brush the hair off my eye. "You don't deserve this."

I blinked at him in surprise. "Those aren't my emails."

"No. But all I would have to do is hit Reply and say it's fake. Then I get to go on living my life as a straight man and it's fine. But for you... there is no getting out of it. That's what makes it unfair. It just is what it is. And why do people fucking care? I mean... why do they care who I sleep with in the first place?"

I snorted out a laugh. "They care because they wish it was them."

Now it was his turn to be surprised. "I'm just a redneck nobody."

"Hardly. You're sexy as fuck. Didn't we talk about this already? You're like a walking wet dream, lumberjack-style."

For a split second, I regretted saying something that might make things even more awkward between us in bed at night, but then I saw the red streaks down his neck and thought it was worth it just to see that blush.

"Anyway," I said with a sigh. "I'm sorry you had to see the horrible side of people. Homophobia sucks. And not in the good way."

I sat up straight and stretched my shoulders. "Come on. Let's make those videos like I said. Then we'll figure something out for lunch, and I'll let you talk me into some manual labor afterwards." I stood up and reached for his hand to pull him up, which was comical since he was so much bigger than I was. He chuckled at my attempt. "Where's that fancy camera you talked about? That bad boy needs to start earning its keep."

The mention of his new camera did the trick. His body relaxed and his smile returned. "Hell yeah. Let me grab it. I have a tripod too. Maybe we can do it sitting on the log here. It's kind of a nice backdrop with the trees and the columns of sunlight through the trees."

A few minutes later we were all set up, but I could see the nerves coming back. I tried to think of something I could do or say that would help.

I snapped my fingers. "You ever heard of method acting?"

He crinkled his forehead. "Um, maybe? But I'm not sure what it is."

"A guy named Stanislavsky in the early part of the twentieth century came up with this concept of acting in which you get into the mind of the character by sort of taking that character on as an identity and going deep into their mindset so that the acting comes more naturally. In other words, to act like a Russian spy, try to convince yourself you *are* a Russian spy. Think through what that would be like and all that entails. Then it makes the acting less like acting and more like just... being."

His lip turned up in a cute smirk. "So... instead of just acting like it, I *am* a gay guy in love with a cocky smart-ass?"

My heart fluttered a little bit like a stupid fucking idiot. Maybe my heart was eager to method act this role, but my brain shot up warning flags everywhere. This was Eli's baby brother. Straight baby brother. Naive, small-town boy from Wheatland, Wyoming. I shook my head to clear it of what I was coming to refer to as beard brain. I was so absurdly attracted to that dark beard, it was making me stupid.

Acting. That was all.

We briefly talked through what we wanted to say, but then I decided to ad-lib a little.

"So that's me in a nutshell. I moved back to Colorado from LA a few months ago to be closer to this guy." I leaned against his strong, sturdy frame. "I went to college with his older brother, and we kind of had a..." I shot him a flirty look. "A flirty thing for a while. Not until he was over eighteen, mind you, but—" I stopped when Nine buried his face in his hands.

"Oh my god," he moaned.

I kissed him on the cheek. "He's shy. It's one of the things I like about him actually. I'm a talker."

"No shit," Nine said with a soft snort. He pulled his hands down and looked into the camera. "He could make friends with a ham sandwich. In fact, I think he did exactly that yesterday."

I shrugged. "So... we fit. He's quiet and I'm not. Match made in heaven."

Nine looked over at me with a smirk. "There's more to it than that. You're also bossy, so when you told me we were dating, I didn't have much choice." He looked back at the camera lens. "I'm still not quite sure how it happened. One day I was going through life normal as can be, and the next I was mixed up with this guy. It's... it's been an adventure to say the least."

I opened my mouth to take back over, but he beat me to it.

"I wouldn't change it though. He's easy to be around. Makes me laugh and stuff. And..." He looked down at the dirt where he'd scuffed lines with the toes of a boot. "And you know you picked a good one when he's sweet to your dog, you know?"

I must have swallowed a whole coconut. My throat was tight and dry. Nine looked from me to the camera and chuckled. "Make a note, ladies and gentlemen. This is a historic moment when Cooper is at a loss for words. It won't ever happen again."

Did I dare do what my brain was screaming for me to do?

When he winked at me, I knew without a doubt, the answer was yes.

So I leaned over and kissed him full on the mouth.

9

NINE

It had been exactly six hours, eighteen minutes, and twenty-three seconds since Cooper Heath kissed me on my mouth.

I could still remember the strawberry taste of him... the whiskery feel of him... the utter liquid heat of his relaxed body against mine.

And my brain couldn't stop replaying all of it over and over.

I'd kissed a guy. Which wasn't as big a deal as the fact it had been Cooper Heath. I'd kissed *Cooper*. Well, more like he'd kissed me. Yeah, it had been for the camera, but still. It had happened. It had been a real kiss, even if it hadn't meant anything to him. I hadn't had all that many kisses in my life, so this one was going in the hall of fame whether I wanted it to or not.

Because I'd felt that kiss in my belly. And other places.

Being physically turned on by a man didn't surprise me as much as being physically turned on by anyone. I'd really never thought of myself as all that sexual. I'd even googled things like "not interested in sex" and "when your friends seem to care about sex more than you." I'd learned terms like gray, asexual, and demisexual even though I'd never really "diagnosed" which one I was. I didn't like the idea of being any of those things because I felt like that meant something in me wasn't quite right. Even though my brain knew that wasn't true, society kind of felt that way, especially where I lived. If I'd said I was "gray" in Wheatland, Wyoming, everyone would have told me to get outside in the sunshine and get some more vitamin D. Or just "cheer up."

Feeling this way about Cooper confused me even more because I hadn't ever thought that it would be a guy who finally flipped my switch. And what did that mean, exactly? Did that mean that I *was* a sexual person, I was just gay? And maybe because gay wasn't all that well-known where I grew up, I just... didn't have that option?

It reminded me of the time my dad had brought home a baby goat and we'd all gone nuts over how damned cute it was. The little puffy-coated guy hopped around without a care in the world and made me feel all bubbly inside. Up to that point, I'd never seen a baby goat and hadn't known what I was missing. But now... now that I knew baby goats were a thing... I'd begged my dad for more of them. I couldn't stop thinking of them. They were so cute and fun to watch. How had I spent several years of my life without knowing the joy a hopping little goat kid could bring to a farm? If I'd had any idea, I would have been begging my dad for one way sooner than that.

That's kind of how I was feeling now after kissing Cooper. Was I gay? And now that I was in a situation where I was kind of "allowed" to be gay, was it something I wanted to find out about for sure? And then... what if I liked it? What if I discovered I really was gay and then I went home to Wheatland and my family? What would my life be like then? What would my family think?

"Pretty sure you got all the lumps out, big guy."

I blinked up at Cooper, who was cutting up some vegetables on the little kitchen counter for dinner. I'd been stirring a bowl of brownie mix like he'd asked, but who knew how long I'd been at it. I looked down at the shiny brown batter. "Okay."

I stood up from the booth bench to pour the batter into the pan Cooper had prepared. Once I slid it into the little propane oven, I sat back down and reached for my laptop to distract myself with some video editing.

"Hey." Cooper squatted down next to me with a concerned look on his face. "You've been in a funk all afternoon. Did I do something to upset you?"

I shook my head and went back to my work.

"Is it the kiss? Are you pissed about that?"

Definitely not. I'd really liked the kiss. But I sure as hell wasn't telling him that. He'd tease me like crazy. So I shook my head again without looking at him.

"Will you please say something?" He didn't sound angry so much as exasperated.

I glanced at him from the corner of my eye. "I'm fine."

He groaned and stood up, throwing his hands up dramatically. "Fine. He's fine. A man of few words, this guy. Fine. You're fine. We're all fine. Jesus."

He went back to fixing our dinner.

"You like to cook," I said, trying to make a better effort. "Eli cooks too. Kind of surprises me. He's not really the cooking type."

"Yeah. Remember when we moved into that apartment junior year and those two guys bailed on us?"

"I think so. They were supposed to help pay rent?"

He nodded. "Money was so tight after that, Eli and I had to cook at home. We got sick of ramen and shit, so we started getting creative. Your mom brought us a box of cookbooks from the thrift store to help us out. Then it kind of became a competition to see who could cook the best shit."

I chuckled. "Everything with you two is a competition."

"True. But I'll tell you... the man cooks a damned fine brisket. And some day you need to get him to make you his sweet potato fries. He puts some kind of spice on them that he won't reveal, but it's legendary."

My eyes followed him as he moved around the tiny space. "He made the brisket for Jessica's high school graduation party. It was a big hit. What's your specialty or, like, your favorite thing to make?" This was me trying harder not to be a grunting Neanderthal.

Cooper grinned. "I do a chicken rice bowl that I've perfected over years of tinkering. It's definitely something I'll be making this summer multiple times. Oh, and I also make a mean banana bread."

"I love banana bread." For some reason, I felt my ears heat. Why were we talking about bananas again?

The evening air blew in on a gentle breeze through the screen-covered windows. It was cooling off quickly, which was good since using the stove and oven heated up the RV.

We'd ended up spending the afternoon clearing debris from inside the cabin so I could start repairing the subflooring first. After that, I would work on the framing and external walls and then the roof. Hopefully by then the windows would be here.

We'd hauled a ton of crap out to the large construction dumpster that had been delivered near the end of the gravel drive but out of view of the cameras. I knew Cooper was probably sore from all the bending and lifting, but he hadn't complained.

We'd both taken quick showers and were now happily decked out in our pajamas, anticipating a big dinner. It was kind of like a sleep-over in a weird way. Cooper had even suggested watching a movie on the big screen TV in the bedroom. His mom had sent him with an old DVD player and a stack of movie discs.

"So I was thinking," Cooper began. His back was still turned to me as he continued putting together a salad to go with the chili baked potatoes he'd made. The RV smelled amazing, and Nacho was drooling a little puddle on the floor from it.

"Yeah?"

"I know you wanted to work on the flooring tomorrow."

"The subfloor," I corrected.

"Whatever. But I was also thinking we could take that drone for a spin and get some good aerial shots I can use to do an intro post on the project. I was watching some YouTube videos today and they have these great clips as part of their opening bit. But I don't really know how to do any of that since I'm not used to working with drones or video editing. So I thought if you showed me how to do both—work the drone and do some basic video editing—it would help me take some of that load off you."

Cooper seemed uncomfortable, so I hurried to reassure him. "But I like doing that stuff."

"No, I know. And I don't want to take it away from you. That's not what I'm saying at all. But I feel like..." He sighed and stopped talking. I didn't push since I figured everyone needed a little time to get their thoughts together sometimes. When he brought our plates to the table and sat down, he finally continued. "I feel like I don't really bring anything to the table here except being gay."

"You brought chili baked potatoes to the table. That's good." My attempt at a joke didn't seem to work.

"Nine..."

"You bring a lot to the table." So maybe I had to think about it before I could give an example. "People like you. You make people laugh and smile. I don't do that. People are watching me to learn a skill, or maybe they're watching me because they like my physical shell, but they're going to watch you because you're funny and you say things that are interesting."

He narrowed his eyes at me. "Hardly."

"No, seriously. Like... like that video post you did earlier today where you couldn't stop laughing because you were telling that story about the boobie balloons from a bachelorette party getting caught on the church steeple. The story itself was funny, but seeing you keep stopping to giggle like that was ten times better. That's you. You're entertaining."

Cooper seemed to relax a little. He took a sip from his water bottle. "Thanks. But I still think it makes sense for me to learn some video editing. And if you teach me how to work the drone, I'll use it to get shots of you working. People will like that."

I nodded. He was right. It made complete sense for him to learn how to do those things, and I certainly didn't want him to feel like he was useless. "Okay. We'll do it tomorrow." I took a bite of the chili and groaned. "This is so good. What did you put in this?"

He laughed. "It's just canned chili with Worcestershire sauce. Heath family secret. Don't tell anyone."

"I make baked potatoes sometimes, but I never thought about

putting canned chili on them. Super easy. Would be good in the winter too. I never know what to make, so half the time I show up at Mom and Dad's for dinner."

"You don't live on the farm? For some reason I thought you did."

"No, I rent a little garage apartment near Walt's. Helps me save on gas since I can walk to work."

We continued to eat in easy silence only broken by the sound of Nacho's desperation.

"I thought you fed him," Cooper finally said with a chuckle.

"I did. But chili is much tastier than dog food. He's no dummy."

Cooper finished his potato and sat back, taking another sip of his water. When he set the bottle down, he crossed his arms over his chest. "We've been getting along all day."

I glanced up at him. "That a problem?"

"No. I just mean... we didn't always get along. I kind of expected us to want to kill each other if we had to be stuck in an RV together."

"It's only day two," I reminded him with a grin.

"Be serious for a minute. What's changed?"

I dug back into my food so he didn't see my hot face. "Well, for one thing, we kissed."

When he didn't say anything, I peeked up at him. Cooper had his pointer finger on his chin and was looking up as if the ceiling had answers. "Hmm... so what you're saying is, if we want to continue getting along... we should kiss more."

I choked a little on my food and grabbed for my water to the sound of his laughter.

"Calm down, straight boy. I was only teasing."

Being labeled, especially after everything I'd been thinking, made me uncomfortable. It was nobody's business if I was straight or not. "Who said I was straight? Who said I was anything? Why does everyone always assume things about people?"

Before he could say anything, I scooted out of the booth, slid my empty plate and fork into the sink with a clatter, and hustled out of the RV.

Turned out, it wasn't just the stove and oven making things hot in there.

10

COOPER

I stared at Nine's back and ass as he blundered down the narrow RV steps and out into the night. Nacho scrambled up and chased after him, assuming there was an adventure waiting.

What the actual fuck?

Had he really implied he wasn't straight? Or... wait. I remembered our conversation earlier about Stanislavski and method acting. Could he be trying to do something like that in hopes it would make things easier on him for this project? Could it be possible he needed to get into a completely different head space to make it okay to pretend he was gay?

Or was he truly questioning his sexuality? And if that was the case, did I want any part of it? No. I needed a floundering bi-curious man right now like a surfboard in the mountains. I had a neighbor back in my old apartment building in LA who'd given his heart to a questioning guy, and the man had shredded the thing and chucked it back at him just before I left town. I'd heard every single scream and cry from his apartment and wanted no part of that kind of roller coaster.

I would focus on the job. I would focus on building our audience and impressing the sponsor. And since Nine wanted the same thing, I assumed we could work together on that common goal without much trouble.

As long as the man in question got his shit together.

If he was going to be awkward about this, it was never going to work. I followed him outside where the moon was doing a good job keeping the clearing bright enough to make things out. Nine was sitting slumped over on the fallen log with his arms around Nacho's neck.

"Hey," I said, approaching slowly and taking a seat next to him. "Do you want to talk about it?"

"No."

I nodded and leaned forward, resting my elbows on my knees and clasping my fingers together. After a few minutes, I let out a breath. "Listen, I'm sorry for teasing you about this, and I'm definitely sorry for making assumptions. You're right. I shouldn't have. It's not fair to you. I just... I feel like the reason you've always been annoyed by me is because I'm gay and that makes you uncomfortable."

Nine turned and looked at me with an exasperated expression. "Are you kidding? I've always been annoyed by you because you're annoying as hell. You teased me relentlessly which only made Eli and my other brothers tease me worse. You made fun of me for being shy. That time you came to visit Eli for his birthday, you hid the keys to my truck, and I was late for work. Walt made me stay four extra hours to clean up the stock room with no pay, so I missed my brother's birthday dinner."

My heart sank. "You're kidding? I never knew that. Your mom said you were probably out with your girlfriend. That's when you were dating Lauren. Jesus, Nine. I'm sorry." I only remembered it was when he was dating Lauren because that was why I'd hidden the keys. I hadn't wanted him going out with a woman who clearly didn't think Nine was good enough for her. Even if I hadn't thought I'd liked him all that much at the time, he was still basically family.

Nine shrugged. "Just don't *assume* I dislike you because you're gay. I don't give a shit you're gay. It's none of my business anyway."

"Well... it kinda is since you're my boyfriend and all." I smiled at him, hoping like hell he'd let the conversation lighten.

The corner of his mouth turned up. His beard was so sexy and his lips were perfectly full, I couldn't miss the tiny smile.

"Why did you hide my keys that time?" He turned his head to watch for my response. I felt uncomfortable under his scrutiny because I was embarrassed by the truth and didn't want him to see it.

"Because I'm an asshole?"

"Mpfh. Try again."

I looked down at my hands. "You... you're a tough nut to crack. Your family is like a tangle of live wires, loud and sparking all the time. But you... you're so quiet and calm. I can't ever figure you out because you just don't say much."

Nine's eyes widened. "I feel like I haven't stopped talking since I got here."

I laughed. "That's true. I don't know why, but I'll take it. Maybe now that you're away from everyone, there's more room for you to speak."

"You didn't really answer my question."

I blew out a breath which got Nacho's attention. He moved over to rest his chin on my knee so I gave him some head scratches.

"I was trying to get a rise out of you so I could figure you out. I wanted you to say something, anything. You were so fucking stoic. Still are. And I can't stand not knowing what you're thinking."

He stared at me so I looked away again, studying Nacho like the answers to the universe were shaved into his coat.

"I'm thinking I liked kissing you."

The softly spoken words sifted through the night air and wrapped around me. Suddenly my throat felt raw and my dick felt very, very interested.

"Really?" I asked, mostly to buy some time.

He nodded. "I kind of want to do it again to see if... if that was just..."

I lurched at him and grasped his face before he could change his mind. I wanted my lips on his. I wanted to feel the thick beard between my fingers and discover how his tongue felt on mine.

Nine grunted when I landed against him, but then his arms came around me and tightened. Before I realized what was happening, I was straddling his thick thighs and kissing his face off.

And it was amazing. Kissing Isaac Winshed made me want to write a letter of apology to my old neighbor explaining that I finally understood why he'd put himself through the torture. Kissing a straight guy was like... eating a molten chocolate brownie sundae after a month of health food. Indulgent, delicious, but a little bit guilt-inducing.

Nine's big hand was in my hair, and the other was on my lower back, holding me tightly against him enough for me to feel the hard dick in the front of his pajama pants. I moaned into his mouth as I surged my hips against it seeking friction for my own out-of-control hard-on.

"Wait," he said against my lips. "Coop, wait."

I pulled back and looked at him in a daze. My lips tingled and I could still feel the ghost of his beard hair against my cheeks. "Huh?"

He grinned and leaned in to peck me on the cheek. "You're kind of cute when you've just been kissed."

"Huh?"

"I just... I don't want to go too far, okay? I feel like I could really screw things up for us, and..."

Enough fresh air made its way to my brain to snap me out of the lust haze. He was right. I couldn't let us fuck up this project. My family was counting on us. If we tried something physical and failed spectacularly, it would be hard to hide the tension from the camera. Plus we'd still be stuck with each other for months. And hadn't I just promised to keep away from the questioning man? Jesus.

"Yeah." I moved off his lap and wiggled my hips to get my dick to stand down. "Of course. You're right. Smart."

He snorted. "Hardly."

I glanced back over at him. "No, really. I mean it."

"Yeah, okay. Hey, you want to take first dibs on the bathroom while I walk Nacho around a little bit?"

I nodded and made my way back to the RV with my brain spinning. I'd just kissed Isaac Winshed. Isaac Winshed had just gotten a hard-on for me.

I pressed my fingers to my lips as I took the steps up into the RV. What would Eli think? Would he be more upset about Nine kissing a man or about Nine kissing *me*?

Thankfully, I had enough privacy for a minute to do something about my aching balls. The minute I closed myself into the tiny bathroom, I spit into my hand and went at it. I thought about how wide and strong his shoulders had been under my hands, how rounded his pecs were... I wondered what his dick looked like and what he would have done if I'd fished it out of his pajama pants right there in the clearing.

"*Fuck*." The orgasm zipped through me hard and fast, sucking away my breath and knocking my head back into the wall. "Fuck, fuck."

Even though coming now would help me control myself when we got into bed together, there was no telling what would happen if I woke up next to him in the middle of the night and knew he might not be so resistant to my advances.

Slow down. He asked you to slow things down.

I quickly washed up and brushed my teeth. Just because I couldn't make those advances tonight didn't mean I couldn't make them ever. We just needed to focus on the job first.

After cleaning up the tiny space and moving to the bedroom area, I pulled out my phone so we could do another end of the day Instagram story. There was a text from my brother on the screen.

Jacks: *Worked a half day at the bakery and didn't die.*

He finished with a winky face. I texted him back.

Cooper: *Proof of life?*

After a couple of minutes, a photo flashed up with Jacks in bed and his cat, Saffy, curled up next to his head. Jacks looked really good. His color was back, and his eyes weren't quite so sunken.

Cooper: *You look like your hot brother again.*

Jacks: *Speaking of hot brothers, holy fuck. Nine Winshed done growed up gooood.*

That one was followed by a shocked face emoji.

Cooper: *I guess. If you like half-crazed mountain man types.*

Jacks: *Which I do.*

I laughed.

Cooper: *Well, keep looking since this one's mine.*

Jacks: *You wish. Wouldn't it be amazing if like... "gay for you" was really a thing?*

I felt my cheeks warm. Another text came through.

Jacks: *I mean those lips... damn. I'd be happy with that beard burn fuckin' everywhere.*

My back teeth clenched so hard they hurt. If Nine was going to rub that big beard against anyone's skin, it was going to be mine. So I pulled the ultimate brother move.

Cooper: *Dibs.*

Jacks: *Fuck. That's not fair.*

Cooper: *Is too.*

Jacks: *Is not.*

The subject of our spat walked in and pulled back the covers on his side. I flicked my phone to mute and snuck a pic of him getting into our bed before sending it to my brother.

Cooper: *Sorry, gotta go. Bedtime.*

Jacks: *Oh Em Gee. JFC. Moar please.*

That one was followed by the little praying hands emoji.

I laughed and clicked out of the text window so I could pull up Instagram. "Ready for our bedtime video post?"

Nine looked up from his own phone and gave me a grin that nearly brought my dick back to life. "Ready when you are."

If only.

We snuggled together and started the recording. I opened up with some thoughts about what we'd gotten done today and was just getting ready to go over what we hoped to accomplish tomorrow when Nine interrupted.

"You have a little beard burn right here." He put his finger on the side of my mouth and grinned at me with such teasing affection, I wondered if I'd swallowed a hummingbird.

When I dropped my jaw open, he used the same finger to lift it closed.

"It's kinda hot," he said in a flirty tone. Didn't he see the camera was rolling?

"Too bad it wasn't your beard that caused it," I said back without thinking. Then I winked at the camera. Nine tackled me on the bed and kissed me again, causing me to yelp and drop the phone. By the time I got my hands on it to stop the video, we were laughing and kissing in a tangled mass of limbs on the bed and Nacho was yipping at us to stop horsing around.

We finally stopped making out long enough to get some sleep, but it wasn't easy. Meanwhile, during the night, that video went viral. When I woke up the next morning to the scent of brewing coffee, I checked my phone to see an absolute avalanche of notifications.

"Um, Nine?" I called to him in the kitchen while he was pouring cream into both mugs.

"Yeah?"

"We hit twenty-five thousand subscribers to our Insta account."

He brought the mugs in and handed me one before sitting back in bed on his side and leaning against the headboard. "Twenty-five hundred, you mean?"

"No, it was eleven thousand yesterday after Stallion shared the project intro post. But after our post last night..."

"Shit, what?" He leaned over my shoulder to look at my phone. "All that's from us goofing around?"

I turned to look at him. "Kissing. From us kissing and being physical with each other. Look. All the comments are about how hot we are together and stuff."

He reached past my arm and scrolled down with a finger. I took the opportunity to lean back into his chest while I sipped the coffee he'd made for me.

"Some of those comments are mean," he muttered. "Those fuckers."

I shrugged. "It's always going to be like that with LGBT content. Just ignore them."

Nine looked at me. "That's not okay. It's not fair."

I laughed at his sheer outrage. "True. But the trick is not to give those assholes any more of your time or energy by worrying about it."

He leaned back again, putting his free arm around my front and holding me against him like it was no big deal, like he held a man against his bare chest any old day.

"It's a good thing we're doing," he said after a minute.

"How so?"

"Showing guys they can be into tools and like kissing boys. I mean, obviously they can, but it's good for them to see examples of it, right? I don't know. Maybe not."

This wasn't the first time he'd talked himself around in a circle. It was almost like he wanted to make a point but then thought maybe his point was stupid.

"You're right. It is good. Especially for boys growing up like you did with guys doing 'guy' things and girls doing 'girl' things. I hope to hell Stallion has plans to support some lesbian representation too."

"Well, they do. I asked them about it during one of the calls."

I sat forward and spun around. "You did?"

Nine blushed. "Yeah, I mean, I said they seemed to be forgetting women and girls in their marketing too, and if they wanted to support some great LGBT content, I did a search and found a really cool lesbian couple in Maine who builds wooden sailboats by hand. They'd be a good vlog to sponsor too. I sent them the link, but I don't know if they did anything with it."

I reached up and cupped his hairy cheek. "You're a magician's hat, Isaac Winshed. I never know what the rabbit's going to pull out of you next."

The grin split his face and made the hummingbird in my stomach beat its wings even faster.

"Good. I like to keep you guessing."

I leaned in and kissed him, coffee breath and all.

11

NINE

The following week went by quickly. Everything was fine for the most part. We'd started to really figure out what kind of Instagram videos captured the most amount of interest and how to use them to feed our YouTube channel. But it wasn't all easy.

Not only were we working our asses off... okay, I was working my ass off... but we'd started getting "helpful feedback" from the people at Stallion. They wanted to talk to us about product placement in video clips and photos, how to mention features and benefits of certain tools, and making sure we were using proper safety protocol since we were representing their brand.

Honestly, it had made me second-guess everything I did, and I was so on edge from it, I'd ended up snapping at Cooper several times even though it wasn't really his fault. That only made me feel like more of an ass which made me quieter. I figured it was better for me to not say anything than to risk snapping at him more.

Things were tense and awkward between us which was the opposite of what I wanted and the opposite of what made for good social media. Even I knew that we'd get more subscribers if we looked like we were having fun than if we looked stilted and weird because we were worried about forgetting to wear goggles when using certain tools.

I wasn't great in front of crowds of people under the best of circumstances, but at least with my own videos on my own channel, I could pretend I was alone. I could pretend I was making the video for Mrs. Anson, who wanted to build a simple birdhouse, or for Mr. Ridley, who didn't know how to make the angled legs of a sawhorse. But the thought of other people watching our videos, of corporate executives at Stallion judging us… That was enough to make me freeze the minute I looked into the lens.

Needless to say, I didn't have much good footage to work with when it was time to put together our first longer-length video.

"Hey, Coop?" I leaned out from the dinette booth and looked back toward the bedroom. We'd eaten dinner a couple of hours ago, and Cooper had gone off to do some kind of yoga routine by himself in the woods. He'd gone straight into the shower when he'd returned, but I'd caught a whiff of his sweaty scent when he moved past me to get there. Now he was supposedly putting on pajamas. I tried not to think about it.

"Yeah?"

He came back into the main part of the RV, pulling a clean T-shirt over his head. I caught a glimpse of his chest and abs which were nice and golden from the afternoons of working outside in nothing but shorts.

I swallowed. "Uh, you wanted me to show you how I got the music for the videos. I'm getting ready to do that part."

"Cool. I'm going to grab a glass of wine first. Want anything?"

I turned around and watched him as he leaned over to dig through our narrow fridge. He had a really nice butt. "Yeah, uh… do you have any of that strawberry kiwi water from earlier?"

He popped his head up and grinned. "You liked that one?"

I shrugged. "Better than the blueberry one. That one tasted the way pressure-treated lumber smells."

His laughter never failed to make me smile. "You're weird."

Instead of using my water bottle that was sitting on the counter, he got out a tall glass from the cabinet, filled it with ice, and then poured the flavored water into it from the pitcher. When he placed it next to me on the table, he even put a paper towel under it to soak up the icy droplets from the outside of the glass.

"Oooh, fancy."

"But wait, there's more." He opened another cabinet and pulled out a package of Oreo cookies and set a few on a plate. "Voilà. Talk about fancy."

I took a cookie from the stack. "Mm, these are my favorite. If I'd known they were in there, I would have been eating them all week."

Cooper slid into the booth next to me instead of sitting across from me. We'd been sitting like this more and more because it made it easier for him to see what I was doing while I edited video. His hair was still wet from the shower, and I caught a whiff of the shampoo we shared.

"I know they're your favorite. That's why I brought them. And that's also why I hid them in my suitcase to save for a special occasion."

I reached for another cookie, and our shoulders brushed together. While I was getting more comfortable with casual touches, we hadn't done anything more than heavy kissing sessions each night before bed. I thought Cooper had probably decided I wouldn't be any good at the sex stuff, and what else could I do but respect that? It was true, I wasn't all that experienced with any kind of sex, much less gay sex. "What's the special occasion?" I asked, trying to refocus on the task at hand instead of follow those Cooper thoughts into a dark place.

"We need to talk."

Well, hell.

"Oh."

Cooper sighed and turned to me, reaching out to clasp my forearm the way he sometimes did when we talked. I liked the touch. My body seemed to crave it.

"Something's wrong. You're being weird."

I shifted uncomfortably and cleared my throat. The second Oreo didn't taste as good as the first one. "I am weird."

"No, you're not. You're unique. There's a difference. Something's gotten into your head, and it's like... when the camera goes on, Nine disappears."

I frowned at him. "I don't disappear. I'm there every time you do a video. We're in this together. I don't shirk my responsibilities."

"Whoa, calm down. That's not what I meant. Of course you're there physically. I'm talking about your personality. The Isaac Winshed I know—the Nine from the popular YouTube DIY channel—isn't showing up right now. What's going on? Are you scared?"

"What? No!"

Cooper blew out a sigh. "Calm down, manly man. That wasn't a dig against your bad-boy image. Not... that's not what I meant. Are you nervous? Or..."

"Yes, no. I don't know. I just... it's too many things to remember all the time." I closed my laptop and pushed it away before pulling the paper towel with my drink on it a little closer. "I feel like everyone's watching. I'm going to say something wrong or hurt someone's feelings."

Cooper let go of my arm and sat back in the booth, studying me for a minute. "Do you always feel this way when you take your videos? Because I gotta tell you, that doesn't come across in your regular ones at all."

I turned toward him and rested my back against the wall. "No, but that's different. With those, I don't talk as much. And I do all the editing so..."

His face lit with understanding. "Shit. So it's the Instagram stuff. The videos we're doing that aren't edited before they're posted."

I hadn't thought about it that way. "Yeah, maybe?"

He thought about it for a minute. "Okay, what about this? What if you focus on doing the talking only when we're recording for the big weekly video? You can speak freely since you'll be doing the edits, or at least you'll have final say if I do the edits. Then, in the Insta stuff, I can take the lead. Or we can keep some of them simple by talking through ahead of time what we're going to say. Would that help?"

I stared at him, unable to grasp how thoughtful that was. He'd confronted the issue head-on and then tried to figure out a solution. Was it because he needed me to be better in front of the camera so we could get more viewers or because he wanted me to feel more comfortable in general? Did it matter?

I fumbled across the bench and fell onto his face with my lips, kind of accidentally kissing his eye and nose before landing on his mouth. He laughed against my lips, but I didn't stop because he also grabbed the back of my head with both hands and held on tight. God, I wanted him. I'd wanted him most of the minutes and hours of the days since the first time we'd kissed. I fell asleep with the memory of it and woke up with a throbbing dick in the bed next to his sleepy, sexy face.

"Fuck, you're so fucking sexy," he mumbled against my face. Cooper moved his fingers into my beard and tugged on it while continuing to kiss me. His tongue pillaged inside my mouth, and I sucked on it like a Popsicle. He was hanging halfway out of the booth from where I'd basically attacked him full-on, but he didn't seem to mind.

"Please," I said, moving down to taste his jawline, his throat, and over to his ear. I wasn't quite sure what I was asking for, but I mostly wanted more. More of him, more of this feeling, more of our bodies as close as we could get them.

Cooper's voice was sexy as hell. "I want to taste your dick so badly."

It took my brain a minute to process what he'd said, but then my brain had instructed all systems to relocate to emergency settings ASAP. "Oh god. Really?"

Ugh, that was stupid. I sounded like a moron.

Cooper pulled back and locked eyes with me. "Really. I really want to suck your dick. I've been fantasizing about it all week."

I must have just stared at him for a beat, because he laughed and leaned back in, muttering, "It's fine. Too much, too soon. I get it."

"No!" I growled, grabbing him up and shoving him out of the booth. "Not too much. Not too soon. Bed. Bed now."

I hadn't had a blow job in years, and even then it had been a furtive, embarrassing encounter in my truck with a waitress who'd come on to me one night after I'd left my brothers at the local roadhouse. I wanted it badly. And the thought of Cooper's full lips around my cock... phew. That... that was enough to make me damn near embarrass myself.

So I pushed him along toward the bed, muttering encouragement for his efficiency and speed. I yanked up his shirt which made him laugh for some reason, but I didn't care. I was mostly brainless at this point and ready to feel his lips on me.

When we got close to the bed, Nacho hopped up and turned in a circle like it was bedtime.

"Out," I barked, pointing back the way we'd come. "Go lie down on the mat. Go."

He slunk off the bed which was almost pitiful enough to make me feel bad, but then I caught sight of Cooper's nipples all brown and hard on his tan chest and forgot all about dogs.

"That poor baby," Cooper teased.

"Mpfh."

I stood there suddenly unsure of myself. How did this work? Was I supposed to sit down on the edge of the bed? Take down my pants a little or get completely naked?

I turned around in a circle, trying to decide, as if there'd be notecards pinned to the wall with instructions.

"You're as bad as Nacho," Cooper said with a laugh. "Get naked and lie on the bed. I can see the big tough guy needs to be bossed around for once."

I was naked and on the bed before he even finished speaking. His delicious laughter continued.

"Why're you laughing?" I grumbled, stroking my dick.

"You're fucking adorable. I'm happy. I like you. I like your body. I like sex. I *love* sucking dick."

My heart ramped up. "You do?"

He bit his lower lip and nodded slowly, deliberately driving me insane while he turned his little strip show into a thing.

I grunted at him again. "You're doing that slowly on purpose."

When he was finally totally bare, I stared at him. My eyes drank him in like lemonade on a hot summer day. He was stunning, marble-smooth and perfectly proportioned. "You look like one of those statues in a museum in Italy," I said stupidly.

His cheeky grin dropped. "Really?"

I nodded and reached out both hands in a desperate gesture to get him to come closer, to see the little cluster of stars tattooed on one of his hips up close.

He knelt up on the end of the bed but kept his eyes on mine. "No one's ever said something like that to me before."

"They should have. C'mere."

My dick was so hard it jumped with every move he made toward me. The movement drew Cooper's attention to my hard-on, and just like that his shit-eating grin was back. "Come to papa, big guy."

I threw my head back in frustration. "Ughhh, you're killing me."

Suddenly, his hot wet tongue stroked up the side of my cock, and I made a combination shouting and choking sound, reaching down automatically to cradle his head in my hands. "Oh. Ohhh. Oh god."

I couldn't believe I was here like this with him. I couldn't believe I was getting head from another man, but more than that, I couldn't believe I was lucky enough to be getting this kind of undivided attention from such a beautiful, attentive human. Even though we argued and kind of bugged the hell out of each other, when we connected like this... it was something else altogether.

It was like wildfire hitting a dry forest. It was like watching Nacho reach that running speed where his entire body seemed more like ocean waves than a racing dog. Being together like this with Cooper was like... watching one of those time-lapse videos of an entire meadow blossoming into a riot of wildflowers.

And it left me reeling because I had absolutely no idea what to do with feelings this big. Especially when I knew I was the only one of the two of us who didn't do casual. I was the only one mixing emotions into this. Cooper wasn't that kind of guy, and he sure as hell wouldn't be that way with a kind of straight-guy dumbass who'd barely ever left his hometown.

"Stay with me, sweetheart." Cooper's voice was rough with want, and it made my throat tight.

I thought I imagined the words, but they were enough to pull me back into the moment—a moment where a sexy man was sucking and licking and stroking me until my balls felt like they were going to explode. How could this be real? It was too good, too unbelievable.

"Coop." It came out in a desperate shout. His eyes met mine, and I lost it, arching back and shoving myself farther into his mouth as the orgasm racked my entire body.

12

COOPER

It took one stroke before I was shooting all over the bedcover beneath me and crying out a curse. Isaac was so hot, so unbelievably wide open and responsive, he'd ramped me up until my lower belly—and the lumberjack thigh I'd been humping—were sticky with precum.

"Me suck you?" Isaac managed to grunt between gasping breaths.

I snorted. "No, baby. I came already. It would have been all over your leg, but you moved just in time."

He lifted his head and blinked down our bodies. "Oh fuck, that's hot." He moved his hand down to feel the precum in the dark hairs of his muscular thigh. "That was you?"

I nodded and moved up next to him, laying my head on his shoulder whether he liked it or not. I was a snuggler. It had killed me lying next to his big, beautiful body every night without being able to slap myself up against him like a cat by a heat vent.

His arms came around me and held me close. Good. If he'd rejected my post-sex cuddle, I would have probably turned very moody on him. He probably wasn't quite ready for full-on queenie bitch mode.

"Wait a minute," I said. "You were willing to suck me off?" I lifted my head up to see his reaction.

"Well, yeah. I mean... I would have probably done it wrong, but it's not fair to just... leave you hanging."

I lay back down. "No such thing as doing it wrong. Not really."

"Mm." Isaac's hands started running slowly up and down my back and arm. I wasn't even sure he realized he was doing it, but it felt really good. Soothing. Caring. "You okay?"

I lifted my head again. "Who me?" It came out a little squeaky. "Of course I'm okay. I'm amazing."

His forehead crinkled. "Oh, okay. Good." He swallowed. "It's just... I kind of attacked you again, and—"

I lurched forward and cut him off with a kiss before cupping his face and staring into his eyes. "Isaac Denton Winshed."

The full-name treatment widened his eyes.

"I find you incredibly sexy and would like to suck your dick pretty much all day every day. In fact, I'd like to have that dick in my ass and your tongue in my mouth and your hands all over my damned body whenever the hell you feel like it. There is not a molecule of regret in my entire body for what we just did. Do you understand me?"

He blushed and nodded. I blew out a breath and sat up, hiking a leg over him until I was straddling him. His wet dick was warm against mine even though they were both temporarily out of order. I leaned down over his chest and dropped kisses on his chin and cheeks before asking the important question. "Are *you* okay?"

His eyes widened again. "I'm the one who got his dick sucked."

"I don't want to make any assumptions here, but I'm guessing it was your first time doing that with another man. I just want to make sure you're not..."

He grinned and it was goddamned sexy, my heart kind of thwacked against my rib cage funny. "Freaking out? No. Not one single bit. I'm kind of..."

He glanced away. His eyes flitted to the window, the lamp, the ceiling, anywhere except at me.

"I'm kind of wondering when I can try it on you."

My dick was no longer out of order. It was very, very interested in the conversation. But I also remembered that this night had started out with a conversation about expectations and Nine's nerves. There was no need to push it.

"Mmm, we'll have to pencil that in soon, I think," I said with a finger to my chin. "In the meantime, though, I think we should do our good-night video."

His eyes almost popped out of his head. "Now?"

"Um. Aren't we going to bed?" I turned around and called Nacho since he was making low whimpering sounds from the other room. He bolted up and took a flying leap onto the bed. I curled my body over Nine's so we didn't get scratched by Nacho's nails.

"We just had sex," he said. "What if they can tell?"

"They'll think we're together. Like... y'know... boyfriends or something." I lifted an eyebrow at him.

He sighed. "Fine, but you have to do the talking. If I do it, I'll probably blurt out something horrible like *blow job*."

I climbed off him and got a towel to clean us up a little before moving to slide under the covers. Nine stared at me. "Are you... are we, um, sleeping naked?"

For such a big, gruff guy, he really was a sweetheart in a lot of ways. This part of him made me want to take care of him, put him in my pocket and keep him safe.

I stopped with one knee on the bed. "Well, we don't have to. I can put back on—"

"No! No, that's good. I mean... if... if it's good for you."

I paused for a beat to make sure that's how he really felt. He smiled, his beard widening in that way that made me want to nuzzle into it. "I kind of like looking at you naked. So I might peek under the covers later."

My laughter was still filling the room when I started the video.

Another week passed and we were starting to see progress in several measures. Nine was proud of the plain-ass plywood floors we'd finished in the cabin even though I thought bragging about not having rotten holes in the floor was setting a particularly low bar.

But the subscriber rates had suddenly shot up as well. The video we'd done the night of the first blow job—because of course there had been more since then—had gone viral which didn't really make sense to me even now, a week later. The video hadn't been anything special. We'd just been joking around about stupid stuff. I'd mentioned making different kinds of flavored water mixes and using Nine as my taste-tester, and then he'd jumped in and started teasing me about it. Then he told our viewers about all the things I'd cooked for him so far, and he'd surprised me by raving about everything one by one.

The comments had been all mushy about how cute we were together and how Nine had "puppy dog eyes" for me when he talked about my cooking. The number of female subscribers was way up which Stallion loved since women made many of the household purchasing decisions.

After that, the flirting came naturally, and our impromptu videos didn't seem to make Nine nearly as stressed as before. He still didn't talk much unless something I said triggered his ability to chime in without fear, so I kept bringing up light things that I thought would keep him comfortable in front of the camera. In one of the videos, I told the story of his pet chicken, and we both started laughing so hard, we had to take two more videos just to get the full story out through the tears.

Besides one visit from a lumber delivery guy, we hadn't seen another human in over two weeks. We were running low on food and needed to head into town to stock back up on essentials. I was hoping that trip included a meal at a restaurant because I needed a break from cooking. Sure, Nine had pitched in and made several meals, but it was obvious cooking wasn't his special skill.

"Hey," I called, walking back toward the cabin from throwing some wood scraps in the dumpster. "I was thinking we could stop early and head into town for some food."

Nine stepped around the side of the house to answer me, and my jaw dropped. He stood there in nothing but his boxer briefs and work boots. His tanned skin glimmered with sweat, and his muscles bulged like something out of my fantasies.

"Dear god," I said under my breath. "And I'm getting paid for this."

"What'd you say?" he asked, tossing his hammer down into his toolbox.

"Dinner, groceries, town," I repeated, walking closer. "You and me. And pants."

His white teeth appeared in a grin. "I was hot."

"That's an incredible understatement."

"And since no one's here but us, I figured I could—"

I didn't let him finish. I stepped into his personal space and plastered my body against his, wrapping my arms around his broad back and tasting his salty lips. Up to now, we'd done a pretty good job of keeping working hours for work and saving our personal explorations for bed time, but there was no way I was missing out on this opportunity.

We kissed and kissed until I felt him grab my ass and pull our hips together. Suddenly, I remembered the cameras in the trees. I peeled my lips off his. "Inside. Shower. Date. Let's go."

Nine froze. His eyes opened wide. "Date?"

I couldn't decide if he was a deer who'd be easily spooked by an affirmative answer or if he was an eager child, too hopeful to disappoint with a negative one.

"I… uh… Do you want it to be a date?"

He glanced down at my chin and seemed to take a second to think about it. "Kinda. I mean, yeah. I do." He glanced back up at my eyes. "If you do. If not, that's—"

"I do."

His entire face relaxed. "Yeah, good. I mean… we can video it and stuff too. Since we're boyfriends anyway."

Even though I knew he meant fake boyfriends for the show, it still made my heart thunk funny in my chest which was happening more and more around him these days.

I leaned in and kissed him again before pushing away and smacking him on the ass. "Go shower so we can hit the road. I already loaded that propane tank in the back of the truck and found a place that can refill it for us."

He flashed me a thumbs-up and jogged across the clearing to the RV at the same time my phone buzzed in my pocket. It was Jacks.

"Hey, how're you feeling?"

"Ugh, stop asking me that. It's all anyone wants to know anymore." He sounded healthy, so that was good.

"Fine, sorry. How's work? How's Mom?"

"All good. The people at her work got together and gave her a gift card to a massage place, so that was really sweet. She's going on Saturday. I'm going to get her one for the nail place next door so she can have a little spa day."

"That's a great idea. I can send you some money to chip in too."

"It's fine. Tips at the bakery have been good. You'll laugh at this. Marchie spilled blueberry syrup all over his uniform shirt one day last week and had to wear one of mine which is two sizes smaller. That day our tips were insane. So I told him he should wear it again to test my theory that it was the shirt. Sure enough." Jacks's laughter was contagious. "The man has killer pecs, and that shirt clung to every muscle on his body. You should have seen the people drooling."

Jackson's best friend was a little bit like Nine. He looked big and tough but was really a teddy bear once you got to know him. "That's pretty funny."

"Yeah, sooo... speaking of pecs... things seem to be going well with you and the lumberjack."

"Mm-hm."

"Tell me."

I glanced back toward the RV. The door was still safely closed against prying ears. "We hooked up."

His screech damn near burst my ear drum. "No shit!"

"Shhhh. Jesus. Don't tell anyone, okay?"

"Not okay. You are publicly in a relationship with him. Of course I can tell people. Don't be an idiot."

Leave it to a brother to speak bluntly. "Fine, but you know what I mean."

Jacks made a sound like he was taking a sip of something before continuing. "I do. So, is this just an experiment thing, or…?"

I ran fingers through my hair and scratched at the back of my neck. "I don't think so?"

"Do you like him like that, or is it just a hookup thing?"

My eyes stayed riveted on the RV door. "Um… the first one?"

He paused for a beat. "Damn, bro. I'm not sure I've heard you this unsure since you were trying to decide whether or not to head out to LA."

"Yeah, well, I don't really see how it could work out, you know?"

I heard Marchie's voice in the background and Jacks's muffled response to whatever it was he'd asked. He came back on the line. "Why not?"

"If you need to get back to work, we can catch up another time."

"Don't be ridiculous. I called you. March just needed to know something about a catering order. It's fine."

I thought through the reasons why I couldn't picture a long-term relationship with Nine. "Well, for one, he's a home boy."

"Says the guy who hates to leave his apartment."

"No. I mean, he's a home*town* boy. I don't think he'll ever leave Wheatland, Wyoming, and I sure as hell can't live there with all those old-fashioned homophobes all up in our business."

"Have you asked him if that's how he really feels?"

I blew out a nervous laugh. "Of course not. Besides, he bugs the hell out of me. Sometimes he barely speaks, and even if I ask him a direct question, he answers with a grunt like some kind of caveman."

"Mm. Sounds hot."

I laughed. "Shut up."

"Does he like you as more than a hookup?"

"Probably not. I drive him even crazier than he does me. I talk too much. I'm prissy and scared of bugs. I don't know the difference between a Phillips and flathead."

"Bullshit."

I kicked at a clump of pine straw on the ground by my sneaker. "Well, I do *now*. But that's not the point. I want to be an actor. That's not the kind of life where a man like Nine would thrive, and I like him too much to see him unhappy. I wouldn't want to put him in that situation."

"But you like him. If there was a solution, you'd want to try."

Damn my brother for pushing and pushing. "Yes, okay? I like him. I like him a lot. And if all of this... shit... wasn't in our way, I'd want to try a real relationship. Okay? You happy now? I like Isaac Winshed. There, I said it. He's sexy and sweet and smart. You'd really like him, Jacks. He's..."

Nacho appeared in my vision, sniffing at the clump of pine straw I'd been kicking around. If the dog wasn't in the RV, that meant someone had opened the door and let him out. I glanced up and saw Nine standing in the open doorway with his mouth set in a firm line and his eyes lasered in on me.

Oh fuck.

13

NINE

I'd heard Cooper talking through the open window, but I hadn't realized it was a private conversation until I'd walked out and overheard him telling someone that he liked me. The sincerity in his voice was hard to ignore, but the words themselves were impossible to believe.

I was almost too scared to ask, but I had to know. "Is that true?"

The whites of Cooper's eyes circled his pupils. "Shit. Sorry, Jacks. Gotta go. Yeah, you too."

He took a tentative step toward me. "Listen, Nine, I—"

I shook my head at him. "It's a yes-or-no question. Don't play word games with me, Coop. I'm not good at them and you know it."

"Yes. It's true. I like you."

When I was little, I'd been poking around in a creek with a stick when I noticed a bunch of tadpoles hatching underneath a little overhang on the bank of the stream. There were a million of them and they wiggled around all over the place, so much so that I didn't know where to rest my eyes. I felt like those tadpoles were hatching in my stomach right now, but I forged ahead anyway.

"I like you too."

Cooper's grin lit up the entire White River National Forest area.

"Good." He strode closer to me. "Then I guess we have an answer about the whole 'date' conundrum, don't we?"

I laughed and shook my head, feeling freer than I had in a long time. "I guess so. But I'm buying. And we're getting steak."

Cooper clapped a hand to his chest. "Wow, look at me landing a big spender."

I closed the final distance between us and drew him in for a kiss. I could hardly keep my hands off him when given half a chance. "But first you need to change that shirt because there's a sweaty Nine-shaped stain on the front from earlier."

Cooper kissed me some more before running to change and meeting me at the truck. We'd decided to bring Nacho along since it was a forty-minute drive each way. I didn't feel comfortable leaving him alone that long with us so far away.

The drive itself was gorgeous. The trees were lush green, and the sky was still bright and blue despite the late-afternoon hour. Cooper hooked his phone up to the stereo and played an oddball selection of music, but managed to throw in some country tunes just for me. We rode through the fading sunshine singing along to the music and feeling the cool mountain air swirling around us with the windows down. It was a moment I hoped I never forgot as long as I lived.

When we got to the tiny town of Shale Falls, Cooper directed me to the hardware store first so we could get the propane refill and pick up a few odds and ends I needed. We pulled into the lot and were preparing to leave Nacho in the truck with the windows halfway down when an old man carrying a bale of pine straw out of the store lifted his chin at us.

"Tim don't mind no dogs inside. Go on."

Cooper shot me a wink and reached for Nacho's leash, eliciting overly excited tail wags and a giant leap down to the ground by the big golden beast.

We entered the store and took a look around. Even though I for damned sure knew my way around a small-town hardware store, every one was different. This one had a nice big camping section since we were close to the national forest, and I even saw a good selection of work clothes and boots. Cooper was going to get some steel-toed work boots even if I had to sneak them to the truck behind his back.

"Don't even say it," Coop said without looking at me.

"You know you need them." I reached for a ball of baling twine and tossed it in the basket I'd grabbed. "What size you wear?"

Cooper stopped to check out a display of novelty duct tape. "They're butt-ugly."

I deliberately misunderstood him. "That's why I stick with the regular gray kind. But we have plenty."

"No, I mean the boots. This tape is awesome. I'm getting this kitty cat one."

I rolled my eyes. "Pink cat tape is fine, but sturdy work boots to protect your toes are a bridge too far?"

He tossed the tape into my basket. "Fine. But I'll have to do an online order for some funky socks to spruce them up a bit."

"Suit yourself," I muttered, yanking him toward the boot selection. I knew I had to strike while the iron was hot and before he changed his mind. "What size did you say you were again?"

After we'd found the right boots, filled the basket with bits and pieces, and paid for everything, I was starving. We asked the man at the counter if there was any place to get a steak in Shale Falls.

The man scratched his stubbled jaw and nodded. "You folks want the Tin Cup. Hang a right out of here, and it's down on the left just past the green brick building. They do a brunch on Sundays too that has a hollandaise sauce that's to die for. Be sure and check it out at some point if you get back to the area."

Cooper tore off a piece of our receipt and reached across the checkout counter for a pencil, scribbling something onto the paper, as if we'd forget such simple directions.

He handed the paper to the guy. "We're in the area all summer renovating a cabin and filming it for a show on YouTube. Stallion Tools is our sponsor. Check it out."

The man's eyebrows went up. "No shit?"

Cooper's trademark grin widened. "No shit. This guy here already has a great DIY vlog too. Your customers might like it, and it'll help sell more stuff if you get them hooked. Nine here works for a store just like this one up in Wyoming and started these videos for his customers there. They love him. I wrote both links down so you can check them out."

The guy was a natural salesman.

"I certainly will. I'm Tim Lemire. You boys let me know if there's anything I can do for you while you're in the area, all right?"

We took turns introducing ourselves and shaking his hand. "Will do, sir. And thanks," Cooper said as we headed out the door. When we finished loading back into the truck, I turned to Coop.

"Why'd you have to do that? Now I'm gonna be embarrassed every time we come back in here."

Cooper punched me lightly on the arm. "No you're not. You're going to sail in there like the Stallion celebrity you are, and he's going to bow down to your highness."

"Be serious. He's going to picture me putting my dick in you."

I hadn't meant to say it, but it just slipped out.

The mood in the truck fell about a thousand notches. "I'm sorry," I blurted. "That was rude."

"I'll have you know you've never, in fact, put your dick in me." The haughtily lifted eyebrow didn't hide the hurt in his eyes.

"Not for lack of trying," I muttered.

Cooper turned so his back was against the door and he was facing me head-on. "Wait, what? You want to have anal sex with me? Since when? And tell me more about this trying you're referring to." He used finger quotes around the word "trying."

I shrugged and began dusting off the dashboard with my bandana. The nooks and crannies were disgusting. "I mean. I, like, hump your butt all the time in bed. And I... did that thing with my fingers and the lube the other night..."

Talking about this stuff made my face feel like it was going to flame up and peel right off.

"Wait. Wait." Cooper held a finger up. "Put a pin in that for a minute. A big one. Go back to Tim. You're worried he's going to find out you're dating a man and he's... what? Not going to take you seriously anymore?"

He was confusing me. "That's not what I meant."

"Fair enough. Then what did you mean?" He crossed his arms in front of his chest which didn't bode well for me.

"I'm sorry," I said again. "I don't want to hurt your feelings."

He softened a little bit. "I know you don't, sweetheart."

The endearment made my eyes feel weird. I swallowed and tried again. "It's just... it's weird because this is the first time I've met someone in person and thought about them seeing me like that. Like in a relationship and kissing and everything. The tools stuff and the hardware projects are old news for me. I'm used to that. But this... this lovey-dovey stuff isn't... it's not the kind of thing I usually share with people. Even my family."

The dust in my truck was everywhere. I tried rubbing it off the little decorative bands around the radio and the top of the gear shift. Cooper finally grabbed my hand to stop me.

"Look at me."

I looked up at him. He was so beautiful even when he had those little cracks of worry between his eyebrows.

"Isaac, do you want to keep our relationship a secret? I mean... obviously there's the fake one for show. That one we can't keep a secret, plus it's too late. But I mean this, us. Whatever this is between us. Do you want to keep that a secret?"

I knew better than to answer his question without thinking it through. After a minute of making sure I knew how I felt, I reached over and opened the truck door to get out.

14

COOPER

Well, that answered that. If he was so annoyed he was getting out of the damned truck, it couldn't mean good things for me. I'd finally pushed Nine past his limit.

Except then he walked around the front of the truck and to my door, opening it and pulling me out until I was standing in front of him on the sidewalk in front of Tim's store.

"No secret" was all he said before gripping the back of my head and hauling me in for an epic kiss right there on the main drag of Shale Falls.

It wasn't a busy town, but there were definitely people out and about, including customers coming in and out of the store right in front of us. When Nine finally let me suck in some oxygen, I wondered if there were any cops around prepared to write my dick a ticket for public indecency.

"Understand?" Isaac grunted at me.

"Mm-hm," I said with a brainless nod.

"Good. Get in the truck. I'm hungry."

"Mm-hm," I said again. And damned if I wasn't hungry too, even though it wasn't for steak.

The Tin Cup turned out to be an old clapboard house set right on the river that ran through town. I could see from the side it had a wide-planked back deck hanging partway over the river with wooden picnic tables covered in white butcher paper and votive candles in fat glass jars. Twinkle lights illuminated the wooden ceiling over the old porch, giving it a sort of shabby-chic look. I loved it on sight.

"You the ones in the truck with that golden retriever?" the hostess asked.

"Yes, ma'am," Nine said. "That's Nacho, but he won't bother anyone, and we left the windows open for him."

The young woman smiled at him with the full dimple treatment. "No, I was going to say, you can bring him in if you're okay sitting outside on the deck."

Nine's face lit up as he turned to me. "That okay with you?"

I rolled my eyes at him. "I can't believe you even asked me that."

He raced out to get the dog while the lady led me out to a table in the corner. It was a beautiful evening, and since it was early in the summer, the water was still moving pretty fast, kicking up some froth around clumps of giant rocks and cooling the air down around us. I was thankful I'd brought a long-sleeved pullover just in case.

When Nine returned to the table with Nacho, they both settled in. Nine took the seat next to me, and Nacho plunked right down on top of my canvas sneakers and let out a deep, contented sigh.

I was pretty much in heaven. These kind of nights were what I loved most about growing up in the Rocky Mountains. Being able to sit outside with someone I cared about as the sun slid down between the evergreens on the other side of the river was like something out of a Hallmark movie. It wasn't something that happened to someone like me.

An outdoorsy-looking dude stepped up to take our order and gave Nine a serious up-down perusal that was impossible to misinterpret. He had brown hair pulled back in a messy bun, and I could see tan marks from sunglasses on the side of his face. He was dressed in what appeared to be the server uniform of the restaurant, blue jeans and a gold-and-white checked button-down shirt with a kind of leather half-apron tied around his waist. He was sexy as fuck, and suddenly I felt a growl of possession rumble in my chest. I bit it down and watched Nine out of the corner of my eye.

He was blushing. Fuck.

“Welcome to Tin Cup. My name is Todd, and I’ll be your server tonight. Would you like to hear about our specials?”

Nine stared down at his menu without responding.

“Sure,” I said.

He rattled off something about a river trout and dressed field greens, but I wasn’t listening closely. I was watching my *boyfriend* get more fidgety and weird around the hot server.

When the guy finished, I kicked Nine under the table.

“Ow!” He glared at me.

I batted my eyes at Todd. “I’ll have a glass of pinot grigio.” I turned to Nine. “*Sweetie*, what would you like? A beer?”

“Just a Coke please and some ice water. Thanks.”

Todd tapped the table. “No problem, guys. Be right back with those.”

Nine continued to glare at me. “What was that about?”

“You can’t flirt with other guys when we’re out together.”

His head tilted the same way Nacho’s did when I made certain sounds. “Flirt? Me? I wouldn’t even know how to flirt if I’d taken a year of professional flirt lessons.”

“Pfft. You flirt all the time at home.”

Well, that was weird. Referring to the RV as our home wasn’t something either of us had had the chance to do before.

He smiled at me, the sexy fuck. “That’s different. That’s you.”

“What’s the difference?” I kind of wanted to kick myself for acting like a child. Why the hell was I staking some claim on him when we were barely even together? “Never mind. I’m sorry.”

“No, wait.” He reached over under the table and clasped my hand, threading our fingers together and bringing them over to rest on his warm thigh. “The difference is, I like you. Flirting with you comes naturally because I want you.”

Oh, he was a smooth talker. I felt a little breathless, but I soldiered on. “Like you want the waiter.” Okay, fine. I was a child.

A loud laugh boomed out of my usually quiet Nine. "No. Not even a little bit."

Of course that's when Todd the Turd returned with the drinks. "Here you go. Are you ready to place your dinner order?"

Nine gave me a knowing smile. "You go first, gorgeous."

Well then. That was... that was new. "Um, oh. I haven't even looked—" I fumbled the menu and nearly dropped it on the floor.

Nine stepped in, smooth as silk. "Sweetheart, if you don't want a steak, they have a vegetarian couscous dish you'd probably like. It's right here." He pointed to it on the menu. He was right. It had all the vegetables I loved in it, including zucchini which was my favorite.

"Yeah. I'll take that. Thanks."

"And for you, sir?" He winked at Nine.

"I'll take the filet medium rare with a potato and salad. Thanks."

Once he asked all the follow-up questions and took off, Nine squeezed my hand. "You're making me feel good right now. I kind of like the cat-hiss look you gave him. No one's ever been like that about me before."

"It's ridiculous. I don't know why I did that. I don't even care."

His face fell and his hand let go of mine. Suddenly, my words hit my stomach like a brick. I scrambled for his hand again, but he'd fisted both of his hands on top of the table. "No. That's not what I meant. Isaac... I'm sorry. That's not what I meant at all."

"It's fine. Really."

I wrenched one of his hands out of a fist and forced him to hold my hand again, squeezing it tight to get him to look at me. "I care about you. I care about how you feel about me. What I don't care about is what a stranger thinks. *That* is what I don't care about. *That* is what I was being stupid about. Not you and not me."

Nine only looked at me from out of the corner of his eye, and he didn't look convinced. My heart was tripping along too fast like I was scared of him leaving. I hated that feeling. I hated being at the mercy of someone else, whether it was for something trivial like a ride home or something more critical like my good mood or, worse, affirmation of my worth.

I steeled my jaw and pulled my hand away. "Never mind."

The stupid server took that moment to pop by with our salads, all cheery-faced and flirty. I kept my eyes on my fork to avoid getting even more mixed-up than I already felt.

Nine mumbled a thanks, and we both dug in. I wasn't hungry anymore, but I ate anyway. The silence was excruciating. Finally, after I'd eaten as much as I could stand, I pushed my plate away and took a deep glug of my wine.

"I care about you too."

His voice was so soft, I almost lost it to the din of the conversations around us. I glanced up at him. The poor man looked miserable. That wasn't the way anyone should look when they've just exchanged "I care about you's" with someone. I pushed my chair back without thinking, almost toppling it and definitely disturbing poor Nacho. I stepped around the corner of the table and leaned down to wrap my arms around his neck.

Nine pushed back his own chair and hugged me back with his strong arms. His beard brushed against my neck, and his familiar honey scent calmed my racing heart. "I'm sorry," I breathed into his ear. "I never want to hurt your feelings, *ever*."

"I was being stupid," he muttered back. "Wasn't the first time."

I pulled back and cupped his face before kissing him on the lips. If we hadn't been in public, I would have stayed like that longer, but as it was, people were already staring, and I thought I'd even seen someone with their phone out taking a picture.

I sat back down in my chair and we both reached for each other's hands automatically. Apparently, Nine wasn't finished talking about it.

"Um... I've never really been good at this kind of thing," he began. "Like, I don't really know why someone would..." He looked around as if worried someone would overhear us. When he continued, his voice was lower. "Would want to be with me like that. So that's why I reacted that way when you said that." He swallowed and steeled his jaw. "Part of me is waiting for you to tell me this isn't real and you're only joking."

"I'm not. And it is real," I said so fervently, it almost came out as a hiss. "But you have to understand I have similar fears."

He looked surprised. "Why would you? How could you possibly think I was that good of an actor?"

"It's not that. I worry that this is all a test, like you're dipping your big toe into that cold river water out there to see if it's swimmable. And you're likely to decide it's not."

Again with the clenching jaw. It made his thick beard move in a way that woke my dick up even though we were having a serious conversation. "Cooper, I've been swimming in frigid rivers my whole life. I'm from hearty stock, and I'll be damned if I'll let a little cold water keep me from something this good." He peeked up at me and gave me a small smile. "I'd make a joke about cold water and hot men right now, but I'm not that clever."

I pulled our hands up to my mouth and pressed a kiss on his knuckles. "That was plenty good enough for me, Shakespeare."

The familiar rumble of his laughter set me back to rights, like the world had been slightly off-kilter until that sound put it back on course. The rest of the dinner passed in the same comfortable, enjoyable companionship we were used to back home in the RV. We discussed the project, joked about some of the video clips we'd taken this week, and made a list of the groceries we needed to pick up after dinner. The more we talked, the more Nine finally relaxed and began to open up.

"You and your zucchini," he said with a laugh.

I finished typing in the last of the grocery list items to my phone. "What? I like it. And we're planning stir-fry. You can't do stir-fry without zucchini and onions."

"You should taste my zucchini."

I glanced up at him in shock. Did Nine Winshed just make a dick joke in public? But his face didn't indicate it had been a joke. "You make zucchini?" I asked.

"Yes, but I meant the zucchini I grow. In the garden."

I set my phone down on the table. "I thought your family grew wheat."

"They do. I'm talking about my garden. When I was in 4-H, my dad let me make a little kitchen garden out past the old tractor shed. I discovered I really liked doing it, so I've put one in every summer since then."

I pictured teenage Nine working in a veggie patch in nothing but a pair of old blue jeans and work boots. I leaned my elbow on the table and rested my chin in my hand. "Go on."

He smiled and his ears turned a little pink. "I'm going to miss it this summer, that's all."

I sat back as someone stepped up to take away our plates. "You could put one in at the cabin."

Nine sat back and stretched. I loved it when he did that at home because it gave me a chance to appreciate his broad shoulders and thick, muscled arms. But this was the first time I'd seen him do it in public where I noticed at least six or seven people actively appreciating the sight along with me. He was a very big man, so he was easy to notice. Plus, he was gorgeous and had a smoking hot body.

Instead of being possessive, I suddenly felt proud and privileged. He was mine. At least for the time being, I was the one who got to take him home and share a bed with him. I was the lucky bastard who got to snuggle up to the hairy, hot furnace of him and sleep safely protected in his arms every night.

Nine's eyes narrowed. "Why are you smiling at me like that? You kind of look like a serial killer."

"You're a sexy motherfucker."

"And you want to eat my corpse?" Nine winked at me before signaling for the bill. It was a small reminder he wasn't exactly shy so much as reserved. He certainly wasn't passive.

I loved flirting with him, especially now that I knew I was the only person he flirted with. "I mean... how am I supposed to answer that..."

When Todd walked up with the bill, Nine's lips and beard were brushing against my neck.

"Oh, sorry," Nine said, clearly flustered at being caught mid-PDA. He took a quick look at the bill and barely made eye contact with the man when he handed over his credit card. If he hadn't been so free with the public affection in the first place, I might have thought he was embarrassed at being caught, but that wasn't it. He was a private guy. Moreover, I was beginning to realize he was used to being overlooked. In his world, he was only a number, pushed aside and forgotten as an afterthought.

Isaac Winshed didn't like being the center of attention, period. It had nothing to do with being perceived as gay. But if he hated public attention, why in the world was he working on this project?

When he looked back over at me, I asked him exactly that. "Why did you say yes to this?"

He looked confused. "To dinner out?"

"No, to *Cooped Up With Nine*. To the project."

He was silent for a moment, and then he looked away. His fingers fiddled with the water glass in front of him, wiping condensation off the side with the length of his pointer finger the way a gas station attendant would wash a windshield.

"Oh, ah... because of the money."

Why did he sound weird, like that wasn't the full story?

"What do you plan to use the money on?" I asked, honestly curious. I was actually surprised we'd never really talked about it before in all the time we'd spent together.

He still didn't meet my eye because the water glass needed attention. "I want to buy some land. Build my own place. And I wanted the new video equipment and stuff."

Nine glanced at me really quickly before looking back at his water glass.

He was a shitty, shitty liar.

15

NINE

There was no way I was telling Cooper the truth. If he knew the real reason I'd agreed to this whole thing, he'd feel responsible or something. I didn't want that. I was happy with what we were doing as long as I didn't think too hard about the people watching our videos. Hell, I loved the work itself, and I even loved taking the video clips and editing them together. Now that Cooper and I did a lot of the editing as a team, it was even more fun.

I didn't regret it.

At first, I'd sworn to myself I wouldn't fake being someone I wasn't, and I wouldn't take advantage of Stallion's generosity and efforts at real LGBT representation by lying to them. But then Eli had given me more information about Cooper's brother, Jackson, and how they needed the money for his treatment. I didn't know what it was like having a twin, but I definitely knew what it was like having brothers and sisters. If any of them needed life-saving treatment, I'd do anything to make it happen.

I knew my brother Eli felt the same way, but he had even less savings than I did. I just had the money I'd been saving to buy some land one day, and it wasn't all that much. At the rate I saved, I'd never have enough to actually buy a decent property with a house already on it.

So that left me and this Stallion thing. Pretending to be gay. Pretending to be gay with Cooper Heath of all people.

And now look at me. No more pretending.

I snorted.

Cooper shot me a look as we walked out of the restaurant. I hadn't dared told him about Todd's phone number being scrawled on the back of our receipt, but he looked miffed enough, I figured he'd already guessed it anyway.

"We're going to talk about this later," he said.

"I thought we already talked about it?" I encouraged Nacho into a patch of nearby grass for a potty break before getting back in the truck.

"You're holding something back, and I want to know what it is."

"Fine. Here." I pulled the receipt out of my pocket and handed it to him.

Cooper looked extra confused. "What the hell is this?"

"His number."

"Who's number? The guy from Stallion?"

"Todd works for Stallion?" I thought about it for a minute. That was a weird coincidence. "What are the chances?"

Cooper put his hands on his hips. "Todd works for Stallion?"

"That's what you just said."

His hands flapped up and down, rattling the thin paper in his hand as it cut through the air. "No I didn't. You did. What are we even talking about right now?"

"Your jealousy. It's kind of cute."

"I'm not jealous," he shouted.

Nacho and I both stared at him until he groaned and rubbed a hand over his face. "We aren't even talking about the same thing, but I can't believe that asshole actually gave you his number."

I pointed to the paper. "Well, if it makes you feel any better, he said you could watch."

His jaw dropped until he actually read the receipt and saw the scribbled message.

If your dog ever has puppies, I'd love to have one.

"Oh," Cooper said.

I tried to bite back the laugh, but it came out as a muffled snort.

"Ohh," he repeated. He looked down at Nacho. "So it was you being flirted with, not your daddy. Huh."

I took the receipt from him and crumpled it up before tossing it in a nearby public trash can. "When you say it like that, you make it weird."

"Hey, we needed that for our expenses."

"No we didn't. It wasn't an expense. It was a date. Stallion doesn't need to pay for me to take my boyfriend out to dinner."

Cooper looked up at me like my words might have been a joke. I gave him a serious face to make sure he knew they weren't. He hesitated another minute before taking my hand in his. "Boyfriend, huh?"

I shrugged. "That's what the website says anyway, so I guess it must be true. You know what they say about things on the internet."

Cooper laughed, and all was right again in my world.

DESPITE THE LONG daylight hours of summer, it was full dark by the time we finished grocery shopping and got back on the road. The rumble of the truck, combined with the good food and glass of wine, must have done their magic on Cooper because he fell asleep just outside of Shale Falls and was slumped across the console onto my shoulder the rest of the drive back. I had to take the mountain curves extra slowly to keep him from sliding the other direction and banging his head against the window.

When we pulled into the clearing, I had an odd sense of coming home. It was like Cooper's and my own little hideaway, something just for us. I let Nacho out of the back seat before going around to the passenger side and opening the door. Cooper blinked up at me and looked around to see where we were.

"Home," I murmured, reaching in to unclip his seat belt. "Come on, let's get you in bed."

He let me help him out of the truck and into the RV which had gotten cold in the night air since we'd left the windows open. Cooper shivered, so I tightened my hold around his shoulders and pressed a kiss to his head. "Just give me a minute to sort Nacho out, and I'll warm you up under the covers."

After we both took a turn in the bathroom and I closed up the RV, including closing and latching all the windows, I stripped down and slid into bed, reaching for Cooper and pulling him close.

"I had a really good time tonight," he murmured sleepily.

"Me too. I should run the heater so we run out of propane more often. I can use it as an excuse to take you to town."

He chuckled. I felt the warm breath of it against my chest. "Don't need an excuse. Next time it's my turn though."

I thought about that for a minute. "I guess with two guys, it's a little different, huh?"

He laughed again. "Guess so."

"No, I mean, it's not like one person mostly does the asking and the paying. Like at home with girls, it's expected to be the guy, you know?"

Cooper snuggled closer and snuck a whiff of my armpit. I'd noticed him do that before. At first I'd thought it was weird, but now I thought it was kind of cute. Anyone willing to put up with my stink was a winner.

"Only because you live in a small town that's still really old-fashioned."

I kissed him on the head again. His hair still held a faint smoky scent from the campfire we'd had the night before even though he'd showered. "Mm. Maybe so. But the women I've gone out with sure expected the man to do all that stuff."

Cooper lifted his head to look at me. "What was it like when you dated those women? I mean, why didn't it work out with any of them?"

I wasn't sure I wanted to talk about it. It was embarrassing. But for some reason, I didn't think Cooper would tease me about it the way my brothers did.

"I mean, it wasn't like there were a lot of them. Mostly just Lauren from a couple of years ago. She's the only one you've met, I think. Before that... I had sex for the first time with my prom date because that's a cliché. She was still in love with her ex-boyfriend, so it never turned into anything between us. Then I kind of dated this woman named Yaz, but my family fucked that up for me."

"Why?"

"She's Black, and my family just couldn't deal. It wasn't obvious stuff like my parents telling me I shouldn't date a Black woman. It was lots of little things like my mother asking her if there was any way to tell ahead of time if a biracial baby would be more black or more white, or the time my brother Aaron told her that he had a Black friend at work and asked if they were related."

Cooper sighed. "Well, honestly, in Wheatland that's probably a reasonable question. I can't imagine growing up Black in small-town Wyoming."

I shot him a look, but I could tell he was joking. "Anyway, I hadn't even deliberately introduced her to my family, they just heard about her and kept showing up wherever we were—the park, the Dairy Queen, the bowling alley. I honestly think that was what drove her away. I didn't even get to a fourth date."

There was a twinkle in Cooper's eye I recognized. "What?" I asked him. "Go ahead and say whatever's giving you that look."

"Maybe she ditched you because you were taking her to the Dairy Queen, the park, and the bowling alley..."

I stared at him for a beat before attacking his ribs with my fingers. "Asshole."

His laughter filled the small room. "What? It's true. You take her to DQ and me to the fancy steak place? What gives?"

"I already told you. I *like* you."

I kept tickling him even though it was making Nacho nervous. He pranced at the end of the bed until Cooper finally called *uncle* and made me stop.

Cooper's eyes shone and his face was flushed. I wanted to jump his bones.

"I like you too," he said softly. He crawled over to me and straddled my lap, sliding his arms around my neck and leaning in until our noses were touching. "And I'm awake enough now to show you how much."

He kissed me then, and I thought maybe my life would never be the same. Now that I'd had a taste of Cooper Heath, how could I be satisfied with anything less? I didn't really think it was the fact he was a man so much as the fact he was funny and sweet and giving. He was just... perfect. At least for me. And I never wanted this to end.

I'd also begun to notice how creative he was and how working with him made the videos we posted so much better than anything I'd done on my own.

"Come back to me," he whispered against my lips. "You go away sometimes."

"No," I said, rolling us over until I had him pinned to the mattress. "I was only thinking about you and how perfect you are."

His arms and legs wrapped around me. The warmth of his skin against mine was heavenly. "Oh, well then keep going."

I reached around to drag a long finger up and down his crease, making him groan. "Want you," I said between kisses.

His eyes locked on mine. "Do you want to fuck me?"

The slightly nervous knot in my stomach tightened. "Um, yeah? But... do you want that? Or..."

Cooper's soft, relaxed smile was the answer. "Hell fucking yes I want that. I just didn't want to rush you."

I leaned in and sucked on the side of his neck while I thought it through to be sure I wasn't feeling rushed. "I want it. I want you. Pretty badly. But... uh... I don't have any supplies or anything."

He shoved at me to get free. "I do. In the grocery stuff we didn't unpack." He jumped off the bed and raced out of the room. His round white butt glowed in the dark like a double moon. I couldn't take my eyes off it, until, of course, he came back and I got to watch his semi-hard dick flopping around instead.

He leaped back onto the bed with a big gold box of condoms and two different kinds of lube. "Ta-da!"

"When did you sneak those in the cart, and how did I not see them?"

"Well, I think I understand now why you asked me why we were getting a box of K-Cups when we didn't have that kind of coffee machine."

I reached out to take the box from him and noticed my hands were shaking. Cooper noticed too.

"Babe. We don't have to do this. I'm very, very happy sticking with what—"

"No! *No*. I want to have sex with you, this kind of sex with you, very badly. I'm just scared of messing up."

Cooper put a hand on my knee. "You can't really mess up."

"Do you remember the first time my dad tried to show you how to feed a calf from a bottle?"

His face scrunched in confusion. "Um, yeah? But can we maybe not talk about your dad right now?"

"Hush. You were nervous because you'd never done it before. But you wanted to try it, right?"

Cooper's face cleared with understanding, and he tried to hide his sudden grin. "So, what you're saying is, wait till he opens up and then just shove the thing down his throat?"

I pounced on him with a growl. He yelped and started laughing, but the minute I began grinding against him and kissing the hell out of him, his laughter turned to whimpers.

"Please," he begged between kisses. "Please put that gorgeous dick in me."

16

COOPER

Having Isaac's big strong body over me was even hotter than feeling his hard dick pressing into my belly. His beard rasped against my cheeks and chest as he dragged his tongue all over me and made little growling sounds when he got to my nipples.

I arched up into him, begging him with my body as well as my voice. He wasn't the only one shaking with nervous anticipation. For two weeks now I'd fantasized about Nine fucking me. It had started out as a lustful daydream born out of basic horniness and proximity to a hot guy. But over time it had morphed into this greater need, a soul-deep longing to feel as close to him as possible and hold on even if just for a little while.

I'd only ever felt like that with one other person, and he'd never reciprocated the feeling. Being with Isaac like this was different. I felt how much he cared about me in every tender touch. Even when he put his huge hand around the front of my throat to hold me in place while he moved his kisses down my stomach, I felt the soft touch of his grip, the slight brush of his thumb across the skin behind my ear as if he couldn't help but cop a tiny sweet feel of me while holding me down.

I was breathless with the pent-up need of him, the desperation to have him inside me. Before we'd even left the property to head to town, I'd planned to add condoms and lube to the shopping list, and when we got home, the first thing I did in the bathroom was some prep.

Now here we were. Isaac held out his free hand, and I scrambled to squeeze some lube on his fingers. He never took his mouth off my happy trail. When he got to the shaft of my dick, he licked up one side while sliding his hand down between my cheeks and slicking me up.

"Mm-hm." I bit my bottom lip and closed my eyes. "More."

"Slow," he grunted.

"Not slow."

He took his mouth off my dick and glared up at me. "Slow."

Oh. Ohh. Bossy Isaac was someone I could get on board with right this very minute. Yes, sir, and thank you.

I blinked at him and nodded which made his face break out in that beard-splitting grin which, honestly, almost made me shoot all over his face.

"Fuck," I said, reaching down and squeezing the base of my shaft. "Don't smile at me like that. Fuck."

The deep rumble of his laugh against my legs was even hotter. What the hell was wrong with me? Was I that keyed up that just the mere presence of the man in my vicinity chambered a few quick rounds in the love gun? Ew, no. No. What even was that thought? Being horny made me stupid.

"Why are you shaking your head? Should I stop?" The finger he had inside me stilled and began to pull out.

"No! Jesus no. I'm... I'm good. I'm just... stop talking. I'm... I need that. Your finger. Yeah. Like that. Shhh."

He went back to work, muttering, "You're weird." And it was so true but also so irrelevant right now.

Finally, I couldn't stand all this prep when really, I'd already prepped myself. He'd probably looked up anal sex on a Gay for Dummies blog or something and thought we needed to spend all day on this. We didn't.

"Put it in," I said as romantically as possible.

"I need to—"

I grabbed his hair and pulled it up until he locked eyes with me. "Put. It. In."

Isaac's eyes widened. His pupils were already blown, and his face was damp and flushed from sucking my dick. There was spittle in his beard, and for a split second I was torn between wanting to come all over that beard and wanting him to fuck me.

The split second was over. "Fuck me before I come on your face."

I regretted being so blunt and worried I'd upset him, but then I heard him say, "Hot damn," before he reached down to point his dick in the right direction. I held my legs back and noticed the moment everything hit him. He paused for a second, staring at my exposed ass. Streaks of red on his neck and chest deepened, and his eyes flicked up to mine to check in. I knew him well enough now to know he was probably making sure I was really, really okay with this. Isaac Winshed would rather jump in front of a moving train than let someone get hurt on his watch.

"I want you," I said softly. "I promise."

When he finally pushed himself inside my body, his entire frame shuddered with his deep groan. He leaned forward, his hands resting on either side of me and my ass propped up a little on his thighs. He leaned even farther down on his elbows, his arms cradling my head.

"You feel amazing. I've never felt anything so good." His voice was low and rough, like he was holding back.

I pulsed my hips back and forth to encourage him to move, and his eyes squeezed closed with another groan. "Coop. Fuck."

I curled my arms underneath his and up over the backs of his shoulders. His body was huge and warm. His dick filled me up just the way I'd imagined and felt even better than I'd anticipated, especially when he finally got the hint and began thrusting in and out. Our eyes met and locked. Through every move of our bodies, we kept eyes on each other. It was simultaneously terrifying and exhilarating.

Neither of us held back or stayed quiet. There was an unexpected freedom in living out in the middle of nowhere with nobody around for miles. I cried out every time Isaac's dick stroked just so, and he grunted with every push into me. I felt his fingers in my hair and his beard against my cheek when he finally leaned down to kiss me. We kissed sloppily until he kissed across my cheek and to my temple.

"Want you to come," he breathed next to my ear. He moved a hand down between us to stroke me off. It didn't take much before I was shouting his name to the ceiling and digging my fingernails into his skin as my whole body shook with its release.

"Oh fuck, oh fuck, oh fuck," he said in a rush, pulling out and ripping the condom off before coming all over my stomach.

I stared down at the combination of our ejaculate on my stomach.

"Sorry," he said, breath still heaving. "I… I don't know why, I just…"

I let out a short laugh. "No sorry needed. That was hot as fuck."

He half collapsed next to me and took in a deep breath before turning his head to look at me with a silly puppy-type grin, all eagerness and joy. "Can we do it again later?"

Now my laugh was long and loud. "Hell fucking yes. But I'm five years older than you are, so I may need a little more recovery time than you do."

Isaac leaned over and kissed me under the chin. "You're so sexy, Cooper. That was amazing. Thank you for… just thank you."

He was so fucking earnest. I adored that about him. There was no guile or subterfuge with Isaac Winshed. It was refreshing.

My entire body felt so deliciously wrung out, I just lay there enjoying it for the moment, not even realizing until it was gone that Isaac's hand had been in mine.

He got up to visit the tiny bathroom and came back with a warm, wet cloth. "Can I… clean you off?" he asked hesitantly.

I almost grabbed the cloth from him to do it myself, but he seemed to want to take care of me this way, like he was asking me permission to have more access to my body.

I nodded.

He began to stroke my stomach slowly with the warm cotton. "I probably should have licked you clean or something," he muttered under his breath. "I'm not really cool enough for advanced moves like that yet, I guess."

Instead of laughing, I sat up and threw my arms around his neck, hugging him as tightly as I could.

"You're the perfect amount of cool," I said, roughly. "You're just right. Don't try to be something you're not, okay? I like you just like this."

I pulled away from him and took the cloth, clearing my throat while I got to the more intimate bits of cleaning before taking it back to the bathroom to finish. When I came back out, I felt a little steadier on my feet. Nine was already under the covers with Nacho curled on his feet. I slid into the bed on my side and turned out the last remaining light.

Suddenly, things felt awkward.

I lay there on my back and looked up at the ceiling which was only vaguely visible in the dim light from the tiny nightlight in the hallway by the bathroom.

After a minute, Nine's pinky finger wrapped around mine and squeezed. "Are we okay?" His voice was soft in the darkness. "Cooper?"

I turned toward him and shot forward until I was pressed up against him in my usual spot. "Yes. Of course."

After laying my head on his chest and feeling his arm come around my shoulders, I let out a deep breath. "Sorry. I think..." I swallowed. Part of me wanted to tell him that was the closest I'd ever felt to anyone during sex, and I was worried admitting that would make me look stupid or needy. While I didn't want Isaac to second-guess what we'd done, I also wasn't one for trusting other people with my feelings, and I sure as hell never wanted anyone to think I needed anything. I didn't. I was fine. "That was really good."

Lame, but true.

"You *think* it was really good? Well, I *know* it was. No thinking necessary."

He sounded happy and light, just what I wanted to hear. I snuggled closer to my furnace bear. "Pfft. Semantics."

Even though I'd slept the entire drive back from town, I fell asleep immediately to the comforting feeling of the near-silent laughter vibrating through his chest.

After a solid night's sleep in which I didn't dream, or at least I didn't have any memories of dreaming, I awoke to the sound of Isaac arguing on the phone. I could tell from his hushed voice he'd been trying not to wake me, but it was almost impossible in the small confines of our little home.

"This *is* real, Mom," he hissed. "It's not some—"

He listened for a while and paced back and forth in the kitchen area with one hand in his hair and the other on the phone. He only wore a pair of boxer briefs, so his body was a bit distracting for me, until I heard the next part.

"What, you want me to pretend not to like him that much? What does that even mean?"

For a split second, I thought he meant he was pretending to like me, that what we had between us was a lie. But then reality kicked back online, and I knew Isaac wasn't that good an actor. He had real feelings in his eyes when he looked at me, and I knew he at least cared enough about my feelings not to use me that way.

"Well, forget it. I do like him, and I like liking him. And I'm going to continue liking him for a very long time, so you might as well get used to it." He pulled the phone away from his face and poked at it, presumably ending the call.

Whoa.

I wasn't sure Isaac Winshed had ever hung up on his mother in his life.

"Babe. You okay?" I called out, suddenly feeling nervous for some reason.

"Shit," he muttered under his breath. "Yeah. Sorry. I tried not to wake you, but it's cold as balls outside and I don't have any clothes on."

I held out my hand. "It's fine. Come here. Get back in bed."

He got back in bed and pulled me on top of him like a blanket. I yelped at the frigid touch of his skin. "Fuck! You're freezing."

"Mm, you're warm."

I let him warm up for a minute before asking, "What did she say?"

Isaac sighed. "She wants me to stop making it look so real. She said she thought she could handle watching me pretend to be gay, but the reality is really bothering her."

My heart dropped. Mrs. Winshed had never made me feel "wrong" for being gay even though there were definitely times when her ignorance about it was apparent.

I kept quiet and let him continue. Lying draped over his furry chest with his large hands running slowly up and down my back was hardly a hardship.

"I told her I wasn't pretending, and do you know what she said? 'Of course you are, Nine, don't be stupid.' Like I don't know my own feelings. Like I'm twelve instead of twenty-four."

"I'm sorry."

His arms tightened around me. "I'm embarrassed to admit I'm more upset about her thinking I'm stupid than about her being homophobic." He took a breath. "Homophobia is like… a symptom of her upbringing and culture. But thinking I'm too stupid to know my own feelings? Thinking I'm so easily led that I'd somehow turn pretend actions in front of the camera to real feelings behind it?"

I kissed his chest before leaning up to kiss his cheek. It was still cool to the touch, so I kissed his cheeks all over to warm them. Finally I pulled back and straddled him with my hands on his chest.

"You're not stupid. Did I ever tell you the time Eli punched a hole in the wall of our apartment when we lived in that shithole orange building our junior year?"

He shook his head.

"Your dad had called and asked him to help Graham apply to UW."

Isaac's brow furrowed in confusion. "My brother Graham? He practically failed out of high school."

I nodded. "Exactly. That's what Eli said. So he asked your dad why he thought Graham should go to college, and your dad said something about how Graham had potential but had never been challenged enough to prove himself. He thought college might help, and he'd be willing to pay for it."

Isaac's entire body tensed up, and some of the light in his eyes seemed too dim. "Oh. Wow."

I regretted telling him this story. Why the fuck hadn't I thought it through before opening my big fat mouth? Clearly my words had hurt him. I tried to get to the good part. "Eli yelled at him. I don't remember any other time Eli yelled at anyone, but he yelled at your dad that day. Told him if any of the ten of you should be going to college besides Beth it was you. Then he told your dad about every single honor you'd gotten in school, every high grade, every bit of teacher praise. I don't know how he knew half of it since he'd been out of the house for a couple of years at that point, but I remember him getting off the phone and saying something that never made sense to me."

His hands stroked my sides as if even hearing hurtful family bullshit couldn't keep him from wanting a connection with me. It made me feel special. Isaac looked up at me with troubled eyes. "What'd he say?"

"'Fuck lucky numbers.' And then he punched the wall."

17

NINE

It shouldn't have come as a surprise to me that my dad had wanted Graham to go to college, but it did. Mostly because I'd never heard the story, and Eli was usually pretty good about telling me everything.

Cooper gave me another kiss on the forehead before moving off me and lying on his side next to me. The soft sounds of Nacho's snores came from the corner of the bed Coop had abandoned when he'd moved closer to me.

"Tell me what he meant."

I picked up his hand and started toying with his fingers so I wouldn't have to look at his distracting face. "Don't you know why I'm called Nine?"

"You're the ninth child of ten."

"Yes, but it's more than that. None of my other siblings go by their birth order number."

He had a point. "I never understood why Tip was short for Francis either."

"That's another story for another time, but remind me because it's a good one." At least that got a smile out of him. "Growing up, everything was numbered to keep things easy for my mom. Our coat hooks, our water bottles, hell, even our underwear had little Sharpie numbers inside the waistband. Naturally, I was nine. I ate off the ninth plate. I got the ninth pick off the cookie plate at dessert. I got ninth choice in board game pieces. You get the idea. Nine. But the thing is, everyone up to me had something about them that made them special, that made them memorable."

I tried not to look at Cooper's face because I absolutely did not want to see him feel sorry for me. But I kept telling the story anyway. Maybe I was a glutton for punishment.

"Aaron was the oldest, the heir to the throne, so to speak. He was Dad's right-hand man, still is. He's the most dependable. Then there was Beth, everyone's favorite. The kindest human on earth. Then Colt, who never met any trouble he didn't want to get into. He was wild, still is. Then Delia, the pretty one. The pageant winner and homecoming queen. Then there was Eli, who was the golden boy. He's everyone's friend and an all-around good guy. And of course Tip, the funny one, and Graham, the lucky one. Then there's me. Obviously, there's Jessie, but she's the baby."

Cooper's voice was different than I'd ever heard it. "But you're the sweet one. You're the kind one. You're the one who saved a baby fox that time when its leg was caught in the fence. You're the one who almost got fired from his job just so you could keep Dee from being stranded on the side of the highway in a rainstorm."

He sounded so offended, so distraught, and it made something inside of me squeeze tight. I let go of his hand and reached for his cheek, cupping it for a minute before sliding my fingers into his hair. "Beth is the sweet one, remember? I'm just me. Nothing special about me. It was actually the preacher at church who started calling me Nine really early on, like at my baptism. He said the number nine was symbolic of the completeness of the Holy Spirit or something, then he said it also represented finality." I laughed. "When Beth told me the story years later, she said it was pretty clear to everyone in the church he meant that as a message for Mom and Dad to stop having more babies. But then came Jessie, so clearly they didn't listen."

"Does it bother you? The name, I mean." The worry was clear in Cooper's eyes.

"No. I'm used to it. Teachers started calling me Nine in kindergarten. I can't remember when my mom started calling me by that name, but my dad got on board when someone thought it was real clever to give me the number nine jersey in tee ball."

Cooper didn't laugh.

I leaned over and kissed his prickly chin. "I notice you call me Isaac more often lately. Is that why? Do you worry about upsetting me?"

He shrugged. "Maybe a little."

"Don't. It doesn't bother me. But… it's nice that you care. I like it when you call me Isaac. But I like it when you call me Nine too. I just like it when you call me at all."

Cooper got a little fidgety under the focused attention and looked away. I'd noticed more and more that he tended to get squirrelly when the subject of him and emotions came up. He'd done it at the restaurant too. Before I could ask him about it, he leaned in and smacked a kiss on my lips before hopping out of bed. "Time to start the day, Winshed. Time waits for no man."

I reached out and pinched a pale ass cheek before he got out of my reach. I just liked hearing him yelp.

"You promised to help me with the kitchen plumbing today," I reminded him as he ducked into the bathroom.

"Yeah, yeah. Start some coffee, would you?" he called back through the thin door.

We got our morning routine started and did the subconscious dance we'd somehow perfected around the tiny kitchen getting our breakfast made and fixing each other's coffee. Once we were finished and cleaned up and Nacho had eaten his breakfast, the three of us headed outside into the cool mountain morning.

"I like it out here more than I expected," Cooper admitted, stretching his arms over his head and then spinning in a circle. His new work boots stood out as too clean and perfect in the pine straw-littered dirt of the clearing. It wouldn't be long before they looked worse for wear.

"It's a far cry from LA." I walked over to my truck to get the plumbing fittings I'd picked up the night before in town. "Sure you're not missing your hot dance clubs and fancy clothes?"

When I turned back toward him with the shopping bag in my hand, I nearly dropped it. Cooper's arms were still over his head, and now he was undulating his hips in a sultry move that made me instantly hard. "Ngh."

His head snapped up, and he shot me a knowing grin. "Wanna dance?"

When I got close enough to set the bag on the makeshift sawhorse table near the cabin's front porch, I tossed it down and came back to him, reaching one arm around his waist and taking his hand with my other one. "I only know how to do this boring boy/girl bullshit," I admitted.

We danced to silent music for a few beats before he made me wait so he could take out his phone and turn on some real music. Sam Smith's "Stay With Me" blasted from the tiny speaker as he slid it back into his pocket. I only knew what the song was because Cooper had played it a thousand times this week and chatted my ear off about how the singer was enby and a proud example of the transformative nature of sexual identity exploration. I didn't really know what any of that meant, but I also didn't care as long as I got to have my hands on Cooper's body while he swayed to the rhythm.

I enjoyed the familiar feel of his body against mine, and I realized that starting the day with his boundless energy and good mood was beginning to spoil me. He was like my own giant ray of personal sunshine, and I wanted to bask in it long after we were done here.

After the second song, I realized I was being had.

"This isn't going to get you out of helping me with the plumbing," I said against his lips before kissing him some more.

Cooper slid his phone out of his pocket and opened the camera, all without stopping our kiss. I heard the familiar ding of the Record button and tried not to think of my mother on the other end of that video when it posted.

"I love you," I murmured against his cheek before moving down to nuzzle his neck. It took a few precious seconds before I realized what I'd said.

The phone dinged again to signal the end of recording just as I froze. An odd numbness hit my body. "I-I..." I stammered. "I was..."

Cooper's smile was easy and confident. "It's fine. You knew we were recording, so you went with it. Don't freak out. I get it."

I let out a breath, but still felt oddly numb. Was that true? Had I been playing it up for the camera? That didn't sound like me, but then again, I also wasn't sure I loved him exactly. It was too soon to think of feelings like that, and even if it wasn't, Cooper wasn't the kind of man you loved. He was the kind of man you tasted and relished before releasing him back to the world. He would never stay still enough to be loved by a man like me, a man more at home in a wooded clearing and half-broken-down cabin than anywhere else in the world.

"Back to work," I said in a gruff voice. "Morning cheese video done. Now it's hustle time."

I didn't say much for the rest of the morning besides grunting out instructions for what Cooper needed to do to help me lay the new piping for the fridge and kitchen sink. When we finished that, we moved right into the bathroom plumbing. By the time we took a break for lunch, we'd knocked out an entire day's worth of work because neither of us had done any of our usual goofing off or joking around.

"I'm going to make us some lunch," Cooper finally said as I began removing all the leftover bits and pieces to the supply area I'd designated on one side of the clearing.

I waved an acknowledgement as I headed out into the trees to take a leak. I was just closing my pants back up when I heard Cooper cry out my name. It sounded different than the bird incident, more like he was in pain. I raced back to the RV and stormed up the steps to find him clutching his side. Underneath his grip was a growing patch of red blood set off starkly against his light pink T-shirt.

"Fuck, what happened?"

"I..." His breath was heaving like he was mid-panic.

"Shhh, slow down and take a breath while I wash my hands." After a quick scrub, I peeled his hands away to see what was wrong. There was a three-inch gash on his side that looked pretty deep. It was right about counter height, so I turned to look for what sharp edge could have caught him.

That's when I saw the big foldable tripod on the floor that I'd left on the counter earlier. "Was it the tripod?" I looked up at him. There were fat tears balancing on the edge of his lower lashes. "Baby, was it this? I'm so fucking sorry."

He nodded, and the tears spilled over. "It's not your fault. I thought I saw another bird in here, and I kind of freaked out and then tripped. Knocked the tripod off and somehow it got me. I don't know. It hurts like a mother."

I grabbed a clean dishcloth and held it in place. "You need stitches. Hold this. I'm going to see if I can butterfly it closed for now, but I doubt it."

When I stuck my head into the lower cabinet to find the first aid kit, I heard him sniffle and let out a shaky breath.

"Just scared me, you know?" he said between breaths.

"Yeah. Those things happen fast." I knelt in front of him and used some supplies from the kit to clean him up and try and bandage it as best I could until I could get him better help.

"You sure it needs stitches? Can't we just—"

"I'm sure. Believe me. We've had plenty of injuries like this on the farm. It's way better to get stitches now and get it over with than hope it stays closed on its own." I finished padding the area with extra gauze before slipping his pants and underwear down off his legs and unlacing his boots.

He just stared at me. "What're you—"

"Getting you clean clothes. Hang tight." I stood up and went back to our room to get a clean T-shirt, a loose pair of sweats, and underwear that weren't covered in blood. I grabbed some socks and his running shoes too. When I got back and finished sorting him out, I loaded us all up in the truck.

I held his hand in mine the entire drive back to Shale Falls, shooting quick glances at him every few minutes to make sure he wasn't too pale. Even though my brain knew he wasn't going to bleed out from the gash in his side, some lizard hindbrain insisted I get him help as soon as possible.

"I think I'm going to die," he said in a shocked voice about halfway down the mountain.

"You're not. I promise." But the conversation made me antsy regardless.

"No, I mean, if you're playing Lady Gaga instead of Kenny Chesney, it must mean I'm on death's door."

I did a classic double take before realizing he was joking. "Haven't lost your sense of humor, hm?"

He gave me a half smile even though he was clearly uncomfortable. "Guess not."

"Shame," I said, shooting him a wink. "We'll be there soon. Close your eyes and breathe deep."

After a few minutes of only the sound of Gaga's voice in the truck, Cooper spoke again softly. "You're a good man, Isaac Winshed."

He'd said that to me before, but it never ceased to make me proud, as if all I needed was for this one human to think that about me and my life would be okay. I'd always wanted to be needed, but as the ninth kid—and the last boy—in my family, no one ever really needed me. Being able to help Cooper was a gift. Plus, the idea of him ever being alone and needing help made my stomach hurt. Thankfully, I'd been there when he'd needed someone.

"Almost there," I assured him, squeezing his hand.

"I don't want stitches. Can't we go home? Please?"

"Mpfh."

When we finally pulled up in front of the emergency clinic, I let him out before parking the truck in a shady spot and cracking the windows for Nacho. "Stay here, bud. I'll bring you some water in a bit." I scratched his head before taking off at a jog to the front slider doors of the one-story building.

Cooper was standing just inside the doors waiting for me. I put my hand on his lower back and guided him toward the reception counter. Thankfully, the place wasn't very busy, so we were checked in quickly and taken straight back.

I helped him onto the exam table and helped replace his T-shirt with a gown. He was shaking and pale. "You okay?" I asked.

"Don't like needles."

I leaned over him and brushed the hair back from his face. "How can I distract you?"

He rolled his eyes, but the tension seemed to bleed out of his face a little. I leaned down to kiss him gently on the lips when I heard the door open behind me.

"Hi, I'm Dr. Rappaport. Which one of you got mauled by a bear?"

I turned to see a tall, slim woman with dark skin and a bright smile. She shot me a wink which managed to put me at ease that quickly.

Cooper let out a soft snort. "I make it a practice to get mauled by this bear as often as possible."

The doc moved over to the sink in the room to wash her hands. "I can see that," she said with a laugh. "And I hope it's not unprofessional for me to tell you I love your vlog. My wife is a schoolteacher, but she fancies herself a construction worker around the house. Thanks to your tutorials, we've saved tons of money on repair people."

I stared at her in disbelief. I'd never met anyone in real life who'd seen my videos outside of my family and the customers at Walt's.

Cooper smiled weakly at me. "He's not used to being recognized for his greatness. Hence the scared-rabbit routine."

My face heated. "Sorry. Thank you. I've never met anyone who's seen my stuff before. Outside of my hometown anyway."

She sat on the rolling exam chair and wheeled closer to Cooper, nudging me out of the way so she could check out his injury. "Well, keep up the great work. I didn't realize your cabin renovation was near here. Tell me more about it. What's been your favorite part so far?"

As Cooper began to talk hesitantly about the project, the doctor peeled off my makeshift bandage and began cleaning his wound. I could tell she was trying to distract him from what she was doing, but he wasn't that easily calmed. His entire body was trembling, and he kept shooting me nervous looks. I moved over to the other side of the table so I could hold his hand without being in the way, and he clutched my hand with a sweaty stranglehold.

As she began putting in the stitches, she asked questions about the camera equipment we used, the kinds of fixtures we were going to put into the bathroom, and finally how we were going to decorate it when it was all done.

"Decorate it?" Cooper asked, flicking his eyes to me. "Shit."

"We obviously haven't gotten that far," I said with a laugh. "But I'm sure Cooper's going to come up with something great."

"Why me?" Cooper asked. He was trying his best to appear normal, but there was a light sheen of sweat on his face, and he was very deliberately not looking anywhere near the needle.

"You've lived in LA. You have style." It sounded stupid when I said it out loud.

Cooper's forehead crinkled. "You mean I'm gay so I must know how to decorate?"

Uh-oh.

I glanced at the doc. "Um, we're both gay, so..."

Cooper's nostrils flared. "You know what I mean."

The doc finished up and sat back. "You should stop by Nick's and pick up some magazines before you head home. Get some ideas that way."

"That's a good idea," I said. "Who's Nick?"

"It's actually called the Nickerie. It's a gift shop at the corner of Corn and Main. Little white house with a deep blue front door. You can't miss it."

Cooper said, "The fact there's a street called Corn in this town makes me irrationally happy."

Dr. Rappaport grinned at him. "Right? I'm only a Shalie by marriage. Wren grew up here and forced me to move back home with her when this job opened. I'm from Seattle. But I wouldn't trade it for the world now. There's something about a small mountain town that's just... special. I don't know. But just so you know, in addition to Corn Avenue, there's also Blueberry Court, Pothole Place, and a neighborhood called Falls Falls. And if you're taking Highway 53 back, you should know that Shalies call it Winding Road and it leads to Frying Pan Road which runs along the Frying Pan River."

Cooper laughed. If I could have given the woman a tip just for that, I would have. After she said her goodbyes and wished us well, I helped Cooper back into his shirt and the zip-up cotton jacket he'd used as a blanket in the truck. "Thank god for Stallion's insurance plan," Cooper muttered. "Otherwise I really would have fought you on this."

I helped him off the table and out to the truck. Nacho had to sniff him up and down to make sure he was still all in one piece. When we started down Main Street, Cooper pointed out the little white house with the blue door. "Let's stop in there."

"I want to get you home."

Cooper flapped his hand at me. "I feel fine. The place where she did the stitches is still numb. Please?"

I pulled into the gravel lot behind the house and helped him out of the truck. "It's just a cut," he muttered when I insisted on keeping an arm around his waist. "I'm hardly dying."

"Yeah, but it's my fault you got hurt, so I'm going to take care of you."

Cooper stopped and turned to me. "You're kidding, right?"

"No, I left the damned tripod there instead of putting it somewhere safe."

"Isaac, it was safe. It was resting on the counter. It wasn't sticking out or anything. I saw something move out of the corner of my eye and flailed. That's what knocked it into a position to gouge me. Nothing about this was your fault. Besides, it was an accident. It doesn't need to be my fault either. No fault, okay. Just... one of those things. Dumb luck. Now I'm all patched up and about to become some kind of gay interior-decorating master." He narrowed his eyes at me and took a deep, dramatic breath. "Fear me, Isaac Winshed. For I will wield all the frou-frou magic in my power once I have… someone else's ideas."

We continued walking toward the building, this time only holding hands. "You kind of petered out there at the end," I teased.

"I really don't know my ass from an occasional table, Nine. We're probably in trouble."

Well, we certainly knew anything he came up with would be better than anything I picked. "You'll do fine. I have faith in you."

When we entered the little shop, a bell over the door tinkled and a blond-haired man popped his head up from behind the counter. "Welcome to the Nickerie. I'm Norman; let me know how I can help. Are you looking for anything special today?"

Cooper studied the man. "Your name isn't Nick?"

"No. Is yours?"

18

COOPER

Nine and I stared at the guy for a beat until he laughed.

"Nicki is my wife. Seriously, gentlemen, what can I help you with? You're those videogrammers, right? Is that the word?"

Being recognized for the second time today really brought home the subscriber numbers we'd been noticing. The numbers were skyrocketing, but until being recognized around this tiny town, it had only been an abstract statistic. It felt strange, but exciting.

"Vlogger," I corrected. "But yes, that's us. We were hoping to find some home decor magazines or books if you have them."

I looked around the store and realized it was all very old-fashioned country. The place was packed to the brim with knickknacks, enough to make my skin crawl with unexpected claustrophobia. Apparently, I did have a preferred aesthetic—who knew?

"Sure, right this way. Nikki keeps the periodicals in a rack in the candle room."

Of course she did. Who wouldn't?

We followed him through the crowded house to a little room full of more stuff, most of it flammable.

"Thanks," Nine said in an apparent attempt to release the man from his duty and free up some space in the tight quarters.

Once he left, Nine leaned down to whisper in my ear. "Norm and Nicki's Nickerie? Really?"

I smiled and leaned back into him, enjoying knowing he was close while I still felt hurt and more vulnerable than I liked. He was such a steady presence, warm and strong, that I felt completely cared for when he was near. It was spoiling me. I knew better than to get used to this, but it was also nice to have a break from always being the one in charge. When I was with Isaac, I could let go.

"Hm," Nine said in the same low voice. "*How to Decorate on a Dime*."

I reached for the one next to that. "*Flea Finds For Less*."

"*Country Tweaks from Grandma's Attic*... these are not what we're looking for, are they?"

I laughed and shook my head. "Don't think so. Let's see..." I reached over to a more modern-looking magazine. "*Millennial Minimalism to Fit Any Budget*."

"Let's just grab one of each and hit the road. Maybe we can find something good in them. Plus, it'll give you something to do while you're laid up. And you can browse online too. Delia uses that corkboard site. We can ask her for help."

I looked over my shoulder to see his sweet eyes filled with serious concern for me. "I'm fine," I said softly.

Nine searched my face, obviously assessing my pain level. "Please let me take you home and put you in bed. I won't be okay until you're off your feet for a little while."

I put my arms around his neck and kissed him gently. "Okay. You get one of each, and I'll go wait in the truck with Nacho. Ask Nicki's Norm where we can get takeout in this one-horse town."

When Nine finally joined me in the truck, he blew out an annoyed sigh. "Sorry that took so long. Apparently I had to hear about every takeout restaurant *and* their owners *and* their backstories *and* what that place used to be."

"What's the verdict?"

"Sounds like there's a health food place you'd like down one of these side streets." He backed the truck out of the parking spot and shifted into Drive.

"Fuck that. Let's get something better. Fried chicken or pasta. I'm starving."

"He said there was a great pizza place just past the gas station."

"Perfect." I searched through my phone to call our order in, but the place was so close, we arrived while I was still on the phone with the guy. "He said it won't be long. Wake me up when it's ready."

That was the last thought I had until I felt the cool breeze on my face from the open passenger door. I blinked my eyes open to see the clearing and the RV. "We're home?"

Nine helped me out and got me inside. The numbness had definitely worn off, and my side hurt like a bitch. I regretted not taking the doc up on her offer of a pain pill prescription. "Hurts and I'm hungry," I said, trying not to whine too much, but I was feeling sorry for myself now because I truly was in pain and I truly was hungry enough to eat the dog.

"I'm going to fix all of that for you. Go pee and then get in bed."

"Love it when you boss me into the toilet," I muttered under my breath.

He went back outside while I moved around like a snail. I finally stripped down to my underwear and crawled in bed, propping myself up in hopes of food. Sure enough, he brought the pizza in. "It's still warm, but I can heat it up more if you want."

"It's fine. I like cold pizza anyway. How the hell is it still warm?"

Nine looked away. "Um, well, I kind of drove fast."

He was so fucking sweet. "Get in here and sit with me."

His beard split with his grin. "Let me grab our drinks and some pain meds for you."

When he got back to bed with everything we needed, including a big bath towel to protect the sheets, we had ourselves a bed pizza picnic. The pizza was amazing, and we both agreed we'd have to order from the same place again when we went back to town next.

After I finished and wiped my hands on the paper towel he'd given me, I reached for my phone to see if I'd missed any messages from home. I had, but there were also a ton of notifications from our Instagram account. I clicked into it and saw a picture of the two of us in the truck. I was asleep on Nine's shoulder, and Nacho was licking my ear. The caption said, "My poor baby had an accident and needed stitches, but don't worry, Nacho and I will take good care of him. #Owie #DocsRule #SnitchesGetStitches #CoopedUpWithNine #DogsOfInstagram #DIY." There were a ton of other hashtags I recognized from many of the posts I'd made on our account.

The outpouring of love and support on the post blew me away. There were hundreds of comments. I looked over at Nine. "You did this?"

He glanced up to see what I was talking about and winced. "Oh. Yeah. Is that bad? I'm sorry."

"No, it's good. It's really good. First of all, it's important to show the good and the bad. We've talked about that. But also, it's... really fucking sweet."

He shrugged and went back to eating his pizza. "I was worried about you, and I kind of felt... I just wanted you to have some nice well-wishes to wake up to, I guess."

I read through the post again. "You even put in the hashtags."

He laughed and tossed his paper towel in the pizza box before closing it. "Yeah, you said it helps us find new followers. I still don't know what I'm doing there, but I tried."

I leaned over and kissed his shoulder before smiling up at him. "I especially like the snitches get stitches one."

Nine huffed and rolled his eyes. "I'm not as funny as you are. You're better at those things."

After shoving everything farther away, I climbed onto his lap and straddled him.

"Careful," he warned, reaching for my hips as gingerly as possible.

I wrapped my arms around his neck and leaned in to kiss him. "Thank you for taking such good care of me, but I'm fine."

"I like taking care of you." He nibbled on my collarbone before nipping at my earlobe.

I sucked in a breath. "I don't like being beholden to anyone."

He snorted. "No shit."

His mouth was distracting. It made me want more. "Let me sit on your dick."

"Nuh-uh. You need to lie down." Despite his words, Isaac continued trailing kisses up and down my neck. My body was covered in tingling nerves ready for action. The pain meds had kicked in, and my side didn't hurt as much as it had before.

"I'm good," I promised. My fingers combed through his beard and tugged when he didn't respond. "I swear."

Isaac gently turned us until I was on my back and he was propped over me. "Stay here while I clean up." He gave me one more searing kiss and then climbed off the bed to take our dinner trash away. He was gone long enough for me to doze a little, but I noticed when he came back because the bed dipped.

"Sit on my face," I slurred.

The deep rumble of his laughter made me smile even though my eyes were still closed.

"How about I rub your feet instead?"

Even though that sounded amazing, it wasn't enough. "There's a hundred percent more orgasms with my plan."

He drew me into his arms until I was curled up in my usual spot with my head on his chest. I inhaled the honeyed scent of him. "Mm, my bear."

Nine must have started reading on his phone because I could hear the faint fingernail tapping sound. "Glad those pain meds are doing you right," he murmured.

"What'd you give me? S'not regular."

"I filled the prescription the doc gave me. After you refused it, she slid it into my hand behind your back and said you'd change your mind. She also said you were going to have a massive bruise there for a while that might hurt worse than the laceration itself."

"Smart Nine."

He laughed again. "Drunk Coop."

My head wasn't putting thoughts together quite right, but I knew there was something missing, something I really needed to do. "Do a vid."

I felt him shift underneath me. "What? Why?"

"Jusss do it."

"Fine." I heard the ding of the recording. "What did you want to tell everyone, baby?"

"I love you too."

19

NINE

Even though I'd known he was under the influence of pain meds and hamming it up for the camera, the words had still hit me like a punch to the gut. I hadn't posted the video. Instead, I'd socked it away as my own little personal treat to replay over and over down the road one day when Cooper was long gone. When he was back in LA pursuing his dream and seeing his own face on big Hollywood billboards one day.

I was in heaven taking care of Cooper. He was the kind of person who never needed help from anyone. It had taken me a while to figure it out, but when I had, I'd noticed it in so many of the things we did.

Like the time I'd tried to teach him how to use the drill as a power screwdriver. He'd ignored me and promptly stripped a screw by going too fast. When I tried to show him how to slow down the drill, he'd thrown his hands up and stormed off in frustration. At first, I'd thought he had a low attention span or maybe he simply frustrated easily, but over time, I realized it was an absolute discomfort with being helped in any way.

After sleeping hard all night on the pain pills, he woke up feeling much better. I still told him to take it easy, but I wasn't surprised when he didn't listen. He joined me in the cabin where I was hanging drywall.

"You need help?" he asked. Normally I would have said yes since it was easier with another set of hands, but I didn't want him to pull his stitches open.

"No, but I made you a little stool so you can keep me company." I gestured over my shoulder to the simple seat I'd made early this morning.

He stared at it like it was something from an alien planet. "That's a step stool."

"Yeah." I went back to adding more drywall screws in the sheet I was hanging.

"You made that? This morning? Like... yourself?"

I turned back to reach for another handful of screws. "Yeah. It's super simple. Just a couple of cuts to the two side boards, add in a middle brace, and then lay the planks on the two steps. It's not sanded or anything, so be careful of splinters. But it should be fine. You could always put a towel over it."

I drilled in a few more screws. When I stepped back to grab the next board, Cooper was still staring at the little stool like it was going to bite.

"You don't have to sit on it," I muttered, hauling the next board over from where I'd propped several on the other side of the room.

"No, it's just... this is amazing. I can't believe you made this for me."

I shrugged and got back to work. After a few minutes, I heard him doing a video about the little stool and how great it was. I turned back around to face him. When he put the phone away, I said, "I recorded myself making it so you could edit it into a little tutorial. The footage is still in the camera. I used the bigger tripod and threw that other one away."

His face broke into a big smile. "Did that tripod offend you?"

"Hey, you don't cut my boyfriend and get to keep your life. Let that be a lesson to all the other tripods out there. I'm watching them."

The sound of his laughter followed me back into the task at hand.

As I worked, I heard him moving around in and out of the main room of the cabin until the familiar click of the computer keys hit my ears. I turned to see him working on the laptop with the camera attached. He'd brought in one of the square folding tables from outside and set it up as a makeshift desk. He'd put both of our water bottles on the table and hooked up his own phone to the Bluetooth speaker before changing out the music I'd been listening to the way he always did when we were both working in here.

I didn't mind it as long as it made him happy, especially because sometimes he gave me a little private dance when his favorite songs came on. I liked that part a lot.

After a while, it seemed he'd wrapped up the video editing and was just goofing around.

"You could always go grab those magazines to look at for decorating tips," I suggested. "And if there's any lemonade in the fridge…"

"Aww, poor baby is thirsty after all of his hard work, huh?" He stood up and came closer.

"I'm a sweaty mess. Stay away unless you want to smell this ripe too," I warned.

Cooper's eyes were full of heat. "Yes. I'm so turned off by the sweaty, muscled construction worker in my midst, whatever shall I do?" He put his index finger in the center of his bottom lip and looked so sexy, I wondered if there was enough clear floor space to throw him down on.

He stalked closer. "Maybe I should remove those sweaty jeans from your poor, overworked body?"

I backed up a few steps. "You're injured."

He shook his head. "I'm fine. I need some dick therapy."

I cringed. "That was awful."

"What can I say? I'm desperate."

Cooper dropped to his knees right in front of me, and I wasn't selfless enough to refuse him. My dick was a steel pipe in my jeans, and the sight of Cooper Heath on his knees for me in a pile of drywall dust and construction materials was like my very own porn scene. And there were no cameras filming inside the cabin.

"Fuck," I breathed as his nimble fingers attacked my fly. As soon as he got my dick out, he began licking it like he was as desperate as he'd claimed. I gently held his chin in one hand and the top of his head in my other. "Oh, fuck. Coop, shit. Like that, just like that."

He sucked and licked and groaned around my cock until the sounds of our grunts were echoing around the mostly empty space. One of his hands grasped the base of my shaft while the other fumbled in the front of his own pants. As soon as I saw him pull his own dick out and begin to stroke it, I was on the edge.

"Coop," I warned. "Coop, fuck." He swallowed me even deeper until all I could feel was his hot, wet throat and his warm breath on my balls. I shot long and deep inside of him, letting go of his head and balling my hands into fists to keep from shoving myself even deeper. "*Nghhh!*"

Cooper pulled off with a final long suck and then threw his head back with a shout. Cum splattered into the plywood subfloor between my work boots, and a primitive part of me relished knowing that we'd marked this place. Maybe it was stupid, but I felt a possessiveness about this cabin now, and I knew it would be hard to leave it when we were done here.

Cooper leaned his head against my thigh and wrapped an arm around my calf. I threaded my fingers through his hair.

"Thank you," I said, leaning down to pull him up carefully. "You shouldn't have done that, but I can't say I regret enjoying it. I think it's time for lunch and a nap though."

He stepped into my body and wrapped his arms around me for a hug. "Mm, only if you come too."

I kissed him softly for a few minutes enjoying the salty taste of him. "I'll lie down with you for a little while, but then I want to get this wall board finished. I thought I'd do a time-lapse video of the rest of it."

We made our way back to the RV, making a list of different video clips we'd taken in the last few days to use for our next YouTube video. I sat Cooper down at the table and began pulling out sandwich stuff when his phone rang. I expected him to take the call outside for more privacy, but he must have been more tired than I'd thought, because he stayed right there at the table.

"This is Cooper. Oh hi." His voice betrayed sudden interest in whoever it was on the other line. I tried not to listen in, but it was impossible with him two feet away from me. "Good to hear from you... wow, that sounds exciting... mm-hm... Would there be an audition, or...? Yeah, sure... Okay... okay... That sounds great. Send me the info... Sure, absolutely. Sounds good."

For some reason, I got a bad feeling about that call. Not a bad feeling for Coop, but for me. Of course I wanted him to have every opportunity to follow his dreams, but if he was being offered an acting opportunity, it probably meant going back to LA. And I would miss him. Terribly.

"Who was that?" I asked, still facing away from him while I finished cutting up some apples to put on each plate.

"Jesus, that was my agent. He heard from a casting director representing Sam Gwan. Do you know Hae Gwan who directed *Red Stone Alpha*?"

I knew the movie, of course. It had been the must-see action movie last summer. "I mean, I don't know movie directors' names, but okay?"

"Well, her son Sam is an up-and-coming director himself who's made a few indie films. One of them is this really cool suspense film where the lead is gay. It's not a big deal in the movie, it's just... the detective has a husband at home instead of a wife."

"That's cool." I didn't really know what else to say. "So this guy wants to talk to you about a part in a movie?"

I finished fixing our plates and set them on the table before sliding into the booth across from him. Our legs found each other under the table naturally and tangled together. Whenever I was within touching distance, my body seemed to seek out a physical connection with Cooper whether it was a conscious move or not.

"I guess. It's still too good to be true. Even auditioning for him would be amazing. Just being in the room, you know?"

I nodded and bit into my sandwich. Cooper deserved my excited support even if I selfishly wished the phone had never rung. "Tell me everything," I said between bites.

He shrugged and took a sip of his water. "I don't know much. It's some kind of medical drama, and the part they want me to come in for is one of the nurses. It's a supporting role, but my agent said it's a big speaking part."

"Wow, that's great. What happens next? Do they... need you to fly to LA, or...?"

He shrugged. "Not sure yet. He's going to send me an email with options. He said they know what I'm working on because that's how they found me."

I snapped my head up. "Really? That's cool. You mean this stuff? *Cooped Up With Nine*?"

He grinned. "Yeah. Super cool. It was one of the things I was hoping for when I agreed to do this, but I never really thought it would happen, especially this soon. Apparently Sam—the director—is a big YouTube watcher. Which makes sense because he's young. In his midtwenties I think."

I made a mental note to search for this guy on the internet to find out if he had a good reputation. Even though Cooper had lived in LA for several years, he was still a small-town Colorado boy at heart. I'd hate for someone to take advantage of him.

Which was stupid since Cooper Heath had way more street smarts than I did and had been taking care of himself and his family for years. Still. I would worry about him regardless.

"That's amazing, Coop. I'm really happy for you." I tucked back into my lunch and tried concentrating on chewing every bite thoroughly so I didn't choke myself in the rush to finish and get out of there. I needed to think. I needed to get myself into a better headspace where I could tell him I was happy for him and really mean it. He deserved that. He deserved my support.

"Thanks. I need to call Jacks and tell him." He picked his phone back up. "Do you mind me calling him even though we're eating?"

"No, of course not. I'm going to finish up and get back to work, but you're going to lie down. Got it?"

He reached across and squeezed my forearm. "Yes, boss. But you promised you'd lie down with me."

"I will after I get a few more things knocked out in the cabin."

He smiled at me with bright eyes. "Okay, good." Then he pressed the button to dial his brother.

The animated way he told Jacks about the opportunity confirmed what I'd already suspected. This was a dream opportunity for him, something he'd never had in the years he'd actively pursued an acting career in LA. If there was anything I could do to help him get this role, including letting him out of this project sooner, I would have to do it.

Because I wanted him to be happy. Whether that was in a life that included me or not.

I shoved my headphones in and got back to work.

20

COOPER

I was too excited to sleep, but I still took Nine's advice and got into bed. Instead of napping, I continued editing the step stool tutorial until I had it ready to upload. It was a good way to keep my mind off the call from Hollywood.

When I heard the RV door open and the clomp of Nine's heavy footfalls on the steps, I called out to Nine. "Hey, I have the stool tutorial ready, but I wanted to talk to you about the best way to use it to cross over your Nine fans with the *Cooped* fans. Since this is more like one of your Nine tutorials, I thought..."

The door slammed closed again and Nine was gone. I stared at the closed door. Only Nacho stood there drinking from his water bowl.

That wasn't like him. He either hadn't heard me, which was possible if he had his earbuds in, or he'd heard me and ignored me. I chose to give him the benefit of the doubt, but it still made me nervous.

I called my brother back even though I'd just spoken to him a little while ago about the call from my agent.

"Hey, miss me?" Jacks said with a smile when he answered.

"Never." I took a breath. "Um, I need—"

"Uh-oh."

"No, it's fine. I just..." Suddenly, and without warning, my eyes felt tight. I flashed a glance toward the main part of the RV to make sure I was definitely alone. "I..." This wasn't easy.

"It's the guy." His voice was full of sympathy which didn't help my eye problem at all.

"It's the guy," I answered in a small voice.

"He doesn't want you to get the job? Because if so, that's a problem, Coop."

"No, it's not that. I mean, I don't even know. But it doesn't really matter because he's not... I mean, it's not... like, between the two of us, there really isn't a future together that I can see working out anyway, so..."

"Oh."

"Yeah." Nacho leaped up onto the bed and settled next to me. I reached out a hand to stroke his long golden fur. I took a deep breath and plastered on a smile. "So it's fine. I mean, it's been fun, don't get me wrong, but going back to LA with a cowboy in tow is hardly—"

"Don't do that," Jacks snapped. "This is me you're talking to. Don't bullshit me."

I let out the breath and sank back down into the covers. "I don't want to want him, and I damned sure don't want to need him."

Jackson's laugh was familiar and comforting even though he was laughing at me. "You don't need anyone, do you? Never have, never will."

"Damned straight. I especially don't need a man to make me happy. I've taken enough of Mom's online quizzes to learn that."

We shared a laugh even though it covered up a huge pile of horseshit.

When Jacks spoke again, his voice was more careful. "You deserve someone to take care of you. You may not need it, but you deserve it."

"Pfft." I knew better than to rely on someone else for my own happiness. I may have been joking about it before, but I really didn't need anyone else in order to live a good life. I'd learned from watching my mother that relying on someone else was a recipe for a whole lot of hurt.

"Not every man is like Dad."

Fucking mind-reading brothers.

"And how do you know that?" It wasn't like Jacks had had any more luck in the relationship department than I had. The minute he'd started having health problems, his boyfriend had hit the road claiming he was "too young and free for this shit." Yet another reason I'd learned not to rely on others. It had wrecked my brother.

I regretted my words but didn't take them back.

"Because there hasn't been a day in twenty years that Marchie Kagen hasn't stood by me and made and supported me in every way."

I flapped my hand in a dismissive gesture he couldn't see. "That doesn't count. Marchie is in love with you. Everyone knows that."

Silence from the other end. "What?"

"Come on. Don't act like you don't know that man is desperate to make babies with you. But back to me. What should I do?"

"Not back to you. Back to me. You think Marchie's in love with me? But that..." His voice trailed off. "That doesn't make any sense."

My brother was oblivious. "Fine. He's not. That's probably why he wasn't the first person to beg me to donate the bone marrow, as if I wasn't going to do it anyway."

"Oh," he said, sounding relieved. "Well, yeah. He was worried about me. And you're right. He does love me. As a friend. Now, back to Nine. Talk to him. Ask him what he thinks about it."

"I already know what he's going to say. He's going to encourage me to follow my dreams. He's going to tell me he'll do anything on earth to help me achieve what I want in life. And then he's going to slink back to Wyoming and fade into the woodwork while I go on to stardom in LA. At least, that's the way it would happen if he had a say."

"Surely he has visions of a bigger life than working at Walt's? Why else would he have taken this opportunity with Stallion?"

For you, I thought. "For me. He knew I wanted to... use it as a platform to get discovered." That sounded lame, but I wasn't going to put more pressure on Jacks by implying Nine had done it for him, for the medical bills. And I knew Nine would never admit that was the reason, but I'd figured it out pretty easily. He wasn't all that great at lying.

"Aww, that's sweet."

I stroked Nacho's silky ear and sighed. "Yeah. That's him. He's the sweetest."

"So talk to him. Tell him you like him."

Nacho's ears perked up. "I have. He knows."

I heard the smile in his voice again. "I'm happy to hear that, brother. Anyone is better than Lee Chambers."

I thought of the man I'd happily left behind when I'd left LA to move back to Colorado. "I was never in a relationship with Lee. Not really."

"Not for lack of trying," Jacks scoffed.

"Listen, can we not talk about Lee, please?"

The RV door opened and Nine came stomping in.

My brother ignored me. "I think Lee is one of the reasons why you won't give this guy a real chance. It's relevant."

My eyes stayed riveted on the big frame in the main area of the RV, kicking off his boots by the door and washing his hands in the sink. For some reason, my heart rate took off. Was he mad at me for the LA thing?

But then he turned his head and searched for me, the concern etched in his face. His eyes brightened when he saw me awake, and his grin split wide, showing off white teeth against his brown beard. "Hey, baby, you okay?"

I couldn't breathe. I couldn't look away from him. My entire body felt oddly frozen with relief. He wasn't upset with me, thank fuck.

"Jacks, I gotta go." My voice came out strangely breathy.

"Okay, but think about what I said. You deserve to have it all, Coop. It doesn't have to be the job or the guy. It can be both."

I ended the call and set the phone on the tiny side table, all the while keeping my eyes pinned on Nine. When he came closer to the bedroom, he ducked his head in. "Gonna take a quick rinse to get the sweat and drywall dust off. You need anything? Ice water? Pain meds?"

I shook my head and held out my arms for him. He frowned for a minute before stepping into the room. "What is it?" he asked, pulling one of my hands to his mouth for a kiss before leaning in and kissing my forehead.

"Nothing," I said. "I just wanted to feel you. Go shower."

He continued to frown down at me, but I plastered on a smile. "You sure?"

I nodded and clamped my teeth together. "Yep."

He narrowed his eyes before turning and stripping off what remained of his clothes. By this time of day he was already down to only jeans and boots, so I had a killer view of his sweaty back muscles as he walked away.

As soon as he was safely in the tiny bathroom with the water running, I closed my eyes and gave myself a stern talking-to.

This. This was what I avoided like the plague. Attaching my happiness to another person was a recipe for fucking disaster. I'd watched for years while my brother didn't reciprocate Marchie's feelings and Marchie suffered in silence. Then I'd met Lee and learned what it was like to be in Marchie's position. Having feelings for someone you couldn't be with was like being the next person to board Space Mountain at Disneyland when suddenly they stopped the line to let a bunch of VIPs on instead. Except once the VIPs were on board, they closed the ride altogether.

Forever.

I laughed into the small bedroom, startling Nacho from his deep sleep. This wasn't me. I didn't pine. And I sure as hell didn't pine for someone I didn't even really have. This was temporary. After we finished *Cooped Up With Nine*, we'd go our separate ways. Hopefully Nine would return home with a hot new Stallion sponsorship to support his vlog, and I would help Jacks and then return to LA to finally start my acting career in earnest.

It was good. Correction: it was great. And I got to have hot sex with an even hotter lumberjack fantasy man in the meantime. Perfect.

The bathroom door opened and Nine stepped out with nothing but a tiny towel wrapped around his waist.

Perfect indeed.

No more deep thoughts. Just sex. And when I went to LA, then I could look for someone more like me. Someone who...

I swallowed. Every feature I'd want in a partner was already present in the big guy standing at the foot of the bed. And if I found someone else in LA, that would mean he'd presumably find someone else in Wheatland. The thought of that made me want to throw an ax at a tree the way Isaac had tried to teach me one afternoon.

"You're glaring at me," he said with a lifted eyebrow. "What's going on? Was that your brother again on the phone?"

I threw back the covers and shimmied out of my underwear, careful not to disturb the big clean bandage covering my stitches.

"Fuck me."

Nine's eyes widened comically before he clutched at his chest and gave an exaggerated gasp. "What, no foreplay? No seduction?"

I turned to reach for the bottle of lube on his side table and felt a giant, callused palm squeeze my ass. Before I could turn back around, his other hand joined in, and suddenly, his beard was scratching down the cleft between my cheeks. "Holy fuck."

Isaac Winshed was going for it.

His hot tongue teased me lightly while his hands squeezed me roughly. The delicious roughness of his beard was something out of my deepest fantasies, but I'd never in a million years imagined Isaac having any interest in rimming me.

"Fuck," I repeated, sucking in a desperate breath. "Don't stop."

I reached back and put my fingers in his thick hair. As soon as that talented tongue landed on the sensitive skin of my hole, I made an embarrassing whimper sound. "Oh god. Fuck."

His laugh rumbled against me. "You like that word."

"Stop talking," I begged. "*Fuck.*"

More laughter. I had to give him credit. He'd never once balked at having sex with a man. Yes, he'd been unsure of himself at times, but he'd never been weirded out about anything we'd done together in bed. But this took the cake. And of course he was a master at it. The beard he had was a bit like cheating though. Bonus points and all that.

"Mmpfhhhh." I bit into the pillow to keep from scaring the dog.

The cool air hit my tender skin when he pulled away. "Hands and knees, baby. Gonna be fast and hard."

Who was this guy? During the day, he was quiet and pliable, but in bed, he suddenly found his confidence and enjoyed taking charge.

I scrambled up onto all fours to do his bidding while he grabbed a condom and flipped open the lube cap. Within moments, he was pressing inside with his hands tight on my hips. Now it was his turn to repeat the same word over and over.

"Fuck, ohhh fuck, *fuck*."

I would have laughed if I hadn't been so busy screaming for more.

21

NINE

Even though the sex with Cooper was still amazing—off-the-charts incredible—something was different. The call from his agent had changed things in some indescribable way. It was like a part of Cooper was no longer here with me. Which made sense, I guess, since he now had an amazing dream carrot dangling in front of him.

But it was even more of a reminder that this wasn't real. He wasn't mine, and we weren't living *my* dream. I'd never really known what I wanted to do with my life before now, but suddenly I'd had a taste of it. This. Him, us, the renovation project filled with DIY tutorials I got to share with others. Late-afternoon sun slanting across the trees while I flew the drone camera to capture nature scapes for the videos. Nacho chasing critters into the underbrush and bounding back happily with a stick in his mouth. Glancing up to find Cooper's head thrown back in laughter over finding another hillbilly decorator trick in one of the magazines from the Nickerie.

I was living my dream right here, but it wasn't going to last. Which, of course, made *me* different. I didn't even realize I was holding back until Cooper called me out on it. I'd walked deep into the woods to find some branches for a trim project I wanted to try. It took much longer than I expected to find enough of the length and width I needed, but I'd finally gotten enough when I heard crashing through the trees behind me. I turned back to see Cooper storming toward me mad as hell.

"I turned around and you were gone!"

I blinked at him. "I just walked into the woods to get some branches."

He looked around us with crazed eyes. "You've been gone two hours! It took me thirty minutes to find you. I thought you were gone. I thought you'd wandered off and... and something had happened to you."

I wasn't used to having to tell someone when I took a walk. Even though I thought he was overreacting, he was upset enough to need a little calming. "I'm... sorry?"

He threw his hands up. "You don't just fucking walk away without telling someone. There are bears out here. And snakes. There are ravines and... big rocks. You could have at least texted me or, *fuck*, taken your phone with you."

I pulled my phone out and held it up. "No service out here maybe."

His hands were fisted at his sides and tendons stood out on his neck. His hair was sticking out like he'd been running his fingers through it. "You're such a fucking man!" he shouted before turning and walking away.

I didn't take it as a compliment.

He whipped back around. Apparently, he wasn't finished.

"And another thing. Maybe, just maybe, when you're upset about something, talk to me! Don't just do the silent, brooding routine where you storm off into the fucking woods like an asshole."

I blinked at him. The only reason I'd gone into the woods was to look for branches for my trim project.

Cooper threw up his hands. "Are you even going to say anything?"

"I'm... sorry?"

He paced back and forth between two saplings. "When we first met, I thought you were shy or you weren't a talker or whatever, but then I came here. And you're not shy with me. You tell me things. You talk about your thoughts and feelings. But now... ever since the call from my agent, you've gone back to being the guy who grunts."

I made a noise in my throat, disagreeing with him.

"See?" He clutched at his hair. "See what I mean? That. You grunt at me when you're holding back your true feelings. Just fucking tell me what you're thinking! I hate this. I hate not knowing what you're thinking."

I stared at him, unsure of what he wanted me to say.

"*Fuck*," he shouted and turned around and stormed off.

I stared after him wondering what had just happened. He'd seemed overly upset for me simply taking a walk in the woods. Granted, I could see his point. If I was going to be this long, I could have given him a heads-up, but then again, I didn't know it would take this long to find what I wanted. And it wasn't like I was far from home. He probably could have shouted for me and I would have heard him.

But then all the talk about me being a talker. I'd never been a talker, mostly because people didn't seem to need yet another opinion about something. There were enough talkers in my family to meet the needs of anyone for the rest of infinity. So why would I talk for the sake of talking?

Nacho had taken off after Cooper, so I trudged behind them with my armload of branches until I could deposit them in a pile by the cabin. When I climbed up into the RV, I smelled something amazing enough to snap me out of my thoughts.

"What are you cooking? It smells amazing."

Cooper had his back to me at the refrigerator like he was looking for something, even though the fridge was small enough not to need that much scrutiny.

"Chicken tikka masala," he muttered.

"What's that? I've never had it."

He still didn't look at me. "I know. That's why I made it. It's an Indian dish."

Even though I was nervous he might reject me, I walked up and closed the fridge door before turning him around and pulling him into a hug. "I'm sorry. I didn't think I'd be gone that long, and I sure as hell didn't think you'd worry."

Cooper scoffed. "I didn't worry."

I bit back a smile. "Okay. I didn't think you'd be mad." I kissed the top of his head and secretly relished the fact he was nuzzling into my neck the way he seemed to like to do. "And I'm sorry if I grunt too much. I'm not used to people caring much about whether or not I talk. I'll try to do better."

"Mpfh. You smell like dirt." His voice was muffled against my skin. Clearly he wasn't all that bothered.

"Want me to shower?"

He didn't answer at first, and that's when I realized his body was trembling slightly. Had he really been that nervous about my disappearance? My truck was still here, so he had to have known where I'd gone.

"They want me in LA," he blurted. His arms tightened around me so I couldn't pull back to look him in the eye.

"That's fantastic!" And it was. Even if it was the end of my little dream world, I was thrilled for him.

"It's just for an audition. I told them I couldn't leave here until at least late July."

I grabbed his upper arms and forcibly removed him from my embrace so I could look him in the eye. "You can absolutely go. You don't owe me anything."

His eyes flicked everywhere but at mine. "Maybe not, but I signed a contract with Stallion."

Oh. He wasn't staying out of loyalty to me. He was staying because he was legally obligated under a contract. Right.

I clamped my teeth together and tried my hardest to remember what he'd said about method acting. I would sink into the role of supportive friend with everything I had.

"Maybe we can look through the contract and see if there's any wiggle room," I suggested.

He still didn't look at me. Maybe the floor or his bare feet were more interesting. "No, it's fine. I probably won't get the part anyway.

But they do want me to come audition as soon as possible. I said I'd talk to you to figure out the best time for me to be gone a couple of days."

"You'll get the part," I said with as big a smile as I could manage. I wanted to punctuate the thought with a kiss, but I wasn't sure if we were still doing that. I'd never been all that great with understanding relationship stuff, but with Cooper, it had been easy. Now, however, I felt like I was navigating uncharted waters. "When do you want to go? My mom always says to strike while the iron's hot. You could go tomorrow, and I could use the time to put in the hardwood floors."

He finally looked up at me. "We were going to do that together."

"It's backbreaking work, and I'd be nervous about you pulling your stitches. Besides, seeing you on your hands and knees would mean the job would take ten times as long." I winked at him which seemed to finally relax him.

He smiled. "Yeah, okay. Are you sure?"

I nodded and kept the smile going. I was a supportive friend. *I was a supportive friend.*

"You can take the truck to Denver."

"What if you need to go somewhere?"

I drew my arm through the room in an arc. "I won't need to, but if there's an emergency, I have this lovely beast."

"You're a good man, Isaac." Cooper put his hands around my neck and pulled me down into a kiss.

Thank fuck.

I lost myself in him for a few minutes, rubbing my hands under his shirt to feel the warm skin of his back and down over his ass. I picked him up carefully and started walking back to the bedroom, but he pulled back.

"Mm, no. Dinner. It's been waiting. Then naked time."

I made a resigned sound and set him down, indulging in one last, long kiss. When I finally let him go, he looked a little dazed for a minute before telling me to take a quick shower while he got everything ready. It wasn't until I was in the shower that his words came back to me.

You're a good man.

It was something I'd heard many times in my life. I was the dependable one. The sacrificing one. The guy who would drop anything to jump a dead battery or help haul heavy furniture from your apartment to your new house. Cooper had said it several times too, and it was like... a backhanded compliment.

Sometimes it felt like all I was was a "good man." I wasn't the fun one, the interesting one, the creative or talented one. I was simply the reliable one. I looked out for others, but no one really needed me. They just needed *someone*.

The water trickled over my body too softly. I wished the RV had better water pressure, but I guessed that was more incentive for me to get the shower installed at the house. Maybe I'd do that while Cooper was gone so he could return home to a palatial bathroom with multiple jets and unlimited hot water.

I dried off quickly and threw on some lounge pants and pulled on a T-shirt while walking back to the table. I leaned over and kissed the top of his head before sitting down. "I don't think I've ever smelled anything this good."

As we sat down to eat, I forced myself to calm down. He wasn't leaving yet, and when he did, it was just for a couple of days. It was fine. I had work to do anyway and lots of it. If I could put my head down and really hustle, I could help speed up our timeline in case the LA people needed him finished sooner.

"You're being awfully quiet," he said after a while.

Oh right. The talking thing. I'd said I would try harder. "Mpfh. Just thinking about what I need to work on next. I think the bathroom fixtures are being delivered tomorrow along with the windows and doors. It'll keep me busy if I finish the flooring."

I served myself a second helping of chicken and rice. "This is amazing. You need to tell me how to make it so I can have it again sometime."

"I'll make it for you." He sounded annoyed and defensive.

"Okay."

"It's not like I'm moving to LA. My family is here."

I glanced up at him. Yep, he was annoyed. I kept my mouth shut.

"And my brother needs his procedure."

I kept chewing.

"And I won't get the part anyway, and even if I do, I'm not sure I want it."

Now that wasn't something I could ignore. "Yes you do."

He blew out a breath and pushed his plate out of the way before laying his head on his arms in a big dramatic gesture.

I took a sip of water.

"Yes I do," he mumbled into the table.

"You're going to do great. How about one day at a time?"

He lifted his head up and glared at me. "Stop being so reasonable."

I reached over and took his hand. "Hey, I was thinking maybe tonight we could browse decorating ideas together. If we see some things we like, you can do some shopping while you're in LA."

Cooper's entire face lit up. "That's a great idea. I can get whatever we need and then arrange shipping for the stuff I can't carry back."

"Exactly. Plus if we don't have any luck with ideas, you can find a place to get decent decorating books and magazines there."

He stood up and began clearing the table. "Okay, you feed Nacho, and I'll get the laptop set up."

I took over with the cleaning since that was our agreement. When he cooked, I cleaned and vice versa. But tonight I took my time with the dishes, trying to get in the right frame of mind to enjoy my last evening with him before everything changed. Because even if he didn't get the part, he would get another one. The fact this opportunity came in so quickly after our project started getting traction meant it was just the beginning for him.

When I finally put the last dish away and made my way to the bedroom, he was clicking away on the keyboard.

"They got me on a flight tomorrow afternoon so I'll be there in time to meet my agent for dinner. Then I guess the audition is the following morning. But I won't be home till the next day since they said they may need another read."

I climbed onto the bed and moved Nacho out of my spot next to Cooper. "That was fast. I guess they're still up working."

Cooper didn't look up. "They're an hour behind us, remember?"

Right. I hadn't really remembered that. I should have, but I'd never really had any reason to talk to anyone in California. Maybe that would change.

I stroked Nacho's coat while I waited for Cooper to finish all of his travel arrangements. When he finally clicked over to the bulletin board website, I leaned in so I could see.

He clicked through some different folders to get to something specific. "This is something I found earlier. It's this really cool mix of color—see here these Persian rugs—and more stark modern pieces like this sofa. Now, before you say you hate stark modern shit, which I already know, look at these pictures..." He pointed to several photos where the modern pieces were mixed in with more colorful, comfortable side things like pillows and pictures on the wall. I wasn't any kind of decorator-minded person, but it looked really nice.

"Yeah. I like that. That's different, but cool, you know?" I probably sounded like an idiot.

Cooper clicked through several more examples of the mix of styles until I could really picture what he had in mind for the main living area of the cabin. "What about the bedroom?"

"Yeah, actually, I was wondering if you thought you could make a big king bed frame to match the trim work you talked about with the branches. See how in this photo they have that rustic frame and then they put the modern bedding on it? It would be like a reverse of what we do in the living room."

I looked over at him. His face was bright and excited. It was the most beautiful version of him even though he was gorgeous in any state. I ran my fingers through his wavy hair. "You're better at this than you thought. It turns out you really *are* gay."

He elbowed me and laughed. "Maybe so. Or maybe I picked up more during my years in LA than I thought."

I slid the laptop off the covers and set it on my little bedside stand before climbing on top of him and forcing him down onto the pillows. "Too bad. For a minute there, I thought we were going to end up with a cabin that would have made Duck Dynasty feel right at home."

Cooper's hands moved around my sides to my lower back and squeezed my ass through the sheets. "Well, thanks to Norm's Nicki and her fancy magazine selection, I do know how to make a wine rack out of a deer antler rack. And I know how to make a coat rack out of an elk rack. And a shoe rack out of—"

I kissed him before he could finish. And then I spent all night making sure he wouldn't forget me very easily in Los Angeles. The late-night sex must have taken more out of me than I'd expected because instead of waking early and starting the coffee the way I always did, I slept right through Cooper's alarm, his shower, and his departure.

I woke up to the sound of Nacho's whining as my pickup truck crunched its way out of the clearing. And just like that, I was alone again with my DIY projects, my camera, and my dog.

Back to the way it had always been and probably always would be.

22

COOPER

I felt guilty for being excited about my trip. In no way did I want to leave Nine behind, and if I could have brought him with me, that would have been ideal. But I couldn't deny how much my mouth watered for the mediterranean salad at Vector's or how relieved I was Kyle could squeeze me in for a haircut on short notice.

Back to the land of civilization. Back to stoplights and late nights. In the Uber to the hotel, I wondered if any of my old friends would be interested in going to a club or even just out for a drink to catch up. I hadn't been back in several months after making the decision to move back home until we figured out what was wrong with Jacks.

In that time, however, I hadn't really missed anyone too much. I'd messaged a few people here and there, mostly my old roommates Evie and Van, and Jarrod, my closest friend from the bar where I'd worked. I texted Evie first, and she responded right away that she'd get some people together to meet up at Low Bar later for drinks. Then I texted Jarrod to see if he'd run lines with me before that.

I settled back in my seat and tried to get excited. Nice visit to the salon, dinner with my agent to go over the project, and then a good catch-up with my friends before getting a good sleep for the audition.

Why wasn't I more excited about it?

When I got to the salon, I let out a sigh of relief and enjoyed every minute of Kyle's pampering. I told him I had an audition the following day, so he slipped me a half-empty tube of styling cream to make sure I looked my best for it. I left the salon lighter in the wallet but feeling so much better. I finally had the smoky, woodsy smell off me and was ready to change into some of my favorite clothes I hadn't worn in ages.

Back at the hotel, I couldn't help but take a minute to check in with Nine. I took a selfie and sent it to him.

Cooper: *Hey, new hair, who dis?*

Nine: *Wow. Sexy. Or as my sister Jessie would say: sexy af. I don't know what the af stands for though.*

Cooper: *As fuck.*

Nine: *Oh, right.*

A photo of him appeared. He was shirtless, tanned, and sweating, and I almost swallowed my tongue. A plaid flannel shirt was tied around his waist, and the jeans he had on stuck to his muscular thighs like spandex. He must have put the phone in the tripod and then stepped back to capture a full-length shot. He was also standing in front of the cabin which had a big swath of sunshine striping across the front porch at an angle through the trees and landing on Nacho, who was dead asleep at the top of the porch stairs. I could just imagine how carefully Nine would step over him with every trip in and out of the cabin so as not to wake the dog.

The photo captured everything I missed: Nine, Nacho, and that rubble pile that was finally starting to look like something worthwhile thanks to all of Nine's hard work. I ran a finger down the image of the man who made my heart throw itself against my rib cage like the damned thing could actually jump out and join Isaac in the photo.

Cooper: *I miss you.*

Nine: *You don't know what missing is. I have to sleep in a bed that smells like you. Been avoiding the RV all day.*

My heart. Jesus, but the man sometimes shot a dart right into it.

My fingers hovered over the keys, but before I could think of what to say, a message popped up from my agent telling me he was downstairs waiting. I glanced at the time and realized he'd probably already been there a few minutes. I raced to finish getting ready and then hustled downstairs.

Mitch Keyes was in his late fifties with a thick head of snow-white hair and dark framed glasses. It had been a while since I'd seen him in person, but he looked the same as always. I reached out to shake his hand. "Hi, Mitch. Thanks for meeting with me. Hope Diane isn't upset I took you away from her."

He smiled and patted me on the shoulder after the handshake. "Nah. She's got some wine-tasting thing with friends tonight, so it worked out."

We walked a couple of blocks down the strip to the Sunset Trocadero. Once we were seated, he pulled some printed pages from his messenger bag. "You got the sides, right? I figured you might not have had a chance to print them out, so I brought you a hard copy just in case. You have someone to run them with?"

I took the papers from him with a nod. "Yeah, my buddy Jarrod. He's meeting me after this."

"Great. Listen, I looked into what you've been working on with your boyfriend, and I gotta say, it's good stuff. I know you were disappointed that we couldn't find you more work when you were here, but that's all going to change with this new exposure."

"You think?"

He took a sip of wine and nodded. "Absolutely. Do you remember the guy who was cast as the dad in that teen movie *Junior Sunday*? He was discovered from a YouTube channel. He'd been trying to get into the business for years. Guy was a high school English teacher, but he was also the drama club sponsor. So he started making drama class videos for his students."

That was interesting. I'd heard of singers getting noticed that way, but not actors. "I never knew that."

An older woman with a thick brown braid and laugh lines around her eyes came over to take our dinner order. After she left, Mitch sat back and stretched his legs out on the other side of the table. "Tell me what you want, Cooper, and I'll see what I can do."

I wasn't quite sure what he was asking. "For this part? Like... compensation?"

His smile was patient as if he was dealing with simple-minded folk. "No, I mean with your career. I can use this. Especially if we get the offer from the Sam Gwan project."

Oh. He was talking about my career in general. "Well, I..." I stopped to think about what I really wanted. In the past, I wanted to act in film. Film acting had been my focus in college, and when I'd moved to LA, the first thing I'd saved up for was a six-thousand-dollar film acting program at the UCLA School of Theater. This had been my dream since I was eight years old and my mom had bought a camcorder before our summer camping trip. Jacks and I had spent the entire trip doing skits in front of the campfire for our mom, and she'd videotaped them one after the other.

That trip was when I'd discovered I was happiest hamming it up in front of a camera. But the real-life aspect of pursuing an acting career had been exhausting. The education classes had been challenging. My professors in college had given me a big wake-up call that acting wasn't as easy as I'd thought. So I'd put my nose down and worked hard to prove that I could do it.

Now that I was finally possibly in a position to get somewhere with it, what did I really want to do? I decided to turn the question back on him. "What do you think is possible?"

"Well, let's be real. We're not talking a lead role in the next Scorsese film, are we?" He let out a chuckle. "But I think it's possible to get you a supporting role in a rom-com, or if you wanted something steadier, I've got a lead on a Netflix series that's looking for some fresh faces. It's a series about producing a reality show, so I think I could sell them on the audience you could potentially bring to the table."

"I'm having a medical procedure at the end of the summer that requires a week of recovery. They say full recovery can take up to a few weeks, but I can't imagine shooting would be that grueling for a supporting role like this. Still, we need to find out what the schedule would be."

Mitch made a dismissive sound. "We'll worry about that when you get the offer. Now, let's talk about these other ideas I mentioned."

I asked him more questions about the pros and cons of each as we finished our wine and waited for our food. Ultimately, I decided the Netflix path might be the smarter choice if I wanted a steadier gig. But nothing said I couldn't pursue both and see what happened. The chances of getting either of them were slim, so the chances of getting both were ridiculous anyway. Still, I had a nervous feeling in my stomach about the way Mitch had dismissed my comment about the bone marrow donation. It truly was a deal-breaker since Jacks was already waiting for my *Cooped Up With Nine* project to finish before he could get the procedure.

When we parted ways outside the restaurant with plans to touch base again after the audition, I tried to be optimistic. It was nice hearing the vlog had made a positive impact on my chances of getting hired. I hoped it made a similar impact on getting Nine the kind of sponsors who would continue to supply him materials and camera equipment since that was pretty much all he wanted besides a place of his own to fix up.

Next, I headed to Jarrod's apartment where he and his boyfriend were just finishing up Chinese takeout. "Hey, stranger," he said with a big smile when he answered the door. We hugged and moved inside. Geoff gave me a smile and wave from the kitchen table where he was clearing off space for us.

"How've you been? We've been watching the show," Geoff said, drying his hands on a kitchen towel. "Your new boyfriend is hot as fuck. Where the hell did you find him?"

I felt strangely proud. "He's my college roommate's baby brother."

"Oooh, robbing the cradle, hm?" Geoff teased with a wink.

Jarrod frowned. "Eli's brother? I thought you didn't like that guy."

"I didn't. He was a total pain in the ass."

Geoff barked out a laugh. "And now he's also a total pain in the ass, just a much better kind, am I right?"

Jarrod rolled his eyes, and Geoff swatted him with the towel. "Anyway," Jarrod said. "It's cute. I mean you guys look like the real deal together. Congrats, man."

My heart gave another lurch. It had been doing that more and more lately when the subjects of Isaac and the future came up. "Thanks. He's… yeah."

Geoff's eyes got wide. "Oh. *Ohhhh.* It's like that, huh?"

I sighed and grinned. "Yeah. It's definitely like that."

Jarrod gave me the big smile that earned him all the best tips at the bar. "That's amazing. Congrats. Now, let's run these lines and get you the part so the two of you can move back here and get out of the godforsaken woods."

"Right on," Geoff said with a nod. "Cooper, you want a beer or something?"

"An ice water would be great if you don't mind."

"Sure thing, sweetie."

When Geoff returned with the water, Jarrod leaned in to take the printed sides from me. "You look really good, Coop. I have to admit you seemed pretty unhappy when you left. Good to see the mountain air and a little dick put everything to rights."

I almost choked on my water. "Big dick, you asshole. *Big* dick."

Geoff laughed. "Told you so, Jerr. Mountain men like that one do not disappoint."

Now my face was on fire. "I don't want to know how you know that. So we're shutting up now. Work. We're changing the subject. Sides. Let's read."

Jarrod laughed while he found his place in the sides, and we finally got down to business running lines. After about an hour, we called it a night and I invited the two of them out for drinks with Evie and me. The three of us made our way to the Low Bar and found Evie and Van right away.

"There he is," Evie shouted from a table they'd managed to save for us. She got up and came in for a huge hug. Bits of her curly red hair escaped from the ponytail it was pulled back in, and her face was scrubbed clean of the makeup she normally caked on for her job at a nearby circus-themed restaurant popular with tourists. The freckles on her nose stood out, and her bright green eyes were a beloved, familiar sight. I sank into the hug.

"Aww, missed you," I said, inhaling her drugstore body lotion scent. "Thanks for coming out."

She pulled back and gestured for me to take the seat next to hers. "Wouldn't miss it. When are you moving back?"

I walked over and kissed Van on the cheek. "Hey, cutie. Where's the bf?"

Van rolled his eyes behind big clear-framed glasses. "Ditched me for some ho. It's fine. He drove a fucking Kia Picanto with undercarriage lighting and lifts. What did I expect?"

Geoff snorted. "Hey, they don't sell those here. That's quite a score."

Van flapped his hand in Geoff's direction. "Believe me, I know all about how rare and exciting his sub-compact piece of shit is. Moving on."

I gave him a quick hug before taking my seat. "Sorry about that, but I gotta say, the first time he asked me to spot him a fiver for condoms *and* beef jerky at the corner market, I had to wonder if he was marriage material. Everyone knows five bucks only buys the shit beef jerky." I shot him a wink, and he laughed.

The rest of the evening was spent downing mixed drinks and catching up. We laughed our asses off as usual, but I still kept thinking of Nine. Was he in bed yet? Was he lonely? Was Nacho keeping him good company? What if he got hurt while no one was around to help him?

"'Scuse me," I mumbled to the group after a while. "Men's room." I got up and made my way to the back hallway before pulling out my phone and seeing several messages from him spaced out a while ago.

Nine: *How long do I heat up these taco things for?*

I held my fingers in front of my mouth. He was so freaking adorable.

Nine: *Never mind. The answer is not eight minutes, in case you were wondering.*

Nine: *How do you treat a burned tongue?*

Nine: *Never mind. I found the strawberry kiwi water you left me.*

Nine: *Sorry to bother you again, but should I still do a goodnight post even though you're not here?*

Nine: *Never mind. Don't text back. Go have fun. I went ahead and did a post anyway. G'night.*

I clicked over to our Instagram account and found the post. After clicking on the white triangle to play the video, I realized my hand was clutching the front of my shirt in anticipation.

He was wearing my favorite T-shirt of his, the one that he'd had for years from the hardware store that had the Stallion logo practically invisible from hundreds of washes. The navy blue had long since faded to a light, mottled denim.

"Hey, it's me. Nine." He cleared his throat. "Oh, and Nacho of course. As you can see, we're missing someone. Cooper had to fly to LA for a couple of days, but don't worry. He'll be back."

His mouth was turned up in a smile, but his eyes were sad. Almost like his heart didn't believe what his mouth was saying.

"Anyway, I'm working on a special surprise for him while he's gone. I really hope he likes it." He looked down at where his hand was idly stroking Nacho's chin. When he looked back up, his face had gone serious. "Coop, if you're watching this... I just want you to know..." He put on a fake-as-shit smile that made my stomach hurt. "You're going to be amazing. I'm so proud of you. And I..." He swallowed. "I... shit, this isn't easy when everyone else is watching."

He let out a little laugh and shook his head before looking back at the camera. This time his smile was totally genuine, and I saw the real Isaac Winshed shine through. "If you were a chicken on my dad's farm when I was growing up, I would have shoved you in my closet too."

The video cut off. The comments and reactions on the post were insane despite the fact it was only half an hour old.

My hand shook as I lifted it up to swipe at my eyes.

Evie's voice cut through the noise around me. "Babe? What's wrong? You're like grinning and crying. Is everything okay? Are we happy or sad?"

I glanced up at her, feeling lighter than I had all day. "I think... I think he loves me."

Her face softened as she cupped my cheek. "Well, of course he does. Who wouldn't?"

I smiled at her until she made her way to the ladies' room, and then I looked back to the other messages I'd missed.

Mom: *Jacks is back in the hospital. I'll let you know what they say.*

Suddenly, the day's roller coaster of emotions took a drastic dive straight down. I dialed her phone with a shaking hand.

"Coop, you didn't have to call. I know you're in LA for the audition. I just wanted to let you know in case you couldn't reach us. You know how they are with phones in here sometimes."

I stuck a finger in my opposite ear to try and block out the restaurant noise. "How is he?"

"He's okay. They're doing blood work to see where we are. Marchie said he had a couple of episodes at work today where he didn't seem quite right. Jacks swears it was just low blood sugar."

"I'll catch the first plane out in the morning," I promised her.

Mom's voice quickly changed to Mother Mode. "You will not. You will stay there and get that part. If he needs another transfusion already, they'll give him another transfusion."

"And if he needs the transplant?" I asked.

Silence. We both knew we couldn't afford the transplant yet, not until I got the Stallion money at the end of our project.

"We'll cross that bridge when we come to it," Mom said.

23

NINE

Instead of working on the bathroom fixtures, I kind of went a little crazy. Cooper had saved a photo on his pinboard where the fireplace was made the big focal point in the room with a mantel made from giant pieces of thick timber. I'd done a little research to make sure I knew how to protect the wood from the heat and everything, and then I'd set off to find the best trees for the job.

Thankfully, the project hadn't taken as long as I'd thought, and I was able to get it finished before midafternoon. I started immediately on the hardwood flooring and busted my ass late into the night, only stopping long enough to fix dinner and get in bed for the good-night video. As soon as I finished recording, I hopped back out of bed and got back to work. As soon as I walked into the cabin, where I'd left several work lamps turned on, I caught sight of the new mantel with its dominating presence in the room. I could just see a collection of colorful candles or glass jars of fresh wildflowers on top of it once the room was full of comfortable furniture in the style Cooper was concocting.

It was the first time I really saw this place as someone's comfortable hideaway instead of my never-ending To Do list. I stood in the middle of the room and spun in a slow circle, imagining how incredible it would look when it was all put together. I wouldn't have been able to tackle something like this without help. Maybe I could have done the renovations themselves, but not the complete package with the vision for how a couple would truly use the space once it was done.

I strapped on the kneepads and got back to work, taking breaks every so often to run back to the RV and refill my water bottle from one of the four pitchers of flavored waters Cooper had left for me. When I got back to the cabin after a water break, my phone buzzed with a text.

Cooper: *You're the only person I'd live in the closet for. The chicken closet.*

I laughed, the sound echoing in the open room.

Nine: *Did you have fun tonight?*

Cooper: *Yes. It was nice seeing my friends. I missed them.*

My smile dropped even though, of course, I was happy for him.

Nine: *Good. I'm sure they missed you too. They'll be happy to have you back.*

Cooper: *Jacks is in the hospital.*

I reread that last text before clicking the button to call. Cooper's sleepy voice answered. "Hey."

"Baby, how is he? What's wrong?" I snapped to get Nacho's attention and then led him back to the RV. If I was going to drive to his mom's place in the morning, I needed to get some sleep.

"No, it's fine. He just might need another transfusion."

I opened the door and climbed up into the RV. "Do you want me to head over there to be with them?"

He didn't say anything for a minute, and I thought I'd lost him.

The town of Caswell was less than three hours away, so I could be there in no time once I got a little sleep and packed up the RV.

Cooper's voice was soft and sweet, the way it was in the moments before he drifted off to sleep. "No, but thank you. And Nine...?"

"Yeah?"

"I'd put you in my chicken closet too."

My chest filled with warmth. "Get some sleep, baby. Tomorrow's a big day."

After we signed off, I stripped down and took a quick shower before finally sliding into bed. Nacho moved up to sleep in Cooper's spot, but I stole the pillow before he could put his doggie head on it.

I spent the rest of the night breathing in the faint scent of gardenias and praying Jacks would be okay. When I finally forced myself to get up the next morning and get going, it was only the thought of knocking out as much work as possible before Cooper got back that forced me on my feet and out the door.

The morning went by fast. I turned the Bluetooth speaker up high and left all the doors open so Nacho could wander in and out of the cabin while I was finishing the flooring. My back was killing me from all the time spent on my knees, but I managed to get it all done. Thankfully, the cabin was very small, only one open room for the combination of kitchen and living area, one bedroom, and one bathroom. For the bathroom, we were laying tile over a floor-warming mat hard-wired into the light switch. Since that was such a small space, it wouldn't take much time at all, but I needed to get the shower in before I could tile the floor in there.

When I returned to the RV to fix a quick sandwich, I finally heard from Cooper about the audition.

"It went great," he said with a big smile in his voice. There was still a thread of uncertainty, but I chalked it up to worry about his brother. "Everyone was amazing and the vibe was incredible."

"That's really good, Coop. Tell me all about it. I mean, unless you're busy."

"No, no. It's fine. I'm headed back to the hotel now to change. I'm meeting my friend Evie for lunch and shopping."

He sounded right at home, like LA was the place he was meant to be. I was happy for him. I knew how long he'd waited for things to come together for his career.

"That sounds fun. Are you going to pick up some stuff for the cabin?"

I heard the city sounds of people talking and car horns honking in the background. "That's the plan. Evie says she knows of some great places that have unique pieces but aren't too expensive."

We had incentive to keep the reno budget low, but I hoped it didn't keep him from picking up what he wanted for the project. "Don't worry too much about the money. I saved a bunch on the flooring and the windows, remember?"

"Oh shit, that's my agent calling. Okay if I call you back?"

"Of course."

But he didn't. Not then and not later that evening either. I'd gone back to work, more motivated than ever to knock these projects out so that Cooper would be free to accept any offer he might get. By the time I finished tiling the shower and installing the fixtures, my body was done for the day. I cleaned up as well as I could and headed for the RV. Thankfully, Cooper had left a mountain of delicious leftovers for me, so all I had to do was warm something in the microwave again.

I fed Nacho, got my own dinner started, and stepped in my shitty RV shower. Since the cabin's water heater would have to be installed by someone licensed to work with the gas line, I couldn't take advantage of the new shower just yet.

Once I was finally settled at the kitchen table with my dinner and my phone, I checked again for any messages from Cooper.

Nothing.

Nine: *Just checking in.*

Did that make me sound too needy?

Nine: *Don't worry about it if you're too busy to message back.*

Shit. I tossed my phone down right as it buzzed. I scrambled to pick it back up just to see it was my brother Eli calling.

"Hey," I said in a rush, wondering if somehow he was calling with news about Cooper. If Coop had been in an accident and the hospital had called his mom, his mom would call Eli, right? "Everything okay?"

"Yeah, fine. How's it going there?"

I let out a breath in a whoosh and tried to get my heart rate to calm back down to human levels. "Fine. Just, you know, working."

"Coop's in LA, huh? I saw it on your Instagram."

"He had an audition. For a part in a movie. Speaking part." Why did I sound like a lunatic? Maybe because I could hardly catch my breath. I hadn't realized just how worried I was from not hearing back from him.

"That's great. What happens if he gets it? Would they need him in LA before you finish your thing with Stallion?"

I pushed my plate away and leaned back in the booth, enjoying the cool breeze coming in through the open window. "I don't know, but I'm trying to hurry up the work here just in case. He still has to do the procedure for Jacks though."

"Shit, right. And he can't do that till he has the money from your thing."

"No. He told me Jacks doesn't need it yet. I'm sure if he did, they'd go ahead and do it."

Eli was quiet for a beat before coming back on the line. "No, they don't have the money. That's why he's doing the Stallion thing. I thought you knew that."

"Well, yeah. I mean, I know he doesn't have insurance and they need the money to pay for it, but..." I thought about it. "Surely the hospital would give them a medical loan or something for it and let them pay it back over time, right? I thought he needed this money to pay back the loan when the time comes or help out with other things like Jacks being out of work."

"They don't have any credit because of Cooper's dad. That means no loans and no credit cards to help. They can't do the procedure until they have the cash."

I felt tingles under my skin as awareness washed over me. "Wait, wait. So, Jacks needs this procedure right now but they can't do it yet?"

"No, I don't think it's like that exactly. They're buying some time with blood transfusions until they can save up the money for the bone marrow thing. How do you not know this? Haven't you guys talked since you've been living together? Jesus, Nine. On social media it looks like you're so close." He chuckled. "You're a damned fine actor, dude. Mom will be happy to know."

That was laughable. I couldn't act my way out of a paper bag. "Mom will be happy to know what?"

"That it's an act. She started to think it was real. You and Coop. I told her she was crazy, but she didn't believe me."

The tingles in my skin turned to live-wire nerves. Was this what it felt like coming out to your family?

"It is real. I told her that."

He laughed again. "No, I mean you and Coop. The boyfriends thing. If you only knew how weird it was for me to see my brother and my best friend kissing in front of the whole world. Christ, it's like CGI or something."

I closed my eyes and counted to three. *Calm down.* "It's real, Eli. I'm falling in love with him."

Now the laughter was loud enough for me to have to pull the phone away from my ear. I couldn't decide if I was angry or sad at his reaction. And then there was the little devil on my shoulder trying to convince me none of it mattered. Why try and convince Eli when Cooper was going to move to LA anyway?

"Nine," Eli said when he finally calmed down enough to speak. "You're not gay. You're what a magician would call highly suggestible. If you really do think you have feelings for Cooper, it's probably from spending too much time around him. He's awesome, don't get me wrong, but you're not gay."

"You're right. I'm not gay," I admitted, but before he had a chance to gloat, I continued. "I'm something else. Gray, demi, I don't know really. But what I do know is that I have strong feelings for Cooper Heath, and those strong feelings have led to sex. Lots and lots of sex. *Gay* sex."

The silence on the other end was satisfying. Finally he said, "You're pulling my leg."

I sighed. "Can we talk about this later? I haven't heard from him all afternoon and I'm starting to worry."

"I'm sure he's fine. He's probably lost track of time because he's having such a good time out there. He's wanted to be cast in a movie since he was a little boy. This is like his dream finally coming true. At least, if he gets it. But he made it sound like the audition went really well."

"You talked to him today?"

"Just text. I messaged him to tell him about a friend of ours from school who's getting married, and Coop texted back he'd just come out of the studio."

I didn't say anything, and after a minute, Eli asked, "You haven't heard from him?"

"No, I did. He said the same. Audition went well. But that was hours ago, and there's been nothing since."

My brother's laugh was easy and free. "I'm sure he's just busy with friends. I know there are some dance clubs he likes there, and it's been forever since he's been able to go out and let off some steam. Calm down and watch a movie or something. Don't work yourself to death. Hear me?"

"Mpfh."

"I mean it. I know you, and this is prime 'Nine tries to be a hero' bullshit. No one needs you to be a hero right now."

Sometimes I hated my family.

"Thanks for the advice." *Asshole.*

I hung up the phone and tried Cooper again, but when the phone rang and rang, I had to admit defeat. Eli was right. Cooper was probably out partying at some loud club. I could just picture his sexy body in formfitting clothes in the middle of a dance floor with colored lights flashing all around. He'd probably draw everyone's attention, and other men would want to dance with him and put their hands on him.

I wanted to punch something. I wanted to throw a fucking boulder across the clearing and smash everything to bits. The idea of having had every fucking thing I never knew I wanted just to have to let it go again was worse than never having known what I was missing.

Nacho let out a loud sigh from his spot on the floor as he settled into sleep. It was late. I cleaned up after myself and stripped for bed. No good-night video tonight. I didn't even want to look at Instagram and see our happy faces. I couldn't bear the thought of acting like I was in a relationship with Cooper right now while he could very well be out dancing with other men. And maybe that was selfish and childish of me, but I was also tired as hell. I just wanted to close my eyes and stop thinking for a while.

But when I closed my eyes, all I could see was Cooper's sweaty skin on the dance floor, his shirtless abs contracting as he moved his hips to the music.

My dick was certainly happy about my brain's obsession, even if my heart wasn't.

I reached down and stroked it. Fucking great. If there was such a thing as an angry jack-off session, this was it. I reached over to the side table and grabbed the lube, grumbling under my breath the entire time about what an idiot I was.

But the images of Cooper's enticing body were too hot to ignore. And the memory of sliding into his tight heat brought me to the edge. Before he'd left, he'd ridden me with his eyes closed and his head thrown back. My hands had moved all over his chest and stomach until I used both of them to jack him off. When he'd come, he'd shot all over my chest and stomach which had been one of the hottest things ever.

I kicked off the covers and stroked myself until the orgasm finally hit hard and fast. But then it was over just as fast.

And I realized it was the first of many, many times I would come alone in bed to the memory of Cooper Heath.

24

COOPER

I hadn't realized my phone was missing until Evie and I had been to at least a dozen different shops around LA. By the time we called around to figure out which one had it, the shop was closing and wouldn't reopen until ten the following morning.

"Let me use your Insta account to send Nine a message," I said to Evie. I stupidly didn't have the man's number. Hell, I didn't even have my mom's number, but at least I could call the hospital and find her that way.

Evie handed me her phone, and I sent two messages. The first was a DM in the Insta account, and the second was an email to our joint email account, both giving him Evie's number and telling him what happened. Then I called the hospital in Caswell and got a hold of my mom.

"He's fine," she said. "They gave him the transfusion, and we'll probably get out of here tomorrow."

I let out a breath and finally let myself calm the fuck down. "Thank god."

"The doc said he needs the transplant soon, Cooper. Like, in a month, no longer." She sounded worried, and who could blame her.

A month. That changed everything. I wasn't sure how we could swing it if we needed the money that soon, especially if that meant not being able to complete my contract with Stallion.

"I'll figure something out. If he needs it, we'll make it happen. I can probably do a GoFundMe online or something now that we have such a big audience." I knew that wasn't actually an option, not with Stallion's contract involved. But I at least wanted to give my mom some hope while I figured something else out.

"Oh, that's a great idea! Wonderful. Let me know how I can help." I could hear the relief in her voice and knew I'd made the right call in suggesting it.

"Tell Jacks I love him and I'll check in when I land in Denver tomorrow afternoon. If you need me in the meantime, call this number."

After Evie and I stopped for my favorite salad for dinner, we went back to my hotel to look at everything we'd bought on Stallion's credit card. We had bags full of stuff and had even begged a big shipping box off one of the shops so I could check it through on the airplane. All the big stuff I ordered was being shipped to us at the cabin.

When I started unwrapping things to repack them into the shipping box, Evie kicked back on the bed and crossed her ankles. I could tell by the look on her face we were getting ready to have a talk.

"Something on your mind?" I asked.

"Why didn't you tell your mom you got the part? I've been thinking about it all afternoon, and I can't figure it out."

"Because they need me by the end of the month, and I can't do that to Nine."

She crossed her arms in front of her chest. Her red hair was loose, and curls tumbled over her shoulders, a little bit crazy from the wind outside. "Sure you can. He'd understand. This is your dream we're talking about."

I put down the shopping bag I'd been holding and glared at her. "Everyone's calling this my dream, but I'm not so sure it is anymore. You know what my dream is? To not have my twin brother die. And so what about my acting dream anyway? I'm not selfish enough to walk out on Nine's dream of finally being able to buy his own place to fix up. What about his dream?"

Evie grinned and lifted an eyebrow. "Six months ago you would have sold your favorite skinny jeans for a chance to even audition for a role like this."

I grabbed up the shopping bag again and began rifling through it. "Yeah, well, shit changes. Besides, those jeans no longer fit since I started doing all this physical work with Nine. My ass is like twice as big as it was," I muttered.

"But you said this vlog deal is supposed to go into August, right? That means you won't get paid till the end of August at the earliest. But if you ditch it and take the film role, you'll shoot in a few weeks and get paid by the end of July. That would mean quicker money for Jacks, right? Just think about it."

"That would mean screwing Nine over," I reminded her. "Not to mention Stallion Tools. Even if I was willing to screw them over, it would fuck up any future sponsorship for Nine with the largest tool company in the country."

"Babe, the way you describe this guy, he'd probably tell you to do it. At least talk to him."

I shook my head and laughed even though it wasn't funny. "No way. He would chop off his right arm if I asked. If he even knew this was an option, he'd insist I take the part."

She tilted her head for a minute like she was thinking. "What if... what if you went back this week, shot a ton of clips in different outfits, and stockpiled them to cover you while you leave to shoot the movie? Meanwhile Nine keeps working on the cabin, and you get to take the part. More money for everyone. Win-win."

The thought of leaving Nine to carry the load for both of us didn't sit right with me, but at least it made me realize there could be a workable solution if I just thought it through a little longer.

"I'll talk to him," I said. "When I get back. There, are you happy?"

She clapped her hands. "Yes! You know I'm just selfishly trying to get you back here, right?"

I went back to packing the box. "And I love you for it. I do."

When I finally pulled the truck into the clearing I was itching to see Nine. I hadn't heard back from him which was disappointing, but I also knew he wasn't the most reliable about checking email since it was mostly fan mail, and those messages made him self-conscious. He preferred to ignore it all and pretend like fans didn't exist.

Nacho came streaking out of the cabin's front door, bouncing and yipping with his tail wagging a million miles a minute. I hopped out and gave him some love.

Nine's exit from the cabin was much more hesitant. He stood on the porch wiping his hands on a rag. The afternoon sun glinted across his legs, showing off the familiar thigh muscles under faded blue jeans. He didn't say a word, simply stood there and watched me as if unsure of what to do.

I gave Nacho one last smooch on the top of his head and took off at a jog across the clearing. Nine's eyes widened and he stumbled down the few steps into the yard just in time for me to fling myself bodily at him. I wrapped my arms and legs around him like a baby monkey and held on tight, soaking in his sweaty, woodsy scent and thanking fate for allowing me to be here in this moment with such a beautiful, kind soul.

His arms tightened around me like thick steel bands, and he let out a desperate sound from his throat that made me want to cry.

"I missed you so much," I admitted against his lips after kissing him hard. I went right back to kissing him without letting him say a word. Finally, I pulled back just long enough to add, "Lost my phone."

His entire body heaved a sigh of relief, and he sank down onto the porch stairs. "I thought... I didn't know. I thought..."

I straddled his lap on the stairs and cupped his face. "I sent you a message in Insta from Evie's account, and then I emailed you, but I know you—"

This time Nine was the one who leaned in for the kiss. "You're here. You're okay. That's all I care about," he mumbled between kisses.

We couldn't keep our hands off each other, but I also didn't want to take the time to move somewhere like inside the RV. So we simply sat like that on the porch and kissed and hugged for a long time, sneaking shy grins at each other between make-out sessions. The afternoon buzzed lazily on as we began catching each other up on the forty-eight hours we'd spent apart. I told him more about my night out with friends and my shopping trip with Evie.

"What about the part? The last I heard, you were getting a call from your agent," Nine said.

"Oh." I flapped a hand like it was no big deal. "Didn't get it. Which is fine. I wasn't really expecting to."

Nine's smile dropped. "What? But you said the audition went well. Shit. Are you sure? Maybe they'll give you a callback?"

I ran my fingers through his beard and tugged at it the way I liked to do. "Nah. It worked out for the best because they needed someone really quickly, and we're doing this. Besides, it gave me an excuse to catch up with my agent, and he thinks he can find me other projects now that I'm getting noticed from our vlog."

Lying to Isaac wasn't great. It felt horrible, in fact, but I also knew that if I told him the truth, he wouldn't let me turn the part down no matter what I said. And even if he did, he'd feel awful and guilty. There was no reason for that. I almost wished I hadn't gotten the part, but I had to admit my ego had been nicely stroked by the offer.

"I'm so sorry, baby," he said, rubbing his big hands up and down my back. "It's their loss. At least you got to see your friends and get a taste of city life again."

I nodded and leaned my face against his chest, snuggling in closer to enjoy the comfort of resting in his arms. "It was weird though. I missed being here with you."

The rumble of a laugh vibrated against my face. "That surprises you? Gee, thanks."

I sat back up and smiled at him. "No. That's not what I meant. I just... you know, I thought I'd be relieved to get to the city and do my favorite things, but... they weren't my favorite anymore."

Nine's fingers brushed through my hair. "Why not?"

I tugged at his beard again. "Because you're my favorite."

For a split second, he looked confused, and then it changed to suspicious. "Me?"

I leaned in and kissed his gorgeous mouth. For some reason, I couldn't exactly bring myself to say the words just yet, but I came as close as I could. "You're my closet chicken."

And then, before he felt obligated to say anything back, I pecked annoying kisses all over his face. "Better than Sir Pecks-A-Lot, right?"

We almost tumbled off the steps laughing and kissing until Nacho made it clear it was dinnertime. Nine pulled me up and led me into the cabin instead of toward the RV.

"Wanna show you something," he said.

When I entered the front door, I was amazed at what a difference the hardwood floors made. "Holy shit. Look at these floors." And then I saw it. Over to the right, surrounding the original stone fireplace, was the most gorgeous custom mantel I'd ever seen. It was made out of big, smooth logs and anchored the room perfectly. I turned to Nine, who was already blushing and twitchy. "You did all this."

He looked away and couldn't seem to figure out what to do with his arms. Finally he shrugged. "Yeah. Well, there wasn't anything else to do, and I remembered you pinned those pictures of the mantels you liked."

I walked right up to him and got down on my knees, yanking his pants open as fast as I could and sucking on his cock before either one of us could even think about it.

"Fuck!" He shouted into the empty space. His deep voice echoed around the room. "Oh god, that's not... you didn't have to... don't stop. *Fuck.*"

I laughed around the dick in my mouth. If I hadn't been busy with other things, I would have made a joke about mixed messages. Instead, I focused on getting him to come as hard and fast as I could.

Nine's hand landed in my hair and held the back of my head tenderly even though the rest of his body was tightly coiled like he was holding back.

He kept grunting out curses as I caressed his sac and peered up at him through my lashes. I could tell when he was close, and I pulled off him and jacked him until he came on my face. It was hot as hell and something we definitely hadn't done before.

"Oh god, fuck, fuck," he grunted. "Babe. Shit." Nine pulled off his shirt and tried to wipe my face off. "I'm sorry. I didn't mean to—"

I yanked the shirt out of his hand and fell down to the floor laughing. He was so goddamned naive in some ways. "It's called a facial. It's a thing. I thought it would be hot. Never mind."

He stared at me for a second before he started laughing. "I'm so stupid. It was hot. Like, really fucking hot. I was just worried I was going to blind you."

Nine pulled me up and into a kiss before reaching down to palm my dick through my jeans. I pulled his hand away. "Not yet. Let's feed Nacho, and then we can start over again in bed."

So that's what we did, and after a crazy, gymnastics-level sixty-nine in the RV bed, we finally slowed down long enough to fix dinner.

"Get out of there and sit down," I told Nine after coming out of the shower and seeing him attempt to cook. "I'm making pasta. Remove your big self from my kitchen."

Before I finished filling up the pot with water though, my mom called. Nine quickly hopped up and took over so I could answer the call.

"Hey, everything okay?"

I could tell right away she was crying, and I reached out to claw at poor Nine's arm. "What? Mom, what is it?"

She sucked in a shaky breath. "Cooper, someone paid for the procedure."

"What? What do you mean?" I peeled my fingernails out of Nine's skin and absently rubbed the little crescent marks to try and get them to go away.

"He okay?" Nine murmured.

"Wait, Mom. Is Jacks okay?"

"What? Oh yeah. He's fine. Back home and watching some kind of drag race, but it's not the car kind."

I nodded at Nine, and he kissed my forehead before going back to the pasta prep. "Mom, tell me what you mean about someone paying for the procedure."

"The doctor's office called and said that they'd found us a grant or something. I'm not really sure. It was all very confusing. But I guess there are people in the community who donate into medical funds for people who need help and they picked us. Can you believe it? It's not even a loan or anything. It's a grant. They said that means it doesn't need to be paid back."

It was too good to be true. "Mom, are you sure?"

She laughed. "I know. That's what I said too. I kept asking them, 'Are you absolutely sure?' But they sent me all the information on email. I'll send it to you so you can take a look at it. Anyway, they said they want to schedule the procedure for the fifteenth of July if that works for you."

I glanced at Nine. "Yeah. Of course. We'll figure something out on our end and make it happen. That's amazing, Mom."

"Well, I'll let you go. Tell Nine hello from us. It's nice to see you looking so happy. Much better than that Lee person."

Why did everyone keep bringing him up? Jesus. "Mom. Lee wasn't a thing. There was nothing between us."

She made a scoffing sound. "Anyway, good riddance."

When we ended the call, I stepped back over to our little stove and nudged Nine out of the way. "Sorry about that. Mom said she got a grant to cover Jacks's procedure. Can you believe it?"

"That's great. Who's Lee?"

I glanced up at him to see furrowed eyebrows. Honestly, I was surprised Eli hadn't already told him all about Lee.

"Nobody important."

I poured the jarred sauce into a small pan and turned the burner on.

"I see." Nine moved over to sit at the table. He didn't say anything else, and the silence wrapped tight bands of guilt around my chest.

I reached into the cabinet for two pasta bowls and then fixed us each a glass of ice water. Finally, I couldn't take it anymore.

"Lee Chambers lived in the apartment above ours in LA. Actually, he owned the building." I continued to find things to do so I wouldn't have to look at Nine while I told this story. "I had a crush on him from the very beginning. We flirted and stuff—no big deal—but then we went out dancing one night with a group of friends and ended up hooking up."

I squatted down to dig our pasta strainer out of a low cupboard, ignoring the little growling sound coming out of Nine's throat. "And then we did it again and again. I developed feelings for him, but he clearly wasn't interested in anything more than physical stuff. Which was fine, I thought. But then I realized he was hooking up with other guys. Which should have also been fine with me because I know tons of guys do that even when they're in a committed relationship, and we weren't even in a relationship or anything." I realized I was babbling, so I stopped and took a breath.

"I should have stopped, but I liked him too much. So I got into this shitty cycle of taking what I could get. He'd call me up late at night and tell me to come upstairs. As soon as we were done, he'd politely but firmly tell me to go." I made a humorless laugh sound. "Drove Evie nuts. She hated him for playing me around like that, but I told her I was a big boy and he was being nothing but totally honest with me about not wanting a relationship."

"Why did you like him so much if he treated you that way?" Nine's voice was rough with frustration.

I sighed. "He was... charismatic. Like one of those magnetic personalities you can't help but be drawn to. He'd traveled everywhere and had amazing stories. His apartment was full of interesting art, and he had this eclectic style that was so... *him*. I envied his life. He lived it on his own terms, and I thought that was somehow brave or bold. Which is why him choosing to stay single and play around was something I had to respect, right? I mean, that was part of what made him so free and desirable to me."

"Mpfh."

I chuckled at Nine's familiar grunt of disapproval. "Anyway, he finally changed his mind one day. Told me he wanted to be with me, that he cared about me. He still wanted an open relationship, but he was ready for an actual commitment where we were there for each other and made each other our top priority."

The timer went off on the pasta, so I drained it into the sink. I quickly dished out big bowls for both of us and sat down across from Nine to continue the conversation. His legs immediately wrapped around mine the way they always did under the dinette table.

I continued. "For like... I don't know... three weeks? It was great. He called me his boyfriend. He introduced me to his friends and coworkers at the studio where he worked—"

"Hold up. He worked in the film industry and didn't help you get a job?"

I appreciated his indignant tone, but I shook my head. "He's a game show producer. Not really my thing."

"But surely he had friends in the business."

I shrugged. "Yes. But I didn't really want to get a job that way. Can you imagine me showing up for an audition that my boyfriend arranged? No. It was fine. My agent was doing a decent job, I just wasn't getting the offers. Turns out, a theater degree from the University of Wyoming doesn't get you as far as one would think."

That got a grin out of him. "Eli told me you went there because of some actor who also went there."

My face heated with embarrassment. "I was a stupid gay kid obsessed with the movie *Copacabana*. Steve Cochran played Steve Hunt in the film, and he went to the University of Wyoming. Also, I was a little bit in love with Matthew Shepherd from his picture and his story. He went there." I shrugged. "I just thought it was the perfect combination of far enough away from home but still close enough to get there in an easy drive."

"So what happened with Lee?"

"I was in a car accident." Before I could say anything more, Nine's head snapped up.

"What? When?" Worry marred his face. Always the caretaker.

I reached over and squeezed his arm. "I'm fine. I didn't have a car when I lived in LA, so I'd taken an Uber down to Culver City for an audition. I stayed in the area afterwards and got dinner with a friend.

When I finally got another Uber home, the driver rear-ended someone because he wasn't paying attention when the guy in front of us slammed on the brakes. Anyway, the car was totaled, and I was stuck on the side of the 405 at night. My head hurt from where I'd banged it on the seat in front of me, and I was scared. The cops weren't being all that helpful, so I called Lee to come get me."

Nine's eyes narrowed because it was clear where this story was going. I tried not to sound too pathetic when I told him the rest. "He was busy. Said he had a really hot guy coming over and if I walked down to the nearest off-ramp, I should be able to get another Uber on a surface street just fine."

25

NINE

My nostrils flared and I felt my back teeth grind together. “Selfish jackass.”

Cooper moved noodles around on his plate without taking a bite. “Yeah, well. I was stupid expecting more than he was willing to give. After my dad left, I’d sworn I’d never rely on another person in my life, so I kicked myself for feeling so dependent on Lee. He was right. I needed to sort it out for myself. I’m a grown man, right? So I did. I walked a mile down the side of the highway and found a coffee shop on Santa Monica Boulevard. Once I fortified myself, I got a car home.”

“And beat the shit out of Lee, I hope,” I grumbled.

“No, but I didn’t see him again after that except in passing. It wasn’t easy, but my friends helped. They kept me too busy to wallow.”

Thank god for good friends. I needed to remember not to be so jealous of them in the future. “What did he say when you broke up with him?”

Cooper let out a laugh. “Nothing. Absolutely nothing. Like he didn’t even notice my absence.”

Selfish fucking prick. “Fuck.”

He shrugged. "I spent a long time buying into the bullshit of happy ever after. I blame Disney, honestly."

He tried to pass it off as a joke, but I wasn't buying it. His father had done a number on him, but Cooper needed to know not all couples were doomed.

I met his eyes. "My parents have been happily married for almost forty years. My dad brushes my mom's hair out every night before bed, and my mom makes my dad's favorite meal every Sunday even though the rest of us hate it. Aaron and Heather are happy as hell. Beth and Gary are perfect for each other and still get starry-eyed when they look at each other. You can't say happy endings are bullshit. My great-grandparents died holding hands."

I could tell he thought I was naive, that those were rare exceptions to the rule.

"Well," he said, clearly hoping to change the subject. "Maybe I'm wrong. I hope you find it."

I jerked back like he'd hit me. "My happy ever after?" Was he kidding? Was this his way of telling me he'd never even hoped things between us would work out in the long run? It was like a blow to the chest. I felt like I couldn't get enough oxygen. Had we just been pretending? What the hell was this if it wasn't real?

"Yeah. Some sweet woman or man back in Wheatland who enjoys this kind of lifestyle. Being outside, fixing things. I'll bet you'll have a line out the door when you get back."

"Line out the door for what? Dates?"

Cooper swallowed, and for a split second it looked like he didn't like the idea of me dating anyone else. But then it was gone under his same old smile. "Of course, dates. Didn't you see the billboard photo I posted?"

I felt like my face had gone numb. Was this what it was like to be dumped by someone you loved? It was excruciating.

"I don't know what you mean," I managed to say as my future dreams caught fire and went up in flames right in front of my eyes. "What billboard?"

"Oh my god, it's so cool," he said, reaching for his phone and scrolling through pictures to show me the one he was talking about. It was a photo of him standing in the back of the pickup on the highway with a giant Stallion billboard in the background featuring *Cooped Up With Nine*. There we were in front of the cabin with our arms around each other like we were the happiest couple in the world.

Except it was all fake.

"Wow." If my heart wasn't busy cracking in half, I might have been excited about it.

"Right?" he asked excitedly, pulling the phone back and scrolling through more photos. "I mean, it's not like it was on a billboard in downtown LA, but it's still amazing. It was on I-70 outside of Denver. But I totally forgot I took a sunset shot in the mountains too. Let me post that really quickly." While he busied himself on his phone, I stood up and cleaned away our dinner dishes. Every move felt like it took five times as long and my body weighed twice as much.

"I need to finish installing the sinks tonight before the plumber's putty dries. I'll be back in a bit," I said over my shoulder. It was total bullshit. That wasn't how plumber's putty was used, but Cooper didn't know that.

I headed out of the RV and crossed the clearing to the front porch of the cabin. I heard the RV door open behind me.

"Nine?"

I turned back to see Cooper's outline in the bright doorway. "Hm?"

"You okay?"

Never. Never would I be okay again. "'Course. Just want to knock these two sinks out so I can install the faucets in the morning before the gas guy gets here and connects the water heater."

Again, it was bullshit. The faucets didn't need to be installed before the water heater was connected, but Cooper didn't know that either.

"You sure?" he asked.

"Get some sleep, babe. I'm sure you're beat from all the excitement and travel."

He smiled and nodded. "Okay. Just shout if you need another pair of hands, okay? And wake me up to do the good-night video."

I lifted my hand to acknowledge what he'd said before I turned and entered the cabin. As soon as the door was closed behind me, I let out a deep, shuddering breath and sat my stupid ass on the floor. I'd allow myself five full minutes to feel like a naive asshole, then I'd get up and move on.

After only a couple of minutes, I realized I'd left the video camera on the table in the RV. I needed it to record the kitchen sink installation, so I headed back across the clearing. When I got close, I heard Cooper's voice through the open window.

"I already told you, I can't take the part. They want me to start filming in three weeks, and I'm already contractually obligated to Stallion."

I stopped in my tracks.

"Mitch, it doesn't matter if you can get me out of the Stallion deal. I'm not screwing over my friend. Nine is counting on this money as much as I am. I don't go back on commitments like that no matter how much I might want a role in a damned film."

I stood there in shock. Not only had Cooper lied to me about not getting the part, but he'd turned it down out of some ridiculous sense of obligation to me. As if me buying a little piece of land in Wyoming was anywhere near as important as him being offered this movie role.

My stomach roiled with a combination of anger and guilt. How dare he make this decision without talking to me? But then again, maybe it was my fault for not telling him he'd been the real reason I'd agreed to do this—the need to pay for Jacks's surgery.

"Fine. Give me twenty-four hours to sleep on it if you want, but my answer will be the same." He listened for a minute. "Sure, tomorrow afternoon. Call me after your meeting."

I snuck back to the cabin without the camera and did the sink installs using my phone camera instead. I focused on talking my way through the tutorials and concentrated on helping other people who might want to know how to install a sink. The familiar cadence of my voice speaking to the camera in an empty room was somehow settling, and when I finally finished both sinks and cleaned up after myself, I felt calmer than I had before.

Before leaving the cabin for the night, I looked around. The windows were in, the flooring was done, the Sheetrock was hung, all plumbing fixtures were now close to being installed and complete, and I only needed to do some tile work before it was time to sand and paint. After that, it wouldn't take long to install the light fixtures, the kitchen cabinets and appliances, and the countertops.

Then all we'd have left would be the interior decorating. I'd fantasized about doing that part of the project together with Cooper, but things had changed.

I made my way back to the RV and got out my phone to record the good-night video from the still-lit kitchen area. I could hear soft snores from the bedroom area.

"Hi, everyone," I said in a semi-whisper. "It's really late. I was still finishing up some work in the cabin, but Coop fell asleep before I got back."

I walked the camera into the bedroom to show him curled up under the covers with Nacho snoring at his feet.

When I returned to the kitchen and pointed the lens back at myself, I let out a soft laugh. "Honestly, I thought it was Cooper snoring, but I guess it was Nacho. Anyway, that's a wrap for today. If you didn't see our fancy billboard, check out the feed for Coop's earlier post. Have a great night, everyone."

I finished the recording and posted it before stripping out of my clothes and sliding into bed next to Cooper's warm body. My feelings were jumbled up like a big tangled ball of cheap yarn, but I knew I still wanted his body next to mine for as long as I could get it. I hauled him over to my side and draped him over my chest the way we normally slept.

"Love you," he mumbled in his sleep.

Neither of us had said those words to each other for real yet, and it figured the first time I heard them would be when he could have been dreaming about anything. For all I knew, he was imagining his old jackass landlord or even dreaming about comforting his brother in a hospital bed.

I felt hot tears well up and spill over. Never had I ever cried over something so ridiculous. I felt like a child.

But it was time to grow up because someone needed to make some difficult decisions around here, and it was time for that someone to be me.

I just needed time to think first.

26

COOPER

Nine was acting weird, and it had started with the conversation about Lee yesterday. Ever since then, he'd gone back to his silent, grunting routine, only speaking to me long enough to teach me how to sand the drywall in preparation for painting.

He was clearly in his head about something, and I finally couldn't stand it any longer.

"Are you going to tell me what has you in such a shitty mood?"

Nine's head whipped up from where he'd been helping the gas guy install the stove. Okay, so maybe I hadn't picked the best time to bring it up, but I couldn't hold back any longer.

Nine looked both confused and annoyed. "What are you talking about?"

The gas installer acted like he wasn't listening.

"You, us, this. You're in a fucking mood today, and I want to know why. You've barely spoken to me all day."

He gathered up the bits of cardboard and plastic that had been packaged around the stove. "Oh, now we're telling each other everything, are we? That's great to know."

Uh-oh.

He took the trash out to the construction dumpster while I followed behind like an annoying little puppy.

"Tell me what you mean by that," I snapped.

"Why should I?" he asked, louder than I'd ever heard him speak. His deep voice rang out through the clearing. He threw his hands out to the sides. "It's not like this is real. It's not like we're actually together. You made your feelings very clear last night. We aren't a thing. This was pretend for the sake of the sponsorship. I get it now, I do."

What the fuck was he talking about? "That's not true!"

"Isn't it? A real couple would have talked about things instead of hiding them. A real couple would have faced a challenge head-on. A real couple—" He stopped and ground his teeth together before turning suddenly and storming off into the woods.

He was so angry, it scared me. Sweet, calm Isaac Winshed never got mad. He never raised his voice. I wasn't scared of him, but I was scared *for* him. I hated seeing him this upset. It was like watching Cinderella being pickpocketed by her favorite fat mouse.

"Stop!" I cried. "Stop. Let's talk about this."

He didn't stop.

Out of the corner of my eye, I saw the gas guy slink back to his truck and drive away. What a shitshow. Hopefully he'd at least done everything we'd needed before we scared him off.

"Nine!"

He stopped and spun around. "But we're not a real couple, are we? We never were. It turns out, you don't even believe in such a thing, which is sad as fuck, Cooper. It breaks my heart to think you don't believe you deserve someone to be there for you." He smacked his chest. "I want to be there for you, dammit. *Me*. But you're just so fucking determined to prove you're a lone wolf. And I get it. You've been hurt. You've been shit on by people who should have done better by you."

He turned his back on me and ran both hands into his hair, clutching at his head in frustration. After a few deep breaths, he dropped his arms and turned back to me.

"You're going to LA and taking the job."

"No I'm not," I said without thinking. I wasn't all that great with taking orders.

His eyes narrowed. "Yes. You are."

Oh. Ohh. Bossy Isaac again. Well, look at that, my dick was hard, as if I needed that bullshit on top of everything else.

"I don't walk out on people who depend on me," I told him.

"You'd better not be including me in that statement, because I don't depend on you and never have. I don't need shit from you, in fact." Nine was angry as hell, and it made me feel untethered and wild. It wasn't until that moment I realized what an anchor he'd been in my life recently.

"But—"

He held up a hand. "No. I don't want you here anyway. I've thought it through, and I've figured out a plan. We've already filmed a shit ton of tutorials in a short amount of time. I was moving as fast as I could in hopes of getting done sooner so you could get back to Jacks."

I opened my mouth to respond, but he cut me off again.

"Hush. Just listen. You're going to take the job. I'm going to keep working and posting videos at a steady pace. We are going to pretend—"

I opened my mouth, but he shook his head.

"We're going to pretend you're still here. We're going to keep the Stallion contract because we're going to fulfill it. And you're going to take the film role. And then you're going to tell them you need a week off for a bone marrow transplant. And they're going to give it to you because—hope to god—they're decent people."

Two could play at this stubborn asshole role. "I don't want the part."

Nine's eyes rolled. "Yes you do. Don't insult me like that. I may be naive, but I'm not stupid, Cooper. Besides, you need the money. There's a chance they could pay you faster than Stallion, and then you can help Jacks and your mom."

How dare he tell me what I needed. I caught myself putting my hands on my hips the way my mom always did when she meant business. "I'm not taking the job."

His eyes bored into mine. "Then I walk. And neither of us gets what we want. It's your choice."

The stubborn fool would shoot himself in the foot to make me whole. "You can't mean that."

His silence echoed through the trees.

"Isaac," I said in a softer voice.

He looked away. "It's for the best, Cooper. You said it yourself. There is no happy ever after here. We're from different worlds. You belong in LA, and I belong in the woods. Go follow your dream and then come back here long enough to close up the project at the end of the summer, okay? Don't fight me on this. You won't win, and I'm not strong enough to keep... to keep..."

There was a pleading sound in his voice, and I realized he'd meant everything he'd ever said to me about love. But maybe he didn't know I'd meant it too.

I walked closer to him, and he looked at me like I was a venomous snake. My hands came up to calm him down. "Just let me hug you."

He looked unsure, like it was some kind of trick.

"Isaac. I'll go. I'll take the job. Just... let me pretend for one more night that we're okay."

He let out a breath, his shoulders sinking down in relief. "Yeah. I'd like that."

I closed the distance between us and held on to him like my life depended on it. He smelled like honey and woodsmoke, sawdust and sweat. I drank it down like sweet wine and let it fill every corner of my soul.

He leaned down and kissed me so softly, his beard tickled my lips. "It's still a workday," he murmured against my mouth. "And we need to take a bunch of good-night video clips and footage of you in different outfits in case I need some stuff to splice in."

He was right, but I wanted some more kisses first. "In a minute," I said before running my tongue along his bottom lip. We kissed slowly for a long time before it was time to either get back to work or find a horizontal surface and some lube.

"Work," he said with a gasp, pulling away and reading my mind at the same time. "Work. But first you make the call."

He clasped my face and leaned down to press a firm kiss to my forehead. "Make the call," he said again in a softer voice.

I nodded and stood there alone in the woods while he walked away from me.

27

NINE

The first two weeks without Cooper were excruciating. I wandered around in a daze feeling like something important was missing, and it was. My heart had flown to LA, and I was never getting it back.

The RV was quiet as fuck without the chatterbox there, so I'd begun playing country music softly through the Bluetooth speaker when I was fixing and eating dinner. After dinner, I usually went back to work and took the speaker with me. Sometimes I listened to podcasts, and sometimes I even played some of the pop music Cooper liked.

So when my phone rang one night, the ring trilled loudly through the speaker, damned near scaring me to death.

It was Eli.

"Hey," I said, disconnecting the phone from the speaker and turning off the music. "What's up?"

"Why didn't you tell me Cooper left?"

Just the sound of his name made my chest tight. "I didn't think we were telling anyone."

"I'm not everyone. Besides, Cooper wanted me to check on you. He said you aren't answering his calls."

I put him on speakerphone so I could start cleaning up the paintbrushes for the night. "I'm fine." I certainly wasn't telling my brother about how hearing Cooper's voice over the phone had become too hard for me to handle.

"Sure, sure. So then tell me why you missed Beth's birthday."

I dropped the brush in the sink with a clatter. "Oh shit, what? I did? Fuck. What day is it?"

If there was one thing you could rely on me for—besides everything—it was celebrating my siblings' birthdays and special moments. I hated being lost in the shuffle, so I made a big deal out of helping each of my siblings feel special whenever I could. That meant birthdays were a big deal to me. I never forgot them. Ever.

"It's June twenty-ninth, Nine."

Fuck. "Really? Her birthday was three days ago and you're just now calling?"

"It didn't occur to me you missed it until she mentioned it tonight at Mom and Dad's cookout. Even Mom said she's tried calling you several times and you haven't answered."

I picked up the paintbrush and continued rinsing it out. "Because I don't want to hear any of her 'I told you so' bullshit," I admitted. "I just need some time alone."

"Well, too bad. I'm coming there tomorrow to help you."

I stood up straight and looked at my reflection in the big picture window over the cabin's new kitchen sink. "No you're not. I don't need help. In fact, I need to slow down the work I'm doing and make it take longer. So, no. You're not coming."

"Cooper sent me the address. He thinks it's a great idea."

"Cooper can go to hell," I growled. "I don't need any of Cooper's bright ideas."

There was silence for a beat and then, "Oh."

"Stay away, Eli. Please."

"Nope. See you bright and early around noon."

The call ended. Fuck.

I finished cleaning up and then headed to the cabin's bathroom to take advantage of the big shower where I'd already put all of my things. The hot jets felt good on my tired body, but my dick had absolutely no interest in any action. It had been on strike since the day I'd taken Cooper to Denver for his flight.

And that was fine.

Totally fine. I hadn't needed sex before, and I could survive without sex now.

I turned off the jets and dried off with a towel before wrapping it around my waist and slipping my feet into my open boots to trek back across the clearing. When I finally settled into bed with Nacho taking up Cooper's spot, my brain wouldn't shut off.

I wondered how Cooper was doing in LA. I worried about him juggling his family's needs with his job. And I welcomed any news of him my brother might bring with him tomorrow. I finally fell asleep to thoughts of seeing him on the big screen one day, happy in the knowledge that there was a reason I'd told him to go. And that reason was him finally getting a chance to live the life he'd always wanted.

WHEN ELI PULLED into the clearing, I had to admit I was happy to see him.

Eli stepped out of his SUV and opened the back door. Out shot his two black labs, Barnaby and Rose. Nacho let out a yip and went tearing across the clearing to join in the excitement. The three of them had spent plenty of time together over the years, so they were thrilled to see each other.

"You look right at home here," he said as he approached me with a bro hug. "You got the woods, the dog, the cabin full of fix-it needs. Seems like your kind of paradise."

I nodded. "Definitely." Even though it was missing something pretty important. But I was choosing to ignore that for the time being so as not to be a depressing son of a bitch. "Let me show you around."

When I took him into the cabin, he was visibly impressed. "Shit, Nine. This is amazing."

I puffed up with pride at his words. "Thanks." I took him through the bedroom and bathroom, showing him the projects I'd already completed and pointing out the things that still needed to be done. "And then, of course, the roof."

"I can help with the roof if you have the supplies," Eli said. "Without Dad here to boss us around, we can actually get it done much faster than we did their house."

We shared a laugh over the remembered summer we helped Dad reroof their house. "That sucked. It was like working for a drill sergeant," I said. "But what about your job? Won't your boss be pissed if you take time off?"

"Nah. He told me to go. It'd be different if it was tax season, but summer's easy. We already have Fridays off in summer to make up for all the overtime in the first quarter."

Eli was an accountant for a small firm in Wheatland. Considering he was dating the boss's daughter, I wasn't surprised he was allowed a little leeway.

"Isn't Rissa going to miss you?" I teased. Everyone knew his girlfriend had him whipped.

"She went to Vegas for a bachelorette thing with the girls at work. Trina Chisolm is marrying that guy Pete who works at the radio station."

"Mpfh." I didn't much care for his girlfriend or her friends. Rissa was always trying to set me up with one of the ladies from that group, and every time I said no thank you, it just seemed to make her double down and try harder.

"She told me to tell you that they all think you and Coop make an adorable couple. I told her it was all for show, but she insists it's real. Says you look at each other the way she wishes I looked at her." Eli studied me out of the corner of his eye. "Did you mean what you said before, that you really feel something for him?"

I threw my arms up. "Yes, dammit. Why doesn't anyone believe me? Is it too much to imagine that one of the ten of us wouldn't be straight? Christ, Eli. People are gay and bi and... whatever else, okay? Stop acting like this isn't believable. I know you're not that ignorant of the world around us."

He held his hands up. "No, no, I know. It's just... I mean... you and Lauren. And then you dated that other chick, what was her name? Never mind. Doesn't matter. But you have to know how weird this is for me, not... not because he's a dude, but because he's Cooper. And you're my brother."

"Yeah, fine. I get that. And it's not like I expected this to happen or anything." I rubbed my hands over my face. "Besides, it's over. He's gone. Whatever."

Eli reached out and clapped a hand on my shoulder. "Nine..."

I glared at him. "You don't have to tell me. Whatever warning you're going to give me about how Cooper would never want to be with someone like me long term or he's meant for greater things. Just... don't. Okay? I already know all of that."

I walked over to the makeshift kitchen counter and began closing up the boxes of finishing nails that I'd left there so they wouldn't scatter everywhere if someone knocked into the board they were sitting on.

"Actually," Eli began hesitantly. "I was going to say the opposite. Cooper is my best friend, and I love him. But you deserve better."

I opened my mouth to argue with him, but he stopped me.

"Hear me out. Cooper's kind of... fucked-up. His dad did a number on him, and then he fell for this asshole who confirmed some false assumptions he had about relationships. The bottom line is, Coop is never going to trust a man to be there for him. He refuses to need anyone. And you're the kind of guy who needs to be needed."

"Not true."

He laughed, but his eyes were soft with affection. "Nine. You're the steadiest man I know, even steadier than Dad. You're going to make someone an amazing husband one day because you're reliable, hard-working, giving, and attentive. It's why all of Rissa's friends are constantly begging to score a date with you. You're a catch. You just don't know it. And Cooper's never going to be ready to make a life-long commitment to anyone, much less a quiet, steady guy from Wheatland, Wyoming."

Well, that part was right, anyway, but it sure as hell hurt to hear it said out loud.

"Thanks for that," I grunted, tossing the boxes of nails into a big plastic bin full of supplies. "Super fucking helpful. Glad you're here."

I headed outside to put the bin of supplies under the tarp with the rest of them, and then I rifled through the stacks of trim pieces to select the ones I needed for the kitchen. Once I took them back inside, I realized I needed the finishing nails to actually install the trim work.

"Fuck." I turned around to head outside again when Eli stepped between me and the door.

"Stop for a minute. I get that you're pissed, but talk to me. Are you mad at me or at Cooper?"

"I'm not mad at anyone," I said. And it was true. "I just want to work, okay? I want to focus on getting this shit done so I can move on with my fucking life."

It wasn't until the words were out of my mouth that I realized they were true. I needed to move on. The only way I was going to get over Cooper was to finish this project and leave this place. Memories of him and the two of us together were everywhere: in the clearing, in the cabin, in the RV, and in the woods around us. Hell, even my truck and the nearest town had memories of Cooper's smiling, snarky self-embedded in them.

Eli studied me for a beat and then nodded with a smile. "Okay. Then let's get to work. I can't promise I'm in decent shape after all these years behind a desk, but hopefully I can still keep up."

That got a snort out of me. Eli took great pride in working out religiously, and he helped Dad and Aaron almost every weekend on the farm. He was in fine shape.

I cranked up the music on the speaker, and we got to work. It was nice having Eli's easy, silent companionship while we worked. It felt somehow like a step in the right direction, away from this crazy temporary life I'd been living with Cooper and back toward my normal life—my real life—at home near my family.

With Eli beside me and the sun beating down on my skin while I worked up a good sweat preparing the roof for the new shingles, I felt like maybe I would be okay.

Five days later, when Eli and I were finishing up repairs to the exterior timbers, I finally got something new to focus on. It was a call from a marketing executive at a big vacation booking website.

"Hi, Nine, this is Adrian Walsh with MyCabin dot com. We were hoping to talk to you about some sponsorship opportunities we have."

I waved to get Eli's attention and then took the call in the cooler air of the shade over by the RV.

"Hi, Adrian. Good to hear from you."

"Yeah, listen, we're actually really impressed with your programming on YouTube, and we'd like to talk to you about an idea we have, but first we needed to find out about your commitment to Stallion. Are you exclusive to them, or are you free to do other projects when this one is over?"

I wasn't sure if they needed the both of us or not, but I decided to find out before this conversation went any further. "Well, I'm available in August for another project, but Cooper isn't. Were you hoping to get both of us, or...?"

"That would be ideal, yes, but... hmm... Come to think of it... you are the one who does most of the heavy lifting, so maybe that would be okay. We're more interested in the renovation-type content anyway. Don't get me wrong, we're LGBT owned, so we'd love to bring an LGBT partner on board, but the content doesn't need to focus on that. Let me go ahead and tell you what we have in mind, and then I'll confirm with our team that we're okay with a solo deal."

He explained that their company was essentially an Airbnb-type site specifically for cabins. They were looking for a vlogger to develop a web series on how to take an old cabin and turn it into a rental for supplemental income.

"Wow, that sounds exciting," I said. "I'd definitely be interested in hearing more about it." We finished the call with a plan to speak again in a few days. When I finally put the phone away, I made my way back to the cabin to tell Eli, who was getting off his own call.

"Guess what?" I called across the clearing. But he didn't answer. Instead he turned to face me.

I could tell the minute I saw his face something was wrong.

28

COOPER

When I'd first arrived in LA, I'd been in heaven. There hadn't even been much time to miss Isaac because I'd immediately gone into some group fitness classes Jarrod had roped me into since I had a scene in the movie where I was changing out of my scrub top in the hospital locker room. Evie convinced me to do some spray tanning to even out the farmer's tan I'd apparently developed in Colorado.

By the time the meetings started for the film, I was already tired and a little overwhelmed. The noise and pace of the city took some getting used to, which was weird because they hadn't seemed to bother me during my short visit before. But then again, maybe knowing that visit had been temporary had been different from thinking of this as my life again.

I was sure a large part of my mixed-up mood was not being able to communicate adequately with Nine. At first, he replied to my messages just fine, but then the responses got shorter. Finally, they were so few and far between, I got up the nerve to call him even though I knew hearing his voice on the phone would probably make me cry like a baby.

He hadn't answered.

And then he'd stopped texting too. I'd been wrong. It wasn't hearing his voice on the other end of the line that made me cry like a baby, it was *not* hearing it.

Evie had been the one to find me curled up on the floor between the sofa and the corner of the room.

"Who do I need to kill?" she'd asked in a growl.

"Me," I'd admitted with a wet sniff. "It's just my own chickens coming home to roost, is all." Which of course made me think of Sir Pecks-A-Lot which only set me off more.

Needless to say, I was a mess. The emotional upheaval of everything with Nine on top of the tenuous medical situation with Jacks was wearing me down quickly. Thankfully, Nine had been right and the production crew had managed to schedule my filming to be done in time for the bone marrow procedure in mid-July. But it had meant working extra hard to get all the scenes in by then.

Despite feeling overwhelmed, I was grateful. I'd spent almost eight years fantasizing about being an actor in LA, and I'd finally landed a decent part in a film. Not only that, but the other cast members were cool as hell and super professional. Bane McKenner played the male lead, and I had to admit I was a little awestruck. He'd just wrapped the film version of a bestselling book called *Colt* which I remembered Eli joking about since he had a brother by the same name. The book had been a huge teen hit, and being cast as the lead in that movie meant Bane McKenner was already on his way to being the hottest celebrity among teens in the world.

Filming with Sam Gwan was also a dream come true, or it should have been. He was brilliant and eager, open and genuine. He was young enough not to have the strong opinions of a seasoned director, but he'd been in the business long enough to really know what he was doing. I was surrounded by talent and energy.

But it was hard fucking work, and I wasn't great at it. Not in this particular role.

I wasn't just saying that to be modest. Pretending to be a nurse to a dying young man was not a great choice for me.

Not at this time in my life anyway.

Thankfully, Jarrod worked with me almost every night to help me prepare for the following day. Without him, I would have probably been escorted off the set as both a third-rate actor *and* a basket case. I had no business being involved in a group of such talented actors in the first place, and being there with them brought home to me just how naive I'd been. I'd honestly thought getting a decent role in a film would fill the hole in my life.

What a joke. Landing this role made me realize that I'd pinned all my hopes and dreams on a myth. It was like finally grabbing hold of the brass ring and finding out it was a hologram all along. I came home every afternoon no more fulfilled than I'd left that morning. And why would I? I'd just come from a monthlong stint of being on camera every day, only with the Stallion vlog, I'd been able to be on camera as myself.

Discovering this wasn't the life for me was freeing in a way. Like finally I didn't feel torn between two places anymore. I knew I wanted to be back home, at least until Jacks was completely recovered and my mom wasn't stretched so thin.

As long as I'd been at the cabin near Shale Falls, I'd known I was only a few-hour drive from my family if they needed me. Being in LA made me feel a million miles away.

And then there was Nine.

I remembered my mom telling me what it was like when she'd finally taken off her wedding ring for good after Dad had left the last time.

She'd said, "I keep reaching for it with my other fingers and finding it missing. It's like a part of me has been left behind and my body somehow senses the loss and can't get over it." It took her a year before she stopped reaching for it with her other fingers.

That's how I felt about Isaac Winshed. He was a part of me, ingrained into my skin like the tiny cluster of stars tattooed on my hip, except he was missing. My body reached for him every fucking night, and I landed with a crash on the floor from where I'd been sleeping on Van and Evie's sofa. Every morning Evie would give me a tally of the number of times she'd heard me hit the ground. Van had even offered to switch with me so I could have his bed.

I'd told them the truth. "I'll only keep rolling across your bed until I fall on the floor anyway."

Because my body wouldn't ever stop looking for him.

"Hey, cutie pie, heads up," Bane said, chucking a balled-up paper napkin at my forehead.

I blinked up at him, trying to shake off the morose mood. My yogurt sat untouched on the craft services table in front of me. "Yeah, sorry. What's up?" For someone playing a dying guy, he was awfully chipper between takes.

"A few of us are getting takeout back at my place after this. You want to come? Willow's desperate to meet you. She follows you and your boyfriend on Insta."

I pushed the yogurt cup away from me. Bane was dating a famous singer. Having dinner at their place was another surreal moment. "Yeah, sure. Of course," I said automatically. "Thanks."

I brought Evie with me after she almost burst my eardrum with squeals and begging when I told her about it. When we got to the large beachfront condo in Santa Monica, I was sufficiently impressed. It was obviously professionally decorated and cool as hell. The walls overlooking the ocean were all glass, and some sliding doors were open to let the sound of the surf inside along with the sea breeze.

Bane introduced me to Willow right away, who chatted excitedly with me about *Cooped Up With Nine*.

"How are you doing both projects at the same time? I asked Bane, but he said he didn't know," Willow asked, leading me over to the long table full of finger foods and wine.

"Nine is still there. He's posting prerecorded stuff and catching up on some of the more mundane work." I took the glass of wine she handed me. "Thanks. He, ah… he insisted I take the role. I didn't want to ditch him but—"

"Isn't he the sweetest thing? I could totally see him doing that. The way he looks at you is like…" She put her slender hand against the vee of her low-cut blouse. "Swoony." She sang a little snippet I recognized from an Ed Sheeran song called "Perfect."

Your heart is all I own. And in your eyes you're holding mine.

I tried smiling and nodding, but my hands began to shake. "He's a good man." I heard the words come out of my mouth, but I felt outside of my body. It was the phrase I knew he hated even though it was a thousand percent true.

Evie must have sensed my discomfort because she immediately began asking bullshit questions about the apartment like where had they found that sofa and who had done that painting on the wall. I took the opportunity to walk out onto the balcony to catch my breath.

I pulled my phone out of my pocket and looked up our Instagram account for the millionth time. There was a new post. Isaac's handsome face was red from sunburn. If I'd been there, I would have reminded him to use sunscreen.

"Hi, everyone. Another day of my brother's help with the roof. Coop's still laid up in bed not feeling well, but he promised he'd put together a great video for you guys as soon as he's feeling better. In the meantime, Nacho and his friends have a new trick for you guys."

He stepped back from the camera into the clearing. The phone was probably in the bendy tripod around the porch railing. The fingers came up to Nine's mouth, and the Winshed Whistle came pealing out. Nacho raced toward him from wherever he'd been in the woods, and Eli's dogs came running as well. All of them sat immediately at Nine's feet.

I didn't blame them.

"Okay, stay," he said, holding out the palm of his hand to calm them. He grabbed a can of tennis balls off a nearby sawhorse and tossed one a few times in the air. The dogs' eyes followed it like it was a juicy steak.

He crouched down with his back tilted at an angle and threw up a ball, calling for Rose. She took off, leaped on his back, and then caught the ball in the air before landing on the ground. He immediately threw up the second ball and called for Barnaby. Then the third one for Nacho. But when Nacho leaped off Nine's back, Nine stood up and caught him in midair as soon as he'd gotten the ball in his mouth.

Nine looked so damned proud of himself. He grinned wide into the camera. His white teeth stood out against the dark brown of his beard. The sun streaked through the clearing at an angle, picking up the reddish highlights in his beard. Eli stepped into the shot and made a crack about Nine slacking off to play with his balls when the video faded out.

Every single cell in my body cried out to be back there with Nine and Nacho in that clearing, goofing off and playing with Nacho between jobs. I was happy to see Nine wasn't alone. From the looks of things, Eli had been there several days already.

I let out a breath and looked out at the waves. After a minute, I could hear Willow belting out a snippet of a song from Hamilton.

I will never be satisfied.

A soft snort escaped me. That was it. That was me. Here I was with everything I'd ever wanted, and I still wasn't happy. Well, fuck that. I needed to get a grip and learn how to be grateful. I turned around and rejoined the party. This was the life I wanted, I just needed to embrace it and stop being a fickle prima donna.

Bane and Willow turned out to be genuinely good people, who did their best to make everyone feel at home in their place. Evie and I found a comfortable spot on a love seat and laughed half the night away when Willow drank enough to start doing singing impersonations of Bane and other actors. I looked around the room at some of the cast and crew I'd gotten to know over the past couple of weeks and decided this was good enough.

If I couldn't have Nine and the Cinderella cabin in the woods, I would be content here in LA with new friends. It was enough.

It had to be.

"Fourth of July fireworks on the yacht at Marina del Ray tomorrow night," Willow said, getting everyone's attention. "Who's in?"

Evie elbowed me hard, getting my attention. When she gave me big eyeballs and a head tilt, I knew we were going to be spending the

Fourth on Willow's yacht. I raised my hand. "Never been on a yacht before, but I've binge-watched *Deadliest Catch.* Does that make me a greenhorn?"

Willow's laugh was punctuated by the twin dimples she was famous for. "I promise we won't make you swab the deck."

Bane walked behind the love seat to get another beer and patted my shoulder on the way past. "You'll love it. It's the best view of the fireworks, and the chef on board makes killer sushi."

When Evie and I finally caught an Uber back to the apartment, she turned to me with huge eyes. "Holy fucking shit, Coop. We're friends with Willow Ex and Bane McKenner. We're spending the Fourth on their fucking *yacht.*"

She sat back and blew air up into her bangs.

"They're so fucking nice. So real. Did you hear Bane when he was talking about teaching his baby brother to ride a bike? That was so sweet. And when Willow found out I worked at Trapeze, her whole face lit up. She says it was her favorite place to go when she was a kid. And that guy Lou who works with you guys as a production assistant? He grew up like twenty miles away from me in Lanton. Isn't that crazy?"

She continued chattering excitedly about our night and the other people she'd met there. I closed my eyes and felt the warm wind coming through the open car window. The sounds and scents of the city were as far away as you could get from my little mountain clearing in Colorado, but the feeling of a warm breeze on my face wasn't. It reminded me of the day we'd brought a blanket outside into the sunshine and had our lunch as a picnic. I'd lain down with my head in Nine's lap and closed my eyes to enjoy the warm sun on my face for a little while. The breeze had blown softly through the trees, making the familiar rattling *whooshing* sound that aspens made in the wind.

Nine's fingers had played in my hair while the soft sounds of his old-fashioned country music came from the speaker we'd left inside the cabin.

"Your phone is buzzing," Evie said, rousing me from my half-asleep state. It was after two in the morning, so if someone was trying to reach me, it couldn't be good news.

"Mom?" I said, fumbling the phone to my ear.

"You need to get here, baby," she said in a frantic voice. "He fell at work and won't stop bleeding."

29

NINE

Somehow I knew it was about Jacks. "What is it?" I asked Eli, striding across the clearing.

"It's Jacks. He had an accident and is in ICU."

"Are they letting Coop go?"

Eli shrugged. "He doesn't know yet since it's a holiday. But he's going anyway."

"Good. He should." I stood there in the clearing like an idiot, like... like I needed to do something or go somewhere.

Eli tilted his head at me. "Are you going to Caswell?"

My entire body wanted to shout *yes*. "No. Not unless he needs me there, and we both know he doesn't need anyone for anything." But I wasn't content knowing he'd be there without plenty of support. "You should go."

Eli's eyes widened. "I can't go. I have to get back to work."

My heart rate ramped up. "He doesn't like needles, Eli. If they need to do the bone marrow thing, he'll need someone there to hold his hand and stuff."

"Dude, it's like a two-hour procedure at most, and it's done under general anesthetic. He'll be fine. I think his part of it is even outpatient."

He didn't understand. It didn't matter how long the procedure was once he was under, it mattered how they *got* him under in the first place.

"He's going to freak out. He has that fainting response to needles where he gets pale and stuff."

Eli picked his hammer back up and hopped back on the ladder. "He's a big boy, Nine. He'll be fine."

He was right, of course. But there was a difference between being fine and being *good*. As I got back to work, I thought about Cooper's little family. With both boys in the hospital, would his mom have any support? Would she even have anyone to bring her food and hold her hand while she waited? And how was her own employer handling the time she needed off work?

After an hour of more repairs to the timber, I finally couldn't stand it any longer.

Nine: *I heard about Jacks. Is he okay?*

The dots seemed to take forever to turn into words.

Cooper: *They got the bleeding under control. As soon as he's strong enough to start the chemo to kill off his bone marrow, they'll do the transplant.*

My stomach twisted, and my brain couldn't stop mentally packing a bag.

Nine: *Do you need me there? I can be there in three hours.*

This time the dots took ten years.

Cooper: *I'm fine, but thank you.*

I stared at the text. Of course he was. He was always fine.

Fuck fine.

I gathered up my tools and took them inside the cabin to where the bigger toolbox was. Suddenly, I had clarity I'd never experienced before. When you loved someone, you showed up regardless of whether or not they wanted you there. I already knew that from years of being part of my big family. It was something I'd taken to heart at a very young age thanks to my parents setting the example.

When you loved someone, you showed up.

"Eli," I shouted. "Let's go. We're packing up and heading to Caswell. You're going to be there for Coop whether you like it or not, and I'm going to... I don't know. Mow his mom's lawn or learn how to cook a casserole. Something. Get your ass in gear."

He clattered his way down from the ladder and poked his head into the cabin with a giant, shit-eating grin. "Little bro has a bossy side. Who knew?"

I cleaned up and secured all the tools and valuable supplies inside the cabin, taking advantage of the new dead bolt locks. Then I went to the RV and packed everything that needed packing. Finally, I was ready to go.

Eli gave me a big, clap-on-the-back hug before whistling for the dogs to load up.

When I finally got on the road, I felt lighter. At least this way he'd have Eli to hold his hand, and I would find a way to make myself useful behind the scenes. Maybe I could even help out at the bakery or do some laundry—anything at all to make their lives easier while Jacks was going through this.

When I got partway down the mountain, I followed Eli into the gas station at Shale Falls to fill up the tank. On a whim, I put in an order for a pizza next door. It would be after seven at night by the time we got to Caswell, but if Coop was hungry, I knew he'd like the pizza even if it was cold. Eli could take it to him at the hospital.

While I was waiting for it to be ready, my phone rang. It was Cooper.

"Hey," I said tentatively, wondering if Eli had told him I was coming and this was Cooper calling to tell me not to.

I could tell right away he was crying, which immediately shot my heart rate into the stratosphere. His voice sounded small and afraid which set my teeth on edge. "Isaac? I don't know if I can do this."

"You can. You absolutely can."

His voice was a hoarse whisper. "I'm scared."

My heart couldn't take it. "Eli's on the way. He'll be there in a couple of hours. Did something else happen?" I was almost too afraid to ask.

He sniffed. "No, I'm just scared, and... and I don't want to be alone... and—" His voice was breaking, and with it, my heart.

"Shh, it's okay, sweetheart. Eli's on his way." I couldn't bring myself to tell him I was coming too. What if that upset him even more? Or what if this was just a temporary moment of fear and he'd regret having me there? "Is your mom there?"

"Mm-hm. She's in with Jacks right now, but they're making us take turns and wear all this protective gear since his immune system is being shut down for the transplant. They said one bad infection and he could be in real trouble. It's freaking me out."

The pizza guy handed over the big box, and I gave him a tight smile in response. When I got back behind the wheel, the call switched over to the Bluetooth speaker. If Coop was alone in the waiting room, he needed a distraction.

"Did I ever tell you about the time me, Graham, and Tip convinced Eli we were all going skinny-dipping in Trandle's pond but then the rest of us snuck in swim trunks?"

He let out a soft, wet laugh. "No, but I can picture it."

"The water was cold as shit. School had already started, so it was probably September. I want to say I was ten, so he would have been sixteen. It was Tip's idea, of course, to see who could cross the pond the fastest. Anyway, Tip had also told his girlfriend at the time, who was head of the cheer squad. They all came down there to the beach side with their bikinis and whatnot. We'd put our trunks in a little baggie that Graham managed to hide in the water. When we swam over to the beachside of the lake, all the girls were there. Graham hands Tip and me our suits, and we all walk out of the water dressed like it's no big deal."

Another soft laugh. "If God loved me, there'd be pictures."

I described Eli's historic hissy fit and then went on to tell him several more Eli stories he'd never heard before. By the time his mom came out of Jackson's room, he sounded much better.

He said something to his mom and then came back on the line. "Thank you."

"Yeah," I said. "Anytime."

"Isaac?" He sounded so tired. All I wanted was to hold him.

"Yeah, baby?"

"Um... I just..."

"Go be there for your mom right now. Everything's going to be okay. I... Eli will be there soon."

30

COOPER

I was so fucking tired. Hearing Nine's sweet voice over the phone had drained all the remaining energy out of me, and now all I wanted to do was sleep.

"He's resting peacefully," Mom said, taking the seat next to me on the little sofa in the private family waiting room they'd given us.

I put my arm around her shoulders and leaned my head against hers. "Why don't you head home and get some rest? You've been up all night. I'll stay here in case he wakes up."

For a brief moment, it looked like she might argue with me, but then she smiled and stood, leaning back down just long enough to kiss me on the top of the head. "Okay. We'll take turns, but only if you agree that means you take a turn when I get back."

Ah, the Mom trick. "We'll see."

She promptly sat back down and crossed her arms. I sighed and waved my hand. "Fine. Go. I promise."

After kissing me again, she was off. I settled back onto the little love seat and tried closing my eyes for a while. There was no telling how long I dozed for before a young nurse came in to wake me.

"Mr. Heath? Dr. Levine wants you to visit the lab for some blood work if you're up for it. I have the orders right here." She handed me a plastic sleeve with some paperwork in it. "I can show you to the lab when you're ready."

I rubbed my face and stood to stretch. My entire body ached from napping on the hard piece of furniture. "I'm ready now. Thanks."

I followed her down the hallways to the lab before remembering that the blood draw would involve needles, and I hated needles. My body went tingly, and I suddenly felt nauseous.

Get it together.

Beads of sweat formed on my upper lip, and my throat felt topped up with acid sludge. I stupidly wished my mom had stayed. How the hell did Jacks withstand all of this medical stuff? He'd never had a problem with needles the way I had.

When a tech led me to a chair with special blood-drawing arms, I clapped my hand in front of my mouth. "Might need bed," I mumbled through sweaty fingers. "Sometimes faint."

The tech nodded and gave me a reassuring smile as he led me farther back to a narrow exam table. "Vasovagal response. It's more common than you think. Go ahead and lie down here."

By the time he pulled out all of his supplies, my body was trembling. I hated feeling this way. I despised acting like a child, being out of control. Adults shouldn't have the same fear responses as toddlers for god's sake.

It took him five tries to find a vein.

By the time he finally found one, both of my arms were mottled with fresh bruises, and hot tears ran down my neck. I missed Nine. I missed him so badly, and I just wanted him there to hold my hand and keep telling me it was going to be okay.

"You need to hydrate," the tech muttered as he stuck the labels on the test tubes. "Would make this a lot easier. You're going to be dealing with a lot of needles if you're donating bone marrow. Hell, the one they put into your hip for the harvest is—"

I didn't let him finish before I was turning and throwing up into the little plastic bowl he'd handed me after the second failed needle stick. The tech took it all in stride, even finding me a travel-sized toothbrush and toothpaste kit to use in the lab's bathroom. I closed my eyes and imagined Nine's big strong body standing behind me and holding me up while I brushed my teeth and washed my face. Maybe imagining him giving me strength would be enough to help me get through this.

By the time I recovered enough to head back to the family waiting room, I was weak, shaky, and so very, very done. I felt sorry for myself way more than I should have considering Jacks was going through so much worse. But that only made me feel even weaker and stupider. And guilty. Very guilty.

Who the hell was I to need anyone? I wasn't the needer here. I was the need-ee. I was here because Jacks needed me, and I needed to be strong. For him. For both of us.

When I got back to the little waiting room, I was surprised to see Eli there. "You came," I said stupidly.

His face lit up, and he stood to give me a hug. He wasn't as big as Nine was, and he smelled different, but there was the faintest hint of woodsmoke in his clothes that reminded me of his brother and our little clearing in the woods.

"Yeah. How are you holding up?" he asked, taking one of the seats in the small place. I sat back down on the hard love seat.

"Shitty," I admitted with a tired laugh. "I wish Nine was here, no offense."

Eli blinked at me. "You do?"

I felt like I was on the verge of more tears which was impossible after the day I'd had, so I simply nodded. Eli looked uncomfortable, but I assumed it was because I was talking about his brother in that way.

We sat together in silence for a while, pretending to watch the cooking show on the television in the corner. Eli tapped at his phone a little bit, but I assumed he was texting his girlfriend, Rissa.

"How's Rissa?" I asked, making conversation. He'd come all this way, so I should at least be grateful enough to have a conversation with him.

He chuckled. "Don't know. She's in Vegas with some friends for a bachelorette weekend. Well, it was supposed to be a weekend, but they extended it."

He looked up at me with a grin. "I told Nine as soon as he gets home to Wheatland, she's going to rope him into a shit ton of dates with her friends."

And just like that, the nausea was back. "He's gay," I said stubbornly, even though he wasn't. Not really. It wasn't fair of me to claim him for my team simply because I was jealous as hell.

"Nah," Eli said, not looking up from his phone. "It was just a phase. Like one of those experiments other people do in college, you know? Except he never went to college."

I stared at him. "Are you kidding?" Since when had my best friend been that stupid?

He shrugged and sat back, closing his eyes and resting his head against the vinyl wall behind him. "You gave him a taste, and he got it out of his system. Easy peasy."

I wanted to punch the guy. "It wasn't like that," I snapped. "I cared about him. Still do, as a matter of fact. It wasn't an experiment at all."

He shrugged again without opening his eyes. "Well, Tank Peterson's gay. He owns the fitness center in Wheatland. Maybe he'll give Nine a try. Wonder if Nine likes big guys. Tank does those weight lifting contests."

I clamped my teeth together, but it didn't stop the tears from spilling over. "Stop talking about him with other people," I said in a rough voice. "It's mean."

Eli looked up in surprise. "What do you mean? You're the one who didn't want him, right? You wanted your life in LA. Didn't even ask if Nine might have wanted to go with you?"

I was all mixed up in my head, but there was one thing I knew for sure. "I do want him. I want him right now. I need him here." More tears flooded out with each word. "I need him," I said again softly. I sounded pathetic, but I was tired down to my bones.

"You have me though," Eli said. He seemed to be searching me for something—a reaction of some kind.

"No offense, Eli, but you're not Isaac," I muttered, leaning over and resting my face in my hands.

"You want Isaac here?"

I snapped my head up and glared at him. "Yes, dammit! How many times do I have to tell you? I want him here. I called him, didn't I? I told him I was scared, but he still didn't—"

Eli interrupted me. "He's out in the parking lot."

I stared at him. "What?"

"He wanted to be here for you, but he was afraid you didn't want him. He had grand plans to sneak over to your mom's house tomorrow and trim the rosebushes or something, I don't know. Go talk to him."

But I was already out the door.

31

NINE

I'd just put the dogs back in the RV from a potty break when I heard someone shouting across the parking lot.

"Hey, asshole!"

It was Cooper, and he might as well have had smoke coming out of his nostrils. His pale face was screwed up in anger, and his hands were balled into fists. He strode across the parking lot like he had hellhounds nipping at his heels.

He was so beautiful I wanted to cry.

But he was mad as a kicked hornet's nest. "What the fuck, Nine? What the actual fuck? You're here and you were too chickenshit to come inside?"

I didn't know what to say. Anything that came out of my mouth right now would probably be wrong. So I didn't say anything.

"So now you're not going to even say anything?" His words were punctuated by a thunderclap. "The great silent Isaac Winshed. Why would I have expected any different?"

I forced myself to speak. "You have Eli. I didn't think—"

"I don't want Eli, you asshole!" He came close enough to shove me with both hands, but he was clearly too worn-out to put much strength behind it. "I want *you*! I need *you*."

Once he got that close, I could see he was crying. His face was puffy like this had been going on all day.

I stared at him stupidly, remembering the text where I specifically asked if he wanted me here. "But I asked you, and—"

His balled fists beat lightly against my chest as I felt the first fat drops of rain.

"I hate you," he wailed. "I needed you, and you were just sitting out here like a fucking—"

I grabbed his shirtfront, yanking him toward me and gathering him up in my arms. I squeezed him as tightly as I could, muffling the rest of his words into the front of my shirt. "Shh, I'm sorry. I'm here. I'm sorry."

He continued to fight me, shoving at me but also pulling me close. It was almost like he couldn't decide if he wanted to beat me or wanted to be with me.

"I fucking hate you," he said again, but his voice was angrier this time. "And I hate myself even more for needing you."

The rain started pelting us for real now, and I reached for the door latch to get us inside the RV. As soon as we stumbled up the stairs and closed the door behind us, Cooper barreled into me, shoving me against the full-length cabinet on the opposite wall.

All three dogs whined and hopped around, trying to get our attention, but I barked out a command for them to sit.

Cooper grabbed my beard and yanked my head down until his lips were crushing mine. His teeth scraped my tongue, and his fingers scratched my face through my beard. It was like being mauled by a sexy wildcat, and I simply stood there and took it, afraid of upsetting him more by restraining him and trying to calm him down.

Suddenly his hands were everywhere. My shirt came off, my jeans sagged open, and I noticed low muttering coming out of his mouth.

"Fucking asshole sitting out here when I was in there, and did you even know I had to get stuck fifty thousand fucking times just for one blood draw? No. You wouldn't have because you were out here like a goddamned head-in-the-sand idiot while I was in there having my fucking veins fed into a wood chipper. Well, you know what? I'm going to fucking tell you what, asshole. This stops now. You belong to me. You're mine. You and me. This is happening whether you like it or not, and you don't get to tell me, *mmmpff*!"

I grabbed his chin and kissed him hard, turning the tables on him and shoving him back across the RV until he was plastered against the back of the door. Now it was his turn to lose some articles of clothing, and when he was finally naked and gasping, I threw him over my shoulder and carried him to the bed, throwing him down on the comforter while I grabbed the lube and a condom.

If he wanted to take out his frustration in sex, I was all too willing. And maybe that didn't reflect great on me, but I knew Cooper and this was clearly what he wanted. What he needed. He needed out of his head if just for a few minutes, and I knew exactly how to do that.

"Get on your hands and knees. *Now*," I said.

"You're not the fucking boss of me," he snapped.

"I am right now. Do it."

Even though he shot me a pissed-off look, he scrambled to do as I said. His pale ass flashed in the dim room.

"You don't get to tell me what to do," he griped into the pillow.

I grabbed an ass cheek and opened him up enough to swipe a slick thumb across his hole. "You're mine. Remember? Your words."

"I said you were mine, I didn't say—*oh my fucking fuck*."

I pressed my thumb inside him hard, and goose bumps raced along his skin.

"Isaac," he said on a gasp. "Please."

I prepped him as quickly as I could and then rolled on a condom, slicking it up before tossing the lube aside. "You want this?" My voice was gruff with need, but I had to be sure.

"Isaac." It was a whimper this time. "Please."

I leaned over his smaller body and pressed my cheek against his. "Tell me you want me inside you. Tell me you want me to fuck you hard. Tell me you—"

"Yes! Yes, okay? Yes. Fuck me. Take me. I need you so badly. Please, dammit. I'm begging you. What more do you—*unghh*!"

I thrust inside of him in one hard shove before rocking back and pushing in again. His body was tight and hot, familiar in a way that made my throat close up. Being back inside him was incredible, and I wanted to stay here always.

I knew he was just desperate for a break, too desperate to really know what he was saying, but I was willing to take it if it meant having him like this again.

As I angled in and out of him, I dropped kisses along his spine until I got to the nape of his neck. He was panting and clutching at the sheets.

"Just like that," he breathed over and over. "Oh god, don't stop."

I grabbed his hands and stretched them up above his head as I continued to fuck him hard and fast. "You feel so fucking good. Gonna make me come."

"Nine!" His shout pierced the room as his entire body locked up. I reached down to stroke him only to find his dick and the sheets below already covered in his release. The thought of him coming without a touch was what pushed me over the edge.

I lost my rhythm and simply held on as my orgasm took over and my mind shattered into jagged pieces. Even after I was finished coming, I stayed like that, pressed inside of him and lying flat along his back. I nuzzled my nose into his hair and kissed the side of his face.

The words were right there on the tip of my tongue, but they wouldn't come out. "I…" *I love you.* "I…"

Cooper's hand came back and sank into my hair, holding my face next to his. "Just hold me for a while. Okay?"

I nodded and tried swallowing back my fear. He deserved to know how incredibly cherished he was, but I was afraid. I was downright terrified he hadn't meant what he'd said earlier, and that this was all the result of his feeling overwhelmed and exhausted. If I confessed my feelings to him and he didn't feel the same way… I wasn't sure I'd be able to get over it.

Besides, he needed me to be his rock right now, steady and sure. It was what I was good at. He didn't need me to be a needy pile of emotional insecurity.

"Stay right here while I clean us up," I murmured, pulling away from him and heading to the small bathroom. When I returned with a rag, he was already asleep. After cleaning us both up and texting Eli that we were napping in the RV, I moved into the bed beside him and pulled him into my arms.

I wasn't sure what any of this meant, but as long as I could hold on to him for a little while, it was enough.

32

COOPER

The next several days were a blur. If Nine hadn't been there to hold my hand through it all, I wasn't sure I would have made it through without turning into an absolute crybaby. There were needles and blood draws, IVs and beeping hospital equipment that all combined to put my teeth on edge.

"Thank you for staying," I said for the millionth time. Nine looked up at me from his laptop. He was kicked back in the big visitor chair in my hospital room with his ankles crossed on the end of my bed. The bone marrow harvest had gone smoothly, but the doctor had admitted me overnight because of a bad reaction to one of the pain meds.

"Stop saying that. Of course I stayed." He went back to his work.

Clearly he didn't need me interrupting him, but I was bored. "What are you editing now?"

He glanced back up at me before folding his laptop closed and sliding it onto my bedside table. "I just posted the tutorial for installing the tile floor in the bathroom. I took your advice and negotiated a discount code for our viewers on the underfloor heating element from Blue Radiant."

I grinned at him. "Look at you, wheeling and dealing."

He shrugged and stood up, stretching his arms up the way he did whenever he unfolded himself from a chair. My eyes immediately darted to the sliver of hairy stomach he exposed whenever he did that. It made me hot every time, even when I was a little fuzzy from prescription pain meds.

"You thirsty?" he asked, reaching for my Gatorade.

I nodded and sat up, wincing with the sudden pain in my hip. "Fuck, I keep forgetting."

A divot formed between his eyebrows. "Stop moving. I'm bringing it right to you."

He was so sweet. The man literally hadn't left my side except the two times they'd kicked him out at night. Even then, it had helped knowing he was just outside in the RV, close enough at hand to get here if I needed him.

I took a sip through the straw, closing my eyes in pleasure as the cool orange drink hit my tongue. When I finished a few sips, I leaned back and asked, "Have you heard from Stallion?"

"Yeah. I told them what was going on and how we had plenty of content to cover our absence. They were cool with it as long as we got back to it as soon as possible. They said to tell you they were rooting for you and Jacks."

"They're a lot nicer than the people in Hollywood," I said with a chuckle.

Nine got the angry-faced look he always did when I mentioned the film. "Those fuckers are uncaring assholes. It should be criminal making you come back before you're barely out of the damned hospital."

I loved it when he stood up for me. I'd never really had that kind of fierce loyalty besides my mom and brother.

"Filming is expensive. They've already rearranged everything to give me five days off."

"Mpfh," he grunted, sitting back down in his chair and moving it closer so he could hold my hand.

I giggled at his caveman routine. The meds were making me high enough to enjoy the easy laughter, but there was a part of me that knew I needed to get off them as soon as possible so Nine and I could work out what this all meant for our future. I assumed he was here because he cared about me. That's certainly the way he'd been making me feel. But was it possible he was only here out of some Isaac Winshed sense of obligation? Had he turned up in Caswell to hold my hand the same way he would show up on the side of the highway with a spare gallon of gas for anyone in need?

I was too woozy to follow those threads of thought for very long. For now, I let myself fall back asleep, dozing in and out for most of the rest of the day. I heard murmured conversations between Nine and my mom. Nine's quiet manners made my mom's voice take on a blushing quality, and if I'd had enough energy to wake up more fully, I would have enjoyed seeing her tittering in response to him.

The following morning, when I was finally lucid enough to think a full thought, I was discharged.

My mom pulled my folded clothes out of the corner cabinet in the room. "Come on, sweetie. Let's get you back to the house where you can rest."

I saw Nine shift from one foot to the other in the corner of the room.

"I..." I glanced at Nine again, trying desperately to read his mind. "I thought maybe I could stay here, with Nine. In the RV."

Nine didn't say anything, so I started backtracking. "I mean, unless you don't want me. I just thought that way I could be closer in case something happened with Jacks and—"

"Of course it's fine," Nine said. "You know that. The RV's as much yours as mine anyway."

I stared at him. Was this lack of enthusiasm some kind of hint that he'd rather me not share the RV with him?

"Honey," Mom said, patting my leg through the blanket. "I just think you'd be more comfortable in your own bed at my house. Your room's all set up, and people from work have been dropping food by. Why don't we let poor Nine get back to work?"

Nine stepped forward hesitantly. "I... I mean, I don't have to go back right away. I could always—"

Mom hustled over and gave him a big hug. "You're such a sweetheart. I can't tell you how much I appreciate you being here for Cooper. I—"

There was a commotion from the hallway, and I recognized Marchie's voice in the same moment Mom did.

She poked her head out of my room. "Marchie, is that you? We're in here, sweetie."

He came storming into the room, eyes red and frantic. "Where is he? Why didn't someone call me? What happened? Is he okay?"

"Where the hell have you been?" I asked. He'd been out of town when all of this had happened, but I would have expected Jacks's closest friend and business partner to have dropped everything and come running when it was time for the transplant.

"Tell me he's okay. Please." His eyes jumped around to all three of us.

Nine was the one who kept a cool head. "Yes. He's still in isolation to keep infection and exposure risk down, but he's doing fine. The transplant was two days ago, and so far everything is going smoothly."

He dashed tears from his face. "He... he fucking told me to go to my cousin's wedding in Vermont. He said the transplant wasn't until the fifteenth, and then he texted like nothing was happening until two days ago. When I couldn't get a hold of him, I called Nan at the shop and she told me. Can... can I see him?"

Once again, it was Nine who stepped forward and offered to lead him to the isolation room where Jacks was. As soon as they were gone, Mom turned to me in surprise. "Did you know he had such strong feelings for Jackson?"

I nodded, pulling the pile of clothes closer so I could put them on under the hospital gown. "He's been in love with him forever. I asked Jacks why Marchie wasn't here for this, and he said he went to a wedding. It never occurred to me Jacks sent him away on purpose."

"Stubborn man," Mom muttered, putting some of my other things in a cloth tote bag she had. "All four of you. Honestly, it's like déjà vu all over again."

"What do you mean?"

Her eyes were shooting lasers right at me. The intensity startled me. "The two of you—Jackson and you—have such a chip on your shoulder about being independent. God forbid you need to ask for help. God forbid you need to rely on someone. But when someone you love is in trouble, you're the first one to want to help. Which is as it should be, but why you can't let others help you when it's your turn is beyond me."

"Hey, wait a minute. That's not fair. I did ask for help. I asked for Nine."

She shot me a look. "No you didn't. Not at first. He asked if you wanted him here, and you said you were fine."

"I *was* fine!"

She dropped the tote on the bed and crossed her arms. Her long floral skirt moved around her legs. "Bullshit. You were scared. You were lonely. And you needed someone who was just here for you. See? You can't even admit it now."

I laughed. "But I do admit it now. I have been lonely, and I've never really had someone just here for me. Having Nine here has been amazing. He's the sweetest man in the world."

She smiled softly. "He is. He takes good care of you."

"Then why didn't you want me to stay with him in the RV?"

Mom rested a hip on the bed next to me. "I just assumed he needed to get back to the mountain house to finish up. That new job he told me about wants him to start by the end of the month, and none of the interior decorating stuff has been done yet at the cabin."

I blinked at her, suddenly feeling the nausea side effect that often accompanied strong pain meds. "What new job?"

"The one with the cabin rental website. You know… their logo is a bear with a big animated heart hopping around it. They have those commercials on TV."

"MyCabin dot com?" I asked incredulously.

"Yeah. Didn't he tell you about it? They want him to teach people how to do over old cabins and turn them into rentals to list on their site. Isn't that perfect for him?"

It was. "Well, yeah..."

"And he said the cabin they found for him is in northern Minnesota, so it'll take him a couple of days to drive out there. I think that's why he needs to get back to the cabin, but don't quote me on that."

When Nine got back to my room, griping again about how they almost didn't let him in since he wasn't family, I felt an odd lump in my throat. The new job explained his reluctance to have me stay in the RV, but why hadn't he told me about the new gig? And how in the hell were we supposed to build a relationship with Nine in Minnesota and me in LA?

"Nine can help you with the rest of this while I go bring the car around, okay?" Mom asked.

I slipped on the flip-flops Nine handed me from the cabinet, but I was still a little too light-headed from all the dressing activity to stand just yet. It was probably time for me to switch from heavy pain meds to over-the-counter stuff.

"You heading back today?" I asked him.

Nine crinkled his forehead. "Uh... I guess so?"

"I just... Mom said you had a lot going on."

He scratched the back of his neck. "I mean... yeah, but..."

"I don't want to be your obligation, Isaac."

His eyes widened. "You're not. Not ever."

I looked everywhere but at him. *Stop being a chickenshit and just ask him about the job.*

"Mom said you were headed to Minnesota."

His feet shuffled. "Oh, uh, I don't really know yet. It's... it's not really a done deal."

I glanced up at him. "Why didn't you tell me about it?"

He looked even more surprised, if it was possible. "Um, because you were in the middle of a crisis and my new sponsorship gig didn't mean anything in comparison to your health and well-being?"

I was tired and confused, half in pain and half bubbleheaded from meds. "Can we... I mean... after the movie wraps and you do what you need to do for the cabin people, can we… talk? Figure some stuff out?"

Nine's fingers brushed through my hair, and his face went all soft. "I would do anything for you. Don't you know that by now?"

I let out a breath. Good. We were good. It was all going to be okay.

33

NINE

I drove back to the cabin in a complete snit. I wasn't normally a complainer, but when Calum Scott's "Dancing On My Own" came on the radio, I wailed out my anger with every word. Poor Nacho probably thought I'd been replaced by an off-key robot of some kind.

As Johnny Cash took over and then Toby Keith and Reba McEntire, I kept on singing. It wasn't until Joe Diffie crooned about a "Texas Size Heartache" that I reached over and slammed the button to shut it off. No reason to wallow anymore. I was a grown man, for god's sake, and this wasn't even a breakup. It was just... two people who obviously cared about each other but had different lives.

Yeah, that.

Every time I tried to picture a life with the two of us, I couldn't figure out how it would work. I could live without the mountains, without the open space of the farm my family lived on. Hell, I could even live without my family. I knew that now. But I wasn't sure I could live without having things to fix, and work to do. After building up my vlog, I didn't really want to go back to a life where I only worked in the hardware store and didn't have something else of my own, something where my own version of creativity could run free, even if just a little bit.

When I finally pulled the RV into the familiar clearing, the cabin was exactly how I'd left it. I parked the vehicle and then followed the instruction pamphlet to make sure I set it up correctly. Nacho raced around peeing on every corner of his kingdom, happy as hell to be back in the woods with all of the animals and interesting smells.

I sent Cooper a quick text to tell him I'd made it safely, but when I didn't hear back, I assumed he was getting much-needed rest.

Since there was nothing else to do, I got right back to work. It only took an hour of replacing rotten front porch boards before I'd worked up a good sweat in the late-afternoon sun. The work was pleasantly distracting, and it was nice to move my body after several days folded up on the visitor chair next to Coop's hospital bed.

The next morning I got a quick text from Cooper thanking me for letting him know I'd arrived. He was more tired than he expected, so if I didn't hear from him, it was most likely because he was sleeping. Then he gave me his mom's number in case I needed it.

I tried not to bother them, but it killed me not knowing how he was doing. I remembered the big bruise blooming on his hip from where they'd taken the bone marrow, and I wondered if it was keeping him from sleeping comfortably.

My father had always taught me to be a hard worker. Growing up on a small family farm meant there was no getting out of it. I was used to hard work. I knew firsthand that working hard on the farm was a direct way of proving your love for your family.

So I threw myself into finishing the cabin and making sure the videos of the project, the tutorials I created, and the actual work itself was as high-quality as I could make them. This project had Cooper's name on it, and I wanted to make him proud.

Four days later, I heard back from Adrian about the MyCabin sponsorship. I was just finishing my lunch at the kitchen table and sorting through some video clips on the laptop when the phone rang.

"We're really excited to get you on board," he said. "My team has already started sourcing a second property in case we decide to renew for another project after the Minnesota cabin. Based on the timeline information you gave us, we think you'll be able to get this reno done before the winter weather hits up there as long as you start by the first of August like we talked about. That would put you at the second property around first of October, and of course we'll pick a mild locale for the winter project. We're thinking possibly the Blue Ridge Mountains or even a lake house in Alabama."

I thought about being that far away from any chance at seeing Cooper, and it was simply not possible. I didn't want this sponsorship more than I wanted him. Suddenly, I knew with great clarity that I would be willing to work at a hardware store in LA if it meant being part of Cooper's life.

"Would you ever consider finding a property in Southern California?" I asked, drawing a design with my fingertip on the smooth table surface.

Adrian actually laughed. "Never in a million years. I hope you're joking. Even a company much bigger than ours wouldn't invest that kind of money into a YouTube campaign."

He went on to remind me that in addition to the primary vlog, they were also offering compensation for print and television ads. "We can shoot all of those at a studio here in Vancouver. We'll fly you out for—"

"I don't have a passport," I blurted. "I don't fly."

He was quiet for a minute, and then he spoke more slowly like he was approaching a live grenade. "That's okay... we can work around those things if need be..."

"Listen. I'm not sure about all of this. My boyf—" I stopped myself. "My... Cooper just got out of the hospital and I... I'm just a little... I'd like to ask his feedback on this first if that's okay."

"Sure. Take the rest of the week if you need it. We're still putting together some of the contract language anyway, so that's not a problem. You know where to reach me if you or your... Cooper have any questions."

He sounded understanding, and I was beyond grateful for it. "Thank you. I appreciate it."

As soon as I got off the phone, it rang again. It was my parents' home number.

"Hi," I said.

"Hi, son, it's me. Dad." As if I didn't recognize his voice. My dad's voice had two volumes: booming and thundering. It boomed on a regular day and only thundered when he was truly angry, like Sir PAL angry. Today he was merely booming. "I was calling to let you know when we're going to need you for the next bit of harvest work. The pinch wheel harvester is having some problems, but Colt is working on it. Won't need that one till September anyway, but the..."

He droned on about farm stuff, and I felt the same, familiar pull of family obligation that was such a part of who I was. There'd never been a question about me helping my family with the harvest. It was simply a fact of life. Even Walt knew I needed time off during harvest times to help Aaron and my dad.

But this year, for the first time ever, I had other things going on outside of my family obligations. I had the job in Minnesota and Cooper in LA. I felt like one of those old stretchy action figures being pulled in three different directions.

"I don't think I'm going to be able to help you this year, Dad," I said, cutting him off midsentence.

There was a moment of silence. "You always help me with the harvest, and I've already had to go through one haying without you. Was a damned mess."

I felt a nervous rumbling under my skin. "I know, but this summer's turning out to be tough. Maybe Colt can get some time off or Tip... or maybe Graham can help out for once in his life. Heck, even Jessie and her friends from school probably wouldn't mind helping as long as you bought them some pizza and beer after."

He scoffed. "The way that girl drives her little sports car confirms she's never getting behind the wheel of my tractor. Besides, she can't lift a bale of hay like you can, and neither can Tip or Lucky as they proved during the first cut. And Colt can't get the time off."

"Dad..."

"Your mother said you should be done with that cabin business by end of the month, so I'll expect you for the second cut right after that. Then we've got the sugar beets to bring in. Hopefully Colt will fix that damned pinch wheel by then."

He rattled off more complaints about aging and finicky equipment which was always a challenge on a small farm. While he spoke, I tried desperately to figure out how to say no. I'd never said no to him in my life.

"I can't, Dad. I have a job in Minnesota, and they want me there first of August," I tried.

"Tell them they can have you by the tenth. That oughta be fine."

I rested my forehead on my palm. "Dad. That's not how the corporate world works. They said the first of the month because that's what the legal contract says. That's when they need me. I'm not the only one who can bale hay in Wyoming. Can't you—"

"What's this really about, son?"

"Sir?"

"Your mother said doing that job down there in Colorado has got you confused about yourself. And I didn't believe her one bit, but hearing you say you're not even coming home to help on the farm? That's not like you, Nine."

"I'm not confused," I said. "I like what I'm doing. I'm excited about fixing up houses like this for a living."

"Is this because of Cooper Heath?"

Just hearing his name made my chest tighten. "No, Dad. He's not even involved in this. He's in LA doing work on a film. The job is just for me."

Which of course made me even more depressed. It was ten times more fun doing this job with Cooper by my side.

"Well, good. At least we got that part straightened out so to speak." He finished that zinger off with a chuckle.

My whole body went tingly and strange. This was the moment whether I liked it or not, whether I was ready or not.

"Dad. I'm in love with him."

Silence.

I hadn't ever been great at withstanding my dad's silence. "I'm sorry if that—"

He cut me off, but he didn't sound angry so much as confused. "I don't understand. I thought this was all pretend for the money."

"It was. But... but then I got to know him and I..."

"Son... it's not that I'm... judging you or anything, because it's not my place to decide what or who makes you happy in this life, but... I guess I don't get how a man can have a girlfriend and then a boyfriend. Like... did he say something to make you change your mind about who you were?"

Now it was my turn to chuckle. "No. I'm the same as I've always been. I just realized that I needed to find the right person before I had strong feelings, and now that I have... well, that person happens to be a man. It was as much a surprise to me as to you probably."

"Well, like I said, I'm not sure I can understand it, but I'll do my best to respect it. You know I've always liked that boy anyway. He's been nothing but friendly and helpful whenever Eli's brought him around."

My nose started to run, and hot tears escaped. If Cooper had been here, he would have made a joke about me being for sure gay now with all this drama. "Thanks, Dad. But I'm not sure it much matters now. He's off in California having a big life as a movie star."

"And?"

"What do you mean, 'and'?"

"And what are you going to do about it? No son of mine just lays down and gives up when the fat hits the fire. You've got to fight for what you want. You remember that time you started your little garden plot for 4-H?"

"Yeah."

"That plot was full of rocks. It was one of the reasons I gave it to you to use. I figured you'd realize how many rocks were in there and give up. I'm not proud to admit it, but I didn't want you wasting resources on a garden I didn't think you'd follow through on. I should have known better than to judge you based on your brother's failed attempt at a similar project the year before. Anyway, you didn't let those rocks stop you one bit. You stayed out there and removed every damned one of them."

"I remember. My hands were shot to shit," I said with a laugh. "But I wanted that garden."

He let the last sentence lie there like an echo.

"Exactly," he said quietly. "You wanted it. So you did what it took to get it. Even though it was hard. Even though it hurt. Some things are worth a little discomfort, Isaac."

My father, the philosopher.

"Thanks, Dad."

He took a breath and snapped back into booming dad mode. "Like harvesting, for example," he teased. "Harvesting is worth the pain, son. Come see for yourself. First of August. See you then."

I got off the phone laughing. And just like that, I knew what I had to do. It wouldn't be easy, but it would be worth the discomfort.

I hoped.

34

COOPER

Getting back into the mindset of my character wasn't easy. I was tired and sore from the procedure and the stress of worrying about Jacks, and I selfishly missed my sexy lumberjack. I planned to return to him as soon as the film cut me loose, but for some reason I was antsy about it, like the more time that passed without seeing him might mean the less chance he'd still be interested in figuring out a future together.

He'd never been the best phone communicator in the first place. Texts and phone calls weren't really his thing, and when you added in the unpredictable nature of my job and his location in the middle of fucking nowhere, it added up to lots of missed opportunities to connect. Not having a chance to see him or hear his voice made me feel at loose ends.

I had it easier than he did, though, because I got to see his posts on Instagram every day. Even though we'd prerecorded a bunch of good-night posts, he posted little tips or snippets each day of himself working on something. He hadn't posted something extra like that in two days, though, so I was beginning to worry about him.

Those two days had been extra long because I'd finished filming my scenes, but I'd still been on the call sheet for a couple more days just in case Sam changed his mind. After wrapping for the day today, the production assistant had finally given me the all clear.

I'd immediately booked a flight to Denver so I could pop in and see Jacks and then head to the cabin to surprise Nine. Hopefully we'd at least have a full week together decorating and finishing the cabin before his new job started.

My friends were eager to take me out to celebrate the end of filming my first decent role. Bane and Willow had reserved the outside terrace in front of a restaurant called Fig and Olive in West Hollywood which sounded like something celebrities would do to show off in front of the press. I leaned over to whisper in Evie's's ear when we arrived.

"Wonder if they even tried to get a private room inside. Would have made it easier to carry on a decent conversation."

Evie's eyes widened. "Babe. You're going to be photographed at a private dinner with two of the hottest young celebrities in LA right now. It's going to be a huge thing for your reputation. I'm sure that's why they booked the terrace. To help you."

That took me aback. It made sense, but... I would have rather had a nice quiet night with friends. The idea of being watched while having dinner gave me the chills. I'd seen the kind of life Bane and Willow lived where their privacy was nonexistent and they felt like they had to constantly be the life of the party. Or maybe it was their "life of the party" personalities that drew them to the world of entertainment. Was it a chicken-and-egg thing?

"I don't want photos," I said stupidly.

Evie laughed. "Don't be ridiculous. Every burgeoning star would kill for exposure like this. I'll bet ten bucks Mitch calls you tomorrow squealing like a pig in shit."

I thought of the calls from Mitch that I'd been avoiding. He'd mentioned receiving several inquiries for me, but nothing that sounded exciting enough to miss out on the final week of *Cooped Up With Nine*. Finally, Mitch had pinned me down and insisted on an early breakfast tomorrow before I left for the airport. I needed to figure out what the hell I wanted to do with my life before then.

We joined the party already in progress on the terrace, and Evie made a beeline for the server who was passing full champagne flutes on a tray.

"Cooper's here!" Willow said, pulling the arm of another young woman who looked vaguely familiar. "Come meet Cooper. He's the one I told you about from Bane's film. Isn't he a cutie?"

The woman blushed and smiled. "Hi, I'm Gillian." Suddenly, my brain served up the answer. Gillian Ivers was a country-music singer I recognized from one of Nine's albums on his phone. She sang a song called "Barn Lights" that he'd played one time when he asked me to slow dance outside in the clearing. After that, we'd played it over and over again on the nights that called for dancing under the stars.

"Oh my god, Gillian. I can't tell you how exciting it is to meet you. My boyfriend is a huge fan."

Her face lit up. "Really? That's so sweet. Do you… do you want to take a picture and send it to him?"

I felt like a total fangirl in that moment, so I tried to keep cool. "That would be amazing."

Willow offered to take the photo with my phone while Gillian turned us around and put her arm around my waist. She was a tiny thing, and it was odd to put my arm around her shoulder when I was used to being the small one in a hug with Nine.

"Tell me about him," she said. "What's his name?"

"His name is…" I spotted a man walking down the sidewalk toward the restaurant with a sandwich board hanging around his neck. He had a beard just like… "Isaac, but everyone calls him…" I squinted at the man. He had a finger and thumb in his mouth and was about to whistle. Could it possibly be… "Nine?"

The whistle rang through the crowd between us, and his beard split in a hesitant smile. "Hi." He looked around nervously. "Um…"

What the hell was going on? The sign hanging on his front had my photo on it and the words "If you see Cooper Heath…" painted on the front in bold letters.

"What is that?" I asked, moving quickly through the crowd

between me and the terrace entrance. My heart was beating fast, and I felt a silly giggle bubbling up in my throat. Nine was here. My Nine.

He turned in a circle. "Oh, um, it's kind of silly, but... I know you wanted a billboard in Hollywood one day, and uh, this is the closest I could come on short notice."

The back of the board read, "Tell him Nine loves him." It had little pink hearts hand-painted all around it. It was the gayest thing Isaac Winshed had ever done, and I fucking adored him for it.

He turned back to face me. My hands had flown to my mouth while everyone around me started chattering excitedly and snapping pictures.

He loved me?

He *loved* me.

Nine's face was red as a fire engine, and his eyes darted around like ping-pong balls spilled on a concrete floor. "I needed you to know," he said in a shaky voice. "I needed... I needed you to know."

Tears streamed down my face. Nine hated attention on him. He hated thinking people were looking at him and judging him. And yet he'd done this for me. Put a damned sandwich board on and walked down the streets of West Hollywood declaring his love for another man.

I let out a mix between a laugh and a sob. "I love you too, you big idiot."

He seemed surprised by my admission. "What?"

I flapped my hands around. "Take that thing off, I want to hug you."

"You do? You love me?" he asked while lifting the boards over his head and setting them down. "But I came here to convince you to give me a chance. I want to be with you. I want—*oof*."

I slammed into him the moment he was free, wrapping my arms and legs around him and holding on for dear life. "I love you so much," I said before kissing his gorgeous fucking face. "Love you, love you."

He held me with those tight bands of muscles and kissed me right there on Melrose for everyone to see, including the clusters of paparazzi gathered just outside the short terrace wall snapping pictures of everything. When I finally pulled out of the kiss, I grinned at him. "You didn't need to come here though. I was flying home to you tomorrow. I already booked my flight."

Nine's face was serious and his eyes intense. "I needed to tell you I'll do whatever it takes. Whatever will make you happy. I'll move here and get a job. I already stopped by two hardware stores to ask if they're hiring."

More tears spilled down my face. "I don't want you to live in LA with me."

His face fell, and I rushed to finish my thought. "No, not that. I don't want you to move here because I want to be with you. I want to go with you to Minnesota and help you fix up houses."

His face finally lit up, and his beard finally split into that sexy grin of his. "Really? You'd do that? What about this? What about movies?"

He let my feet drop to the pavement, but I didn't let him go. I nuzzled my face into his neck and inhaled his woodsy scent. "I don't want this life," I whispered so only he could hear it. "I thought I did, but I don't. I want to keep doing what we're doing with the vlog and social media. I have a lot of ideas and… and I can still be in front of the camera. But this way I can be in front of the camera as me. And I can be with you at the same time. I want our life together—the one in the clearing. Except I don't care where it is, as long as I have you."

He pulled me back and cupped my face. His eyes were locked on mine with a kind of searching intensity. "You sure?"

"I love you," I said, probably beaming up at him like an idiot. I heard Evie's squeal in the background.

Isaac's face softened. "I love you too. More than anything."

"More than your pride, I see," I teased. "I can't imagine this stunt was easy for you."

Isaac seemed to suddenly realize we were surrounded by people and cameras. Now it was his turn to tuck his face into my neck.

"I think I'm hallucinating," he whispered. "There's a woman over there who looks like a famous country singer."

I stepped away and reached for his hand. I felt lighter and happier than I could remember feeling for a long, long time. "Come on. Let me introduce you to a few people. I can't wait to show you off to my friends."

Even though he was painfully shy, Isaac was the belle of the ball. Everyone adored him, obviously. Evie practically attacked him with hugs and squeals over his "grand gesture" as she called it. I caught Willow swiping away a few tears while Gillian seemed to have to fan herself when she caught eyes with my boyfriend. So much for being the cute one in the relationship.

My boyfriend.

Every time I used the term to introduce him to someone, his lips turned up in a tiny smile. Throughout the night, he never strayed far from my side. In fact, his hand held mine in a death grip most of the time which was about the most endearing thing ever. It was clear he was nervous as hell and felt completely out of his comfort zone, but he was here. For me. He'd shown up to prove to me that this was worth fighting for. *We* were worth fighting for.

"That man can handle my wood any damn time he wants," Van slurred into my ear. "You didn't tell me your lumberjack was even hotter in person."

I glanced over at my old roommate, who was staring dazedly at my new roommate. "You should see him naked," I said back to him. "It's even better."

Van's jaw dropped and his eyes stayed locked on Nine as if he was undressing the poor man with his imagination. Nine was too busy talking to Gillian to notice.

"Does he have any brothers?" Van asked. "Someone who might want to plow my field and so forth. Give me a good ride on their tractor, so to speak."

Nine's hand tightened around mine, indicating he'd heard every bit of Van's drunken hopes.

"Oh yeah," I said. "He actually has five brothers. And they all know how to plant a seed if you know what I mean."

Nine choked on the beer he'd been nursing, but he somehow

managed to continue his conversation with the singer on his other side.

I looked around at the LA family I'd gathered in such a short time. They were an amazing group of people, but I knew I didn't need to live here in LA to continue having them in my life. No, we wouldn't make nearly the amount of money with a YouTube gig as we would with actual film work, but we would still make enough to come back for visits. And when we did, I could show Nine all of the things I loved about Southern California.

But then we could return to our little RV in the woods wherever it happened to be parked at the time and enjoy our quiet alone time with Nacho curled around our feet and Nine's cheesy music playing on the Bluetooth speaker. Just the thought of it calmed me down and helped me breathe easier.

I blew out a breath.

Isaac leaned over and kissed the shell of my ear. "You okay, baby? Getting tired? Is it your hip? Are you hurting?"

I leaned over and slid my arms around his neck, pulling him in for a hug. "I'm better than I've ever been in my entire life. Let's go home."

EPILOGUE

NINE - DECEMBER

I almost got away with it. But when you join two lives together, including two bank accounts, nosy boyfriends tended to poke around where they didn't belong.

"Nine!" Cooper shouted from the RV loud enough to make me jump and knock my head into the garbage disposal and sink pipes.

"What?"

"Get your ass out here!"

I sighed and scooted out from the kitchen cabinet where I'd just finished installing the dishwasher. "Coming."

After wiping my hands with a nearby rag, I made my way through the small one-bedroom ski chalet and out into the fresh snow. I could just see the colorful ski parkas on the Vail lifts through the trees in the distance. I still didn't know how Cooper had managed to get us a gig so close to home over the holidays, but I was looking forward to my mom's big turkey dinner at the end of the week. Coop's mom was coming with us to Wheatland since Jacks was spending the holiday with Marchie's family.

I stomped through the snow to the door of the new RV. This one was a fifth wheel that we towed behind the truck which allowed us to travel together from place to place without needing to drive two vehicles. We'd bought it ourselves... well, we'd financed it ourselves... and it was set up much better for the two of us and our business. We even had a big-screen television that we could watch movies on from our comfy leather couch. The bathroom had a shower big enough for both of us. Okay, barely big enough, but still. We could shower together when the mood struck us, and it struck us more often than I'd expected. The absolute best thing about our new home was that it was ours. Cooper had decorated it with his new love of interior shit, and he'd hung up some framed photos from our social media feed.

There was a photo of us dancing in the clearing. When we'd finished the cabin project and watched the time-lapse videos of the clearing, it had been like watching a movie of the two of us falling in love.

There was the slow dancing, the long moments of kissing on the porch, the picnic. Coop had particularly enjoyed the clips of me dashing across the clearing in nothing but a towel and boots after having taken a shower in the cabin. He'd spent plenty of time watching footage from the days when he'd been gone, and he'd time-stamped his favorite parts to watch over and over.

Next to the photo of our dance was a still image from the first Instagram story good-night video we did where I looked spooked and weird. But then there was one of me with my head thrown back in laughter after trying to teach Cooper to throw an ax and he'd flung it deep into the woods. Behind us.

There was a framed picture of me standing on the sidewalk in Hollywood with the sandwich board, looking terrified. One of the two of us in the cheesy tuxedo T-shirts we wore when we crashed Jacks and Marchie's elopement in Vegas. And one of us standing in front of each of the three houses we'd already renovated since starting *Cooped Up With Nine.*

I kicked off my boots in the rubber tray by the door. "I'm here," I called, reaching down to pet Nacho where he was curled up on his favorite blanket. His tail wagged in response, but his eyes remained closed. I noticed the little gas fireplace was turned on and Coop's music was playing softly. Cooper stepped out of the bedroom. He was crying and flapping a piece of paper through the air.

"Baby, what's wrong?" I strode over to him, but he held out his hand to stop me. My heart lurched.

"How could you?"

Was he mad because I'd spent more than we'd agreed on for his Christmas present? No. I'd paid for his new laptop in cash, and it was locked in the toolbox of my truck underneath a bunch of dirty tools. There was no way he could have found out about it.

"How could I what? Help me out here."

He swiped at his face. "You're the anonymous donor?"

Oh. *Ohhh.* I tried to play dumb. That usually worked.

"Anonymous donor for what?"

He narrowed his eyes at me. "Jackson's surgery. The bone marrow transplant. The hospital bills."

Shit. "Um, no?"

He snorted. "You're a shit liar, Isaac Winshed. The hospital sent a final statement to our post office box."

"Oh, that. Well, yeah. I had the money, and you guys needed it."

His eyes glittered at me. "Easy as that, huh?"

I shrugged.

"You were going to buy a piece of property with that money. That was your savings. It was for your future."

I smiled at him and pulled him close, despite his weak attempts to keep me at arm's length. "Yes, I was saving that money for my future, and that's exactly what I spent it on."

"Your future?"

I nodded. "My future family."

He leaned his forehead on my chest. "God dammit. Stop being such a good fucking person. You make other people look bad. *Asshole.*"

I laughed and kissed the top of his head. "Sorry. I'll try to be a shittier person next time."

"Thank you," he said softly into my chest. And I could tell he wasn't joking anymore.

"You're welcome. Besides, I only wanted to buy my own property so I'd have a project to work on and a place to call home. Now I have all of that anyway."

Coop yanked my flannel shirt out of the back of my pants so he could warm his hands on my back the way he always did now that the weather was freezing. I winced when his cold fingers hit my hot skin. "I also called you in here because I just got a phone call from Mitch."

Suddenly, the skin on my lower back wasn't the only thing running cold. I still secretly worried there would come a big film opportunity that would be exciting enough to tempt Cooper back to LA. I knew now that it wouldn't be the end of our relationship, but I still didn't want to be far away from him. "Oh?"

When Cooper pulled back, I saw the giant grin on his face. "HGTV wants to talk to us about bringing our program to their network as a regular show."

"What's HGTV?" I asked with a straight face.

Cooper's smile dropped. "What? You... what?"

"Kidding. That's amazing. What do you think?" I laughed at his dumbfounded expression and stepped away from him to grab some water from the fridge. "Is that something we should consider?"

"Wait!" he screeched, lurching toward me and slamming me bodily against the refrigerator door. We both stood there, with him plastered against my back and my face smashed against the cool surface of the fridge, as the sound of his panicked shout echoed around us.

"Baby," I said carefully. "Is there a reason I can't get something to drink?"

"No... yes... no. Just..."

I turned around and peered at him. He looked uncharacteristically nervous. He had his bottom lip caught between his teeth.

He sighed. "It's just that your Christmas present is in there."

"You got me flavored water for Christmas?" I teased. "That was awfully sweet of you."

He punched my chest with a fist. "Don't make fun of me right now, I'm nervous as hell."

I leaned down to kiss him. "No need to be nervous with me. I'll love anything you got me, especially if it's strawberry kiwi flavored."

He laughed. "Stop."

"Why don't I hop in the shower and wash off the grime from dealing with that old dishwasher while you re-hide my gift? Does that sound good? And maybe you can pour me a water while you're at it." I winked at him and moved away toward the bathroom, reaching for the buttons on my shirt. I stripped down and tossed my clothes in the canvas laundry bag we had on the back of the closet door. Maybe we could head into town to get some dinner tonight while we visited the laundromat.

The water was nice and hot, and we'd paid extra for a robust pump to give us decent water pressure. It had taken me a while to figure out how to create an RV hookup site at each of our cabin renovations, but the result was a much more comfortable stay for us and some added value for the cabin owner when they went to list their rental on the website.

It was with those sexy thoughts in my head that I heard Coop enter the bathroom. Suddenly the lights went out, leaving a lone candle in its place. The light was dim and wavy through the frosted glass of the shower door.

"Get in here, sexy," I growled. A little shower sex would go a long way toward washing away the stresses of the day.

He didn't answer me. Instead, he kept moving around lighting more and more candles until the little bathroom glowed with light.

When he still didn't join me, I poked my head out of the frosted door to see what he was up to. There, on the fluffy gray bathmat, knelt the love of my life with a tiny square box in his hands.

"Merry Christmas," he said in a shaky voice. "I... I hope this is the first of many together. And... I guess what I'm trying to say is..."

The rest of his words were lost to the thunder of the spray as I ducked back into the stall and slammed the water off. When I practically tripped and fell out of the stall, dripping wet and buck naked, Cooper laughed.

"Maybe I should have thought this through," he said.

"Say it again," I growled.

His eyes widened. "I have never met a kinder, more gentle soul than you. You are funny and smart, hardworking and generous. I'm already the luckiest man alive for sharing this life with you, but would it be too much to ask if we made it official? Isaac Winshed, will you marry me?"

I fell to my knees on the mat in front of him and took his face in my hands. "Yes." I kissed him long and hard. My brain spun with all of the exciting possibilities of what marriage would bring, with the relief of knowing he was mine forever, and with the certainty that this was the exact way my life was supposed to go.

When we finally came up for air, Cooper had a smirk on his face. "Did I do okay? Was it good even though you're dripping wet and naked? Because I gotta tell you, that's kind of what makes it for me."

My laugh boomed around the tiny space, reminding me of my dad. "Well, as far as love declarations go, it was no hiding a chicken in a closet, but it'll do."

~

Thanks for reading! Want to know what happens with Jacks and Marchie? Visit my website or sign up for my newsletter to get their free 5k word bonus short!

~

What's next? The brand-new Aster Valley series begins with the story of a hot professional football player and his accidental—very off-limits—personal chef. Order Right as Raine *now!*

~

Want to see artist Lauren Dombrowski's depiction of Cooper and Nine? Turn the page...

LETTER FROM LUCY

Dear Reader,

Thank you so much for reading *Say You'll Be Nine*! This story was inspired by my love for Tyler and Todd's YouTube channel as well as the YouTube channel by My Self Reliance. These channels were inspiration *only*. In no way are the characters or locations in my story meant to represent any real life people or situation. This novel is a work of fiction, including the made-up towns of Shale Falls and Caswell, Colorado.

I loved the idea of two men spending time in an RV together, tackling a renovation project while filming it for an audience. I wanted to add some necessary conflict by making the pair not complete strangers, but also not friends.

The gorgeous videography done by the real-life YouTubers mentioned above was inspirational to me, and it fed into the fantasy of what it would be like to live and work together a little bit off the grid while taking full advantage of gorgeous natural surroundings. I hope I did justice to Isaac and Cooper's story.

If this is your first Lucy Lennox book, please check out *Borrowing Blue* which is my most popular title and the story of two men as sweet as the ones found here.

If you want to read the bonus short featuring Jacks and Marchie, don't forget to sign up for my newsletter here:

readerlinks.com/l/1444197

If you miss the newsletter, you can always find links to the free bonus content on my website.

Be sure to follow me on Amazon to be notified of new releases, and look for me on Facebook for sneak peeks of upcoming stories.

Feel free to stop by www.LucyLennox.com or visit me on social media to stay in touch. We have a super fun reader group on Facebook that can be found here:

https://www.facebook.com/groups/lucyslair/

To see fun inspiration photos for all of my stories, including *Say You'll Be Nine*, visit my Pinterest boards.

Happy reading!

Lucy

ABOUT LUCY LENNOX

Lucy Lennox is the creator of the bestselling Made Marian series, the Forever Wilde series, and co-creator of the Twist of Fate Series with Sloane Kennedy and the After Oscar series with Molly Maddox. Born and raised in the southeast, she is finally putting good use to that English Lit degree.

Lucy enjoys naps, pizza, and procrastinating. She is married to someone who is better at math than romance but who makes her laugh every single day and is the best dancer in the history of ever.

She stays up way too late each night reading M/M romance because that stuff is impossible to put down.

For more information and to stay updated about future releases, please sign up for Lucy's author newsletter on her website.

~

Connect with Lucy on social media:
www.LucyLennox.com
Lucy@LucyLennox.com

WANT MORE?

Join Lucy's Lair

Get Lucy's New Release Alerts

Like Lucy on Facebook

Follow Lucy on BookBub

Follow Lucy on Amazon

Follow Lucy on Instagram

Follow Lucy on Pinterest

Other books by Lucy:

Made Marian Series

Forever Wilde Series

Aster Valley Series

Twist of Fate Series with Sloane Kennedy

After Oscar Series with Molly Maddox

Licking Thicket Series with May Archer

Virgin Flyer

Say You'll Be Nine

Visit Lucy's website at www.LucyLennox.com for a comprehensive list of titles, audio samples, freebies, suggested reading order, and more!

CPSIA information can be obtained
at www.ICGtesting.com
Printed in the USA
LVHW041611190621
690653LV00003B/247